WESLEY KING

G. P. PUTNAM'S SONS · AN IMPRINT OF PENGUIN GROUP (USA) INC.

G. P. PUTNAM'S SONS • A DIVISION OF PENGUIN YOUNG READERS GROUP.
Published by The Penguin Group.
Penguin Group (USA) Inc., 375 Hudson Street, New York, NY 10014, U.S.A.
Penguin Group (Canada), 90 Eglinton Avenue East, Suite 700, Toronto,
Ontario M4P 2Y3, Canada (a division of Pearson Penguin Canada Inc.).
Penguin Books Ltd, 80 Strand, London WC2R ORL, England.
Penguin Ireland, 25 St. Stephen's Green, Dublin 2, Ireland (a division of Penguin Books Ltd).
Penguin Group (Australia), 250 Camberwell Road, Camberwell, Victoria 3124, Australia
(a division of Pearson Australia Group Pty Ltd).
Penguin Books India Pvt Ltd, 11 Community Centre, Panchsheel Park,
New Delhi—110 017, India.
Penguin Group (NZ), 67 Apollo Drive, Rosedale, Auckland 0632, New Zealand
(a division of Pearson New Zealand Ltd).
Penguin Books (South Africa) (Pty) Ltd, 24 Sturdee Avenue, Rosebank,
Johannesburg 2196, South Africa.
Penguin Books Ltd, Registered Offices: 80 Strand, London WC2R ORL, England.

Published simultaneously in Canada. Printed in the United States of America.
Design by Marikka Tamura. Text set in Scherzo Std.
Library of Congress Cataloging-in-Publication Data is available upon request.
King, Wesley.
The Vindico / Wesley King. p. cm.
Summary: When supervillains of the Vindico realize they are getting too old to fight the
League of Heroes, they kidnap and begin training five teens, but James, Lana, Hayden,
Emily, and Sam will not become the next generation of evil without a fight.
[1. Supervillains—Fiction. 2. Good and evil—Fiction. 3. Kidnapping—Fiction. 4. Science fiction.]
I. Title. PZ7.K58922Vin 2012 [Fic]—dc23 2011033410
ISBN 978-0-399-25654-7
1 3 5 7 9 10 8 6 4 2

For Oma
who taught me that youth is
synonymous with wonder

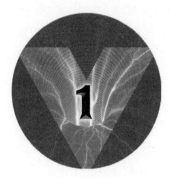

JAMES TIREDLY SLID HIS LEGS OFF THE BED AND LOOKED AROUND in disgust. His room was a mess. Half-finished glasses and plates covered his desk and dresser, while clothes were scattered in a tangled layer across the carpet. Crumpled and ripped photographs had been haphazardly thrown on top of the clothing, along with their now-empty frames. Only the walls had escaped the chaos, and they were almost entirely taken up by posters of his favorite League members. Thunderbolt had his arms crossed on the far wall by the closet, looking down on the room in disapproval.

James wasn't usually so messy; he'd accumulated all this in the last thirty-two hours. He'd spent thirty-one-and-a-half of those in his bedroom.

After digging around for some passably clean clothes, James shuffled into the bathroom. Catching a glimpse of himself in the mirror, he frowned. He focused on his nose in particular, which was small, a bit pointy, and covered with faint freckles. Growing up, his pet name from his mother had been "my little weasel." He'd never found it quite as endearing as she had.

James walked into the kitchen and found his two younger sisters sitting at the table. They both looked up, wearing the same patronizing smile.

"Still moping about Sara?" Ally asked.

"It's only been two days," James said defensively.

He went to get himself a piece of plain bread. It was the only thing he'd been able to keep down.

Jen snickered. "Kids these days."

"I know you like to forget," James said, taking a bite, "but I am your *older* brother. *Older.*"

Jen put down her spoon. "Did you know this?" she asked Ally, sounding shocked.

"Of course," Ally said. "Look how mature he is."

James rubbed his forehead in exasperation. He wasn't getting a lot of sympathy from his family, and he somehow doubted it would be any better at school today.

"Are you hassling your brother?" their mother asked as she hurried into the kitchen. "Give him a break, please. Jen, put the news on. I just heard something on the radio." She glanced at James. "You're going to want to hear this."

Jen got up and turned the TV to the news station. Thunderbolt stood behind a raised podium, looking somewhat old and tired as camera flashes lit up the stage. There were bags under his dark-rimmed eyes. James frowned, his own problems forgotten for a moment. Thunderbolt hadn't held a formal news conference in over two years.

Thunderbolt leaned forward as someone asked a question. "As I said, the exact details are still unknown. All we can confirm is that Nighthawk is missing and has been for about a week now. We wanted to be absolutely sure before we released this information to the public."

James hurried over to the TV. *If a League member is missing,* he thought, *that can only mean one thing.*

"At this time, we suspect that the Villains may be involved," Thunderbolt said gravely, confirming James's guess. This piece of information elicited a new rush of questions, and Thunderbolt held up his hands. "There's no need to panic. The League, combined with local and federal authorities, has been put on alert." He looked out into the cameras. "As before, we want to stress that the public is *not* a direct target of these individuals. All of the casualties in the past, including the tragic Night of Ashes, were unfortunate results of attacks on League members. But this time, the League is ready, and we will do everything in our power to ensure that there are no more civilian deaths."

There was another flurry of questions, but Thunderbolt just shook his head. "No," he said quietly. "I have no idea why they've returned now."

The screen suddenly went black.

"Hey," James protested. "I wanted to see . . ."

"You're going to be late for school," his mother said, putting the remote back on the table. "I'm sure you'll hear more about it there. And just to be on the safe side, I want you all inside well before dark tonight."

"Maybe we should stay home from school, you know, just to be safe," Jen suggested.

Their mother glared at her, and the three of them quickly went upstairs.

Messing a little gel into his chestnut hair, James grabbed his backpack and headed out into the cool September morning. He could worry about Nighthawk's disappearance later: there was a more pressing concern on his mind. He had made a fateful decision last night, and it was time to follow through.

James walked through the front doors of Cambilsford High, and the whispers started immediately. The story had already spread.

He narrowed his eyes and started down the hallway. Everyone watched carefully as he passed, and the whispers grew louder behind him, intermingled with muted laughs. He felt his skin prickling.

"James!"

He glanced to the right and saw his friend, Dennis, abandoning his still-open locker and hurrying toward him. James didn't slow down. He had to stay focused.

"Did you hear the news?" Dennis asked excitedly, almost jogging to keep up.

"Yeah," James said.

Dennis grinned. "We guessed it, remember? When we

saw that footage of the Flame returning to League headquarters alone? We knew that Nighthawk had been with him! Can you slow down?"

"No," James replied firmly.

"I bet the war's starting up again," Dennis said, grabbing his arm. "The League is going into panic mode, you can tell. Will you stop so we can talk about this?"

"I don't have time right now. I have to go."

Dennis scowled and pulled him to a stop. "You don't have time for a missing League member? Is this about Sara? You have to get over it! So she cheated on you. And okay, it was with your former best friend. But it happens. She got hotter, and now she thinks she has to date a football player . . ."

"I'm marching toward my own impending death," James said quietly, continuing down the hallway. "It's slightly more important."

"I hope you don't mean what I think you mean!" Dennis called after him.

James spotted Mark at the far end of the hallway, standing with a group of his football teammates.

All right James, he told himself. *Time to face your destiny.*

He walked up to Mark, grabbed his arm, and spun him around. James's right hand tightened into a fist, and with a sudden, unexpected movement, he launched a surprise attack at Mark's chin.

I'm doing it! James thought excitedly. *I'm beating up Mark!*

Then his knuckles made contact. The punch slid awkwardly off of Mark's broad chin, and pain flared in James's wrist and forearm. To make matters worse, Mark didn't seem the least bit affected. He just smiled calmly, and James knew he was dead.

Mark drew back his fist, and James watched in resigned defeat as it sailed toward his left eye. He felt the punch and the floor seemingly at the same time, and everything slipped into darkness.

Principal Gorm paced back and forth behind his desk, his round cheeks flushing pink with agitation. "This is the third time you've been beaten up this month, James," he said, wagging a pudgy finger.

"I'm not sure I'd consider them all as being 'beaten up' per se," James muttered.

He was perched uncomfortably on a stiff metal chair, where he'd been escorted soon after his bleary awakening on the hallway floor.

"Were you not in my office last week holding an ice pack to your eye?"

James shifted his current ice pack. "Well, that time, sure. But the time before that, I just had a split lip."

The principal shook his head. "You need to stop picking fights, James."

"He started it!" James protested.

"I talked to Mark already," Principal Gorm said. "He says you walked up to him and punched him, spraining your wrist in the process. And then he punched you, and you collapsed like a sack of potatoes." He winced a little. "Those were his words."

"You should be a counselor, Mr. Gorm. You're really boosting my spirits. And my wrist is fine. So he's a liar."

Principal Gorm sighed. "You can go home for the day and rest up," he said. "Keep the ice on. Tomorrow you have detention."

"For getting beaten up?" James asked, outraged. "I'm going to have to sit in the same room as Mark!"

The principal hesitated. "Well, no, actually. Mark has a game tomorrow. He won't be able to serve detention."

James glared at him. "Maybe I'm busy too."

"You don't play any sports."

"I almost made the badminton team."

"I'll see you at three."

James opened his mouth to retort but instead turned and stormed out of the office. He threw open the front doors with his left hand, since he was fairly sure his right one was sprained, and started down the steps. Thankfully, the bell had rung about twenty minutes earlier, and the parking lot was empty.

James hurried down the street. He was so upset that he didn't notice the gray van pulling out to follow him.

Fifteen minutes later, James crept into the house, slipped off his shoes, and tiptoed up the stairs.

"Is that you, James?" his mother called from the kitchen.

"No."

"Your principal called me about the fight. Are you hurt?"

"Only emotionally."

"That's good. Well, go lie down. We'll have a family discussion later."

"Can't wait!" James shouted, and slammed the door.

He stepped over the piles of clothing and collapsed face-first on his bed. He spent the rest of the day in that position, getting up only to use the bathroom and nibble on the bread from the turkey sandwich his mom left by the door. The only positive was that he convinced his parents to postpone the "family discussion" until the next morning, claiming dizziness.

Finally, after everyone else had gone to bed, he got up and went to brush his teeth.

When he finished, James shuffled back to his bedroom but stopped at the door, feeling a breeze.

That's odd, he thought. *I could have sworn the window was closed.*

He stepped into the room and flicked on the light. There, standing right in the middle of his bedroom, was the biggest man James had ever seen. He had to be almost seven feet tall and at least four hundred pounds. Enormous arms protruded from his forest-green T-shirt, like two tree trunks.

"Hello, James," he said.

Then something hard smacked James on the back of his head.

"Ow!" he cried, clutching the spot. A bump was already forming underneath his hair. James spun around to see a handsome young man in dress pants and a button-down shirt. He was holding a strip of hard leather and looking somewhat embarrassed.

"What did you do that for?" James asked sharply.

"I thought that worked?" the younger man said to the giant, ignoring James. "I told you I should have just done it my usual way."

The large man folded his arms. "I don't want you screwing with his mind. You just didn't do it right."

"Well, it's not the same if I just hit him again."

"I agree," James cut in. He knew he should probably be afraid, but he was already feeling a little woozy from the bump on his head. "How about no hitting?"

"Fine, I'll do it," the giant said.

James turned just in time to see a massive fist heading straight for his already-swollen eye.

This really isn't my day, James thought, and once again, there was blackness.

LANA TOOK ONE LAST LOOK AT HERSELF IN THE MIRROR, RUNNING a comb through her blond hair. She had decided to wear it down tonight, draped over the black hoodie she'd picked out for the bonfire. A sweatshirt and jeans wasn't the most glamorous outfit she could find, but that was the idea. She was still a little nervous about going to a party with college kids, even if Tasha's brother was there, and she didn't want to give them the wrong impression.

Satisfied, Lana switched off the light and headed downstairs. She had just reached the front door when a car pulled into the driveway, its headlights cutting through the darkness.

"All right, they're here!" she called to her parents. "I'll see you later!"

"Hold it just a minute!"

Lana held back a sigh as her mother scurried out of the living room. She carefully scanned Lana over and nodded.

"You look cute. Is Tasha going to come in and say hello?" she asked, looking past her at the waiting car. "When does the movie start again?"

"In twenty minutes," Lana said, feeling guilty for lying. "And her brother is dropping us off before he goes out, so I have to hurry."

Lana almost never lied to her mom, but Tasha had begged her to come tonight, and she had finally conceded. Of course, the only way she could go was to lie about it. Her mom was *very* overprotective: she would sooner put bars on Lana's window than let her go to a bonfire.

"Her brother?" Lana's mother asked suspiciously. She went to the door, and Tasha waved at her from the passenger's side. "How old is he again?"

"Eighteen. He's a good driver," Lana said, answering the next question on her mother's lips. "I've got to go. Call my cell if you need me." She pulled open the door. "I'll keep it on."

"Yes, you will!" her father shouted from the other room.

Her mom rolled her eyes. "Stop eavesdropping if you're not going to get up!" Then she leaned in to give Lana a kiss on the cheek. "I still don't think this is the best time to be going out at night . . ."

Ever since the news about Nighthawk's disappearance, Lana's parents had been strongly appealing for her and her brother to stay in the house after sunset. Thankfully, they'd stopped short of demanding it, but only because her brother had outright refused. Lana thought the whole thing was being overblown anyway. She'd never taken much interest in the League; two years ago, after the Night of Ashes, she'd basically been confined to the house for a month, and she was still bitter about it.

"Nighthawk disappeared in *Utah,* Mom," Lana said for the sixth time that day. "We live in Maine."

Her mother pointed a stern finger. "You don't know with those maniacs. People have been murdered all over the country. And you know it's always at night."

"I'll be fine," Lana replied soothingly. "Now put that thing away before you hurt somebody."

Her mother withdrew her finger, wringing her hands together instead. "I'm sorry. You know I worry about you, and . . ."

"I know," Lana said. "I'll be fine, okay? We're going to a crowded movie theater." More lying. *Am I becoming a bad kid?* she wondered. *When did that happen?* "I'll be back by midnight."

Her mother's eyes widened. "You'll be back at . . ."

"Eleven," Lana finished, smiling. "It was worth a shot. Bye, Mom. Bye, Dad!"

She started down the steps, shivering a little. The ocean was only a few blocks away, and a cold wind blew off the water this time of year. Lana's hair flapped around her as a particularly strong gust howled down the street.

Good thing I spent all that time combing it, she thought resignedly.

"Jeremy is at his friend's house," her mother called after her, leaning out the door. "Call him if you need a ride!"

Lana just shook her head and climbed into the car.

"Sorry," she muttered to Tasha's brother, who was wearing a lopsided grin. "She's a bit overprotective."

"I told him," Tasha said as they pulled out of the driveway. She waved at Lana's mom. "Do you think she suspects anything?"

"No," Lana replied, forcing a smile. She glanced at her mother on the porch and felt another surge of guilt. But it was too late now. "As long as I'm back by curfew, it'll be fine."

Tasha laughed. "We'll get you back in time. She'd have the cops looking for you at five after eleven."

"Yeah," Lana said as they drove down the street, leaving her waving mother behind.

Lana sat uncomfortably on one of the fallen logs that had been dragged around the bonfire. The trees at the edge of the beach almost looked like they were moving in the flickering orange glow.

Tasha was sitting beside her, but she was busy talking to one of her brother's friends, who'd been introduced as "Gongshow." Lana still had no idea what that meant, nor did she really care. She was cold, tired, and growing steadily more annoyed by the boisterous hooting from the boys around the fire. That, along with the lingering guilt of lying to her mom, had Lana definitely ready to go home.

"It's ten thirty," she said. "We should start walking back to the car soon."

Tasha turned to her, rolling her eyes. "It's like a two-minute walk and a five-minute drive. We'll be fine. Go talk to someone, have fun!"

"Yeah," the older boy said, grinning, "go have some fun!"

Lana glared at him. "Thank you, *Gongshow*." She shifted a little. "I have to go to the bathroom."

"There's an outhouse," Gongshow said, pointing to a tree. Tasha laughed like this was the funniest thing she'd ever heard.

Lana shook her head. Maybe she needed new friends. "Thank you," she snarled.

But Lana really did have to pee, so she reluctantly walked off into the trees. It was dark beneath the canopy, so she went just far enough that she could still see the fire through the shadows. The wind had picked up, and it was now howling overhead, loud enough that she could barely hear the others. Grimacing, she spotted a particularly large oak and decided to use it as cover. As Lana started toward it, she heard a snap.

She whirled around, terrified, and saw a boy emerge from the darkness, still zipping up his fly.

"Hey," he said. "Sorry if I scared you. You're Tasha's friend, right?"

"Uh . . . yeah," Lana replied awkwardly.

He stuck his hand out, and she looked at it in disgust.

"Oh, right," he said, pulling it back again.

I'll just hold it until I get home, Lana decided, starting back to the fire. A strong hand landed on her arm.

"Wait a second," the boy said. "What's the rush? We didn't even introduce ourselves yet. I'm Kyle."

"Lana," she replied coolly. "Can you take your hand off me, please?"

Kyle stepped in front of her. With his back to the fire, she couldn't really see his face, but it looked like he was grinning. "Sorry. Have I met you before?"

Lana tried to go around him, but he moved in her way.

"No," she said. "Excuse me."

Another strong gust of wind whipped through the trees.

"Stay for a bit," he said, coming a little closer. "Let's talk."

Lana stepped backward, feeling a tinge of fear. She didn't like the way he was looking at her. "We can talk back at the fire," she said, trying to get around him again.

He stopped her, grabbing her shoulders. "What's the big deal?" he asked, and then leaned in, trying to kiss her.

Lana lifted her hand and stuck it right on his forehead. It made a smacking noise when it hit. "The big deal is I don't want to," she said sweetly.

He leaned in again. "I can change your mind."

"I can change yours," Lana said, and kneed him in the groin.

He cursed and bent over. Lana hurried around him, but he snatched her wrist, jarring her elbow. "Wait!"

Without even looking at him, she grabbed one of his fingers with her free hand and wrenched it backward. He swore again and released her.

"I'd rather not," Lana snarled. But she'd only taken a few steps more when Kyle pulled her arm again, and this time, she lost her balance and tripped.

Lana hit the ground, smacking her cheek against the dirt. She lay there for a moment, dazed, and then looked up to see Kyle standing over her.

"Help!" she managed, but her voice was drowned out by the wind. The boys were shouting so loudly that no one could hear her.

She'd never felt so vulnerable, so *weak,* in her entire life. *What was I thinking coming here?* she thought. *I'm sorry, Mom.*

Lana was at his mercy now, and she knew it. Kyle was too strong for her. She thought she could see him grinning again, and she prepared to fight with everything she had.

Then she saw something move behind Kyle. It looked like one of the shadows had come to life, and it was now slinking toward him.

Lana realized it was a woman just as she leaned into Kyle's ear.

"Bad move," the woman whispered.

Kyle tried to turn around, but he didn't get the chance. In one lightning-fast motion, the woman jabbed him in the side of the neck, and he collapsed. Lana stared at his body in shock.

"Get up," the woman ordered Lana. She was wearing a scarlet bodysuit and had long black hair that fell almost to her waist.

Lana shakily climbed to her feet, her eyes still on Kyle. "Did you kill him?" She didn't know whether to be afraid of this woman or just relieved that she'd been saved.

"No," the woman said. "We'll leave that for another time. We'll leave that for you."

Lana frowned. "I don't understand."

"You will. Now, Rono."

Lana felt something jam into the small of her back, and then a numbing sensation flooded through her. She was unconscious before she hit the ground.

HAYDEN SLOWLY DESCENDED THE STAIRS, HIS EYES HALF-CLOSED. He wore only a pair of faded boxers, as was his usual daytime attire, and even they were beginning to devolve back into thread.

Reaching the bottom, Hayden absently kicked through a pile of cans, spilling liquid across the dirty hardwood floor. His bare feet made sticking noises as he walked toward the living room.

I need to start wearing socks, he mused.

Dan and Steve, his best friends, lay sprawled across two stained couches watching TV. They glanced at him as he walked into the room.

"You're alive," Steve observed. His T-shirt was riding up, and his hand was resting on his pale, protruding stomach.

"Sort of," Hayden said, stretching. He looked around the room. "I see you guys have been cleaning."

Empty cans, glasses, and dirty plates were everywhere.

Chips had been scattered in a finely crushed blanket all around the coffee table, which once had a glass top. Now the shards formed another sedimentary layer over the chips. This was of course a hazard, but Hayden had solved that problem by creating a trail of pizza boxes over the glass, which they now referred to as the "Bridge of Doom."

"Yeah, we did some work," Dan said, gesturing at the floor. A tiny space had been cleared away so he could rest his cup. "Looks good, right?"

"Better than ever," Hayden agreed, and then wandered into the kitchen to get a drink.

He found a glass that looked relatively clean and filled it with tap water. The counter was completely covered with dishes, so Hayden started to put them back into the cupboard.

"What are you doing?" a female voice asked.

Hayden turned around and saw a girl sitting at the table, eating a bowl of cereal. She had short brown hair and was wearing jeans and a red dress shirt. A backpack sat on the table beside her.

"Who are you?" Hayden asked.

"Liz. I'm Steve's girlfriend, remember? What are you doing?"

Hayden frowned and glanced at the cupboard. "Putting the dishes away?"

"They're *dirty*," she said, as if talking to a child.

"Yeah, I know," he replied, stacking more plates on the shelf. "That's the rule in this house. If you want to eat, you wash your own dishes. Everything in here is dirty."

Liz slowly pushed the bowl of cereal away from her, looking sick.

Hayden continued piling dishes until he'd freed up a big enough area to cook breakfast. He wiped his hands in satisfaction. "You're looking very put together," he commented, turning back to Liz. "Is it a school day?"

"Yes, Hayden," she replied coldly. "Some of us still go to school. We just came from there."

"Really? Wow, I slept longer than I thought. So Dan and Steve . . ."

"Were there too," she finished. "You should really start going again. I know you don't live with your parents, but . . ."

"Maybe tomorrow," Hayden said dismissively, heading back to the living room. He crossed the Bridge of Doom and plopped down onto a recliner.

Hayden hadn't been to school in two weeks, ever since the incident with his math teacher, Mrs. Hun. All Hayden had done was ask if she was in a bad mood because Attila was giving her a hard time at home. It seemed like a reasonable, and hilarious, comment to him. She didn't find it as funny.

Mrs. Hun had sent him to the office, where the principal had explained that Mrs. Hun was, in fact, getting a divorce, and gave Hayden a three-day suspension. Hayden was thrilled: he lived alone, so it was just a sentence to play more video games. By the time the suspension was over, he'd decided that he didn't want to go back.

"Steve, your girlfriend is yelling at me," Hayden complained. "I forgot you even had a girlfriend. She is cute, though."

"She can hear you," Steve said. "Your kitchen is right there."

Hayden shrugged. "I didn't say anything bad. It was a compliment. Granted, I'm not crazy about the short hair, but she's got pretty features."

"Very nice, Hayden," Liz said as she walked into the room. "You're a charmer. I'm leaving; your house disgusts me."

"Shh," Hayden replied, looking around in dismay. "You'll hurt its feelings."

Liz rolled her eyes and turned to Steve. "Call me later, when you leave. And fix your shirt!"

She marched out of the house, and the door slammed behind her. Steve looked like he was about to get up, but then he just turned up the volume on the TV instead.

"She seems nice," Hayden said. "Do we have to watch the news?"

Steve nodded. "They just released new info on the Nighthawk disappearance. Everyone was talking about it at school today. Apparently someone spotted a huge guy in that town in Utah, the one Nighthawk was last seen in. Didn't get a picture, but they said he matches the description of one of the guys from the Night of Ashes, and maybe even the same dude from the Portersfield Incident. Definitely one of the Villains."

"I'll care more when I get *my* superpowers," Hayden replied. "Until then, let the League deal with it."

"You're turning seventeen in three months," Dan said. "If you haven't got them by now, you're not going to."

"Hey, I still have three months." Hayden got to his feet and flexed. "Besides, I already have powers. It's pretty clear that these are supernatural abs."

"I'm going to be sick," Steve groaned, as Dan chuckled from the other couch.

"Well," Hayden said, "I suppose I should have a shower. It's been a day . . . or three. And I've got people coming over tonight." He looked down at his boxers. "Think I should change, or just go with these?"

Hayden was halfway up the stairs when the doorbell rang, but he ignored it. Despite his best attempts, he couldn't stop thinking about what Liz had said. Hayden had lived by himself for a while now, and though he was used to the fact that he didn't have a normal kid's life, a part of him still wanted one. Now he'd quit school, and his house really was becoming more and more disgusting.

I better go back on Monday, he thought. *One more weekend, and then I'll apologize to Mrs. Hun.*

The doorbell rang again.

"Dan, get it!" he called.

"You get it!" Dan shouted back.

"Fine. Lazy Dan."

Hayden walked the nine steps back to the front door and swung it open.

"Hello," he said slowly.

Standing on the porch was a gorgeous woman with long, strawberry-blond hair and a white dress shirt that was unbuttoned right to the point of interest. She smiled, revealing sparkling teeth.

"Sorry for bothering you," she said in a sweet voice, "but I'm moving in down the street, and I have a really heavy television in my van that I just can't lift by myself. Can you help me get it inside? Someone was supposed to meet me, but they didn't show."

"People these days," Hayden replied, conscious that he was still wearing only his boxers. "It's hard to find good help. Well, this is what neighbors are for."

"Who is it?" Dan shouted from the living room.

"No one!" he called, and turned back to the woman. "Shall we?"

"Thank you so much," she said. "Hopefully I can return the favor one day."

Hayden smirked and strolled outside in his bare feet. "I'm sure an opportunity will arise."

They crossed the street toward a black van that was parked a few houses down.

"Did you know the people who moved out of this house?" she asked, glancing at him.

"I don't even know the people right next door to me, except that they've phoned in two noise complaints."

She giggled. "A bit of a partyer?"

"I have the occasional get-together," he explained modestly. "I'm having one tonight actually, if you want to stop by."

"Maybe I will."

"Lovely. This is quite the van. If you were offering me candy, I might be worried."

She laughed and flung open the side door.

"Here it is," she said.

Hayden looked inside, dumbfounded. Televisions, computer screens, and camera equipment lined the entire interior of the van.

"Do you work in television?" he asked conversationally, eyeing her again.

"I do. Working my way up to be a reporter." She lightly scratched the skin above her cleavage. "The television is right over there. I'll get the other side."

She climbed into the van, pausing just for a moment as she bent to get through the door. Hayden grinned and followed her.

Suddenly, two very strong hands gripped his shoulders and pulled him in.

"What the . . ." Hayden shouted, and then one of the hands clasped tightly over his mouth. The door slammed shut.

Hayden heard duct tape being pulled off the roll, and then the woman stuck it over his mouth. He struggled for a moment and briefly caught a glimpse of a large man before he felt both his hands being tied behind his back. Then he was twisted around and lain on the floor. The metal felt very cold against his bare skin.

"The boss said he wants him sedated anyway," the woman said.

These have to be cops, Hayden realized in alarm. *I'm getting busted for all the skipping!* He'd had no idea it was this serious. Hayden tried to say, "I know my rights," but he couldn't move his lips against the tape.

He felt a sharp prick in his arm.

I should have told them I was going back, he thought sleepily, and then closed his eyes.

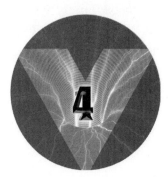

EMILY SAT IN HER BEDROOM, HUNCHED OVER THE COMPUTER.
Her fingers flew over the keyboard in a near blur, and lines of code scrolled across the screen. She was almost in.

Emily's bedroom was entirely black: the walls, the furniture, the carpet. Even the blinds had been taped to the window frame so that the morning sun couldn't sneak in along the edges. The only decorations were two framed photographs on her desk. One was of Emily and her grandfather, standing in the field behind his house with butterfly nets over their shoulders. The second was of a young girl sitting with her parents, all wearing happy smiles. She'd cut that one out of a magazine.

Emily matched her room in many ways. She always wore plain black clothes, but not to make any sort of political or emotional statement. Emily just liked black. Her raven hair blended into her outfit, creating a sharp contrast with her pallid skin. The kids at school called her "emo," but Emily still failed to see how a color choice could indicate a social categorization. She would have preferred to be called "nerd" if she'd had a choice of baseless stereotypes, but she was pretty much stuck with the label.

"Come on," she whispered as she broke through a sixth firewall.

Emily's computer screen abruptly shifted to a navy blue. She almost shouted in excitement but managed to rein it in. Her parents were fairly heavy sleepers, but the rare times Emily had woken them up, they had not been pleased.

Not that they're ever pleased, she thought dispassionately. Emily knew her bizarre family situation upset her teachers, the ones who cared at least, but it didn't affect her anymore. She'd dealt with those emotions as a little girl.

The League of Heroes' golden crest appeared on her screen: a circle surrounding four silhouettes, three men and one woman, representing the Four Founders. It was the most renowned symbol on the planet, and it meant that Emily had done what no hacker in the world had managed before. She'd cracked the League's network.

Her online persona, Black Arrow, was about to become even more infamous.

But Emily also knew the network was heavily policed, and her intrusion would be detected in moments. She had to move quickly.

Bypassing the entry screen, Emily ran a search for the archives. She found a folder called Collected Surveillance Footage and started downloading the most recent file.

A grainy video popped onto the screen, showing a warehouse on a run-down street. For a moment, nothing happened. Then a gray van with tinted windows pulled in front of the warehouse, and a huge man climbed out. He grabbed a metal crate from the back, spared a quick look in either direction, and then hurried inside.

Emily knew she'd just struck gold. Black Arrow was about to break the story to the world before anyone else: the League *did* have footage of Nighthawk's abductor, and he definitely matched the description of the Villain from the Night of Ashes incident. The League was covering it up.

Just then, an error message appeared: *unauthorized access.* Emily tried to override it, but the controls were frozen. The file disappeared, and the screen went black. After all that, she'd gotten nothing.

I'll try again tomorrow, Emily thought. She was disappointed, but it was to be expected. That would have been too easy.

Sighing, Emily glanced at the clock. 3:30 A.M. It was getting late, even for her. It was only Thursday, and she had to be up at seven for school. Rubbing her eyes, she looked down and saw that her black eyeliner had smeared off on her fingers.

After washing the eyeliner off in the bathroom, she brushed her teeth, only to decide she was still hungry.

Emily shuffled down the stairs in the darkness, her feet just skimming over the carpet. She flicked on the kitchen light and began pawing through the cupboards. After stuffing a wide assortment of items into her mouth, including a handful of chips, four Sour Patch kids, a dipped finger of peanut butter, and a leftover chicken wing, she switched off the light again and left the kitchen.

As she walked back toward the stairs, Emily felt her skin prickle. She froze. This wasn't the first time she'd had this feeling: like she was being watched.

Emily was somewhat of a paranoid kid growing up. When she was four, she told her parents that she was going to be abducted by a group of gnome-like people who would need her to save their world. At ten, she'd been convinced that an otherworldly race was observing her through her window, trying to discern if she was in fact one of their own trapped in a humanoid body.

But for the last few days, she had really felt it. This time, she knew someone was finally here for her. But who were they? Could the League have tracked her hacking attempts already? Had they come to arrest her?

Emily backed against the wall, senses alert. Her eyes were accustomed to the darkness, but the kitchen lights had momentarily blinded her. She scanned the hallway, trying to see through the glowing spots in her vision.

Emily stalked forward, bending slightly.

"I know you're here," she whispered. "I'm not afraid. Who are you?"

There was no answer.

"Come out," Emily said, louder this time. "Show yourself."

She thought she heard a quiet voice coming from behind the bathroom door, and she tiptoed toward it.

Emily was just reaching for the door when it burst open.

A short man stepped into the hallway. He was wearing a long brown trench coat, and a silver visor curved around the side of his head, covering his left eye. His dark skin almost made him invisible in the shadows.

"Who are you?" Emily asked. "I don't recognize you. You're not a League member. Well, it doesn't matter, I suppose. You're coming for me."

The short man shifted a little, looking confused, and then a woman stepped out behind him. She was wearing a scarlet bodysuit.

"What are you waiting for, exactly?" the woman asked the man. There was no mistaking the threat in her flashing green eyes.

Emily looked at her. "You're quite beautiful. You have a fantasy look to you, like an elf."

The woman raised one slender eyebrow.

"I'm going to stun you now," the man said, hoisting a gun. "Sorry, it's a formality."

Emily took a step backward. "That's a strange formality. I have to say, I would rather you didn't. And now that I take a second to think about it, you don't particularly look like good guys. It's the odd pairing maybe, or the unspoken threat of the elf woman. After all, why would you be stunning me if you weren't evil?"

"It will all be explained," the man said. "This won't hurt."

"I should probably leave a note. I'm going to my grandpa's house tomorrow night, and he'll be worried if I don't show up."

"I'll send him a message," he told her.

"Please stun her," the woman said.

"Right." He thrust the stun gun toward Emily, but she took another quick step backward and put her hands on her hips.

"It's not very polite to just fly at me with it," Emily reprimanded.

"Sorry," he said. "Can I stun you now?"

"Now I'm not so sure," she said haughtily. She had been inching toward the hall closet, and now her hands found the doorknob.

"Watch her . . ." the woman warned.

The man started toward Emily. "Now, that's enough. Don't make me use this one." He gestured at the rifle slung over his back.

Emily narrowed her eyes. "You'll be sorry, then."

All at once, Emily threw open the closet door behind her and grabbed a wooden cane. The man rushed forward to stun her, but she wheeled out of the way and smashed the cane into his arm. The stun gun clattered to the ground, and he swore under his breath, clutching his wrist. The woman laughed.

Emily circled to the left, the cane pointed in their direction. "I am not a defenseless maiden to be captured at whim."

The man scowled and swung the larger rifle around.

But before he could pull the trigger, Emily's cane lashed out and hit the barrel of the weapon, knocking it from his hands. She took a big step toward him, ready to swipe at his feet. In a flash, the woman was beside her, holding the cane in an iron grip.

Emily glanced at her. "You *are* like an elf."

The man picked up his stun gun and fired into Emily's stomach.

SAM YAWNED AND SLID OUT OF BED. THE SMELL OF BACON WAS wafting in from the hallway, so he quickly grabbed the pre-arranged Friday outfit from his desk chair.

It was his favorite outfit of the week: a pair of crisp jeans and a baggy red shirt that he affectionately called his tunic. Wearing a tunic seemed very heroic and chivalrous, so on Fridays, Sam made a special effort to fulfill those virtues. As a true supporter of the League of Heroes, it was the least he could do. But despite his best efforts at chivalry, Sam was still picked on by just about every kid in school, and he couldn't understand why. Even the younger grades made fun of him.

Sam wasn't about to quit now, though. His hero, Captain Courage, wouldn't let a little name-calling and shoving get to him, so neither would he.

He glanced at the Courage action figure on his dresser, wearing the League's famed navy-blue uniform. It was his most prized collectible. Five years ago, Captain Courage had disappeared without a trace. Sam still remembered that day, even though he was only six years old at the time: the panicked headlines, Phoenix's grave public address. After that, they'd stopped making Courage merchandise.

Once he was dressed, Sam trotted down the stairs, his curly black hair bouncing as he went. He was the shortest one in his entire grade and so skinny that a soccer ball had once knocked him over in gym class. Even the teacher had laughed at him for that.

"Good morning, everyone," Sam said brightly as he entered the kitchen. As usual, his mother was busy cooking, and his father was shoveling down breakfast before work.

"Good morning, Sammy," his mother replied, turning from the stove. "How did you sleep?"

Sam took a seat at the table next to his father. "Perfectly, thank you."

His father stood up immediately. "I'm going to work."

"Bye, Dad," Sam said. "Have a great day."

"Yeah," he muttered, and walked out of the kitchen.

Sam didn't talk to his father very much anymore. He used to coach Sam's baseball team, but now that Sam had given it up, it seemed they had nothing to talk about. Sam would have kept playing, but it got a little boring sitting on the bench all game. He didn't even get to swing the bat.

His mother handed him a plate piled high with eggs, bacon, and toast just as his older brother, Hugh, moped into the kitchen. Hugh shuffled to the counter, saw that his breakfast wasn't ready, and then plopped down at the table. Sam's brother was almost a carbon copy of their father, from his athletic build to his dark skin. Sam had a slightly lighter complexion, like his mother's, adding to the long list of things the brothers didn't have in common.

"Morning, Hughie," Sam said. "How you feeling today?"

He glared at Sam. "Don't call me that. I've told you a thousand times. It's Hugh."

"I like Hughie better."

"I don't care," Hugh snarled.

"Be nice," their mother cut in. "Hugh, your breakfast will be ready in a few minutes."

"Thanks," he mumbled.

As usual, the brothers ate in silence.

"Thank you," Sam said, bringing his empty plate to the counter.

"You're very welcome," his mother replied.

Sam threw on his overfull backpack and headed out the door.

His school was only a ten-minute walk, and homeroom didn't start for thirty minutes. But Sam liked to leave early, just in case he witnessed a traffic accident or some other sudden cause for heroism. He also liked to sit down at his desk before the other kids arrived so he could avoid being picked on in the hallways.

Sam had just started down the sidewalk when he noticed an elderly woman about to cross the street. *And on a Friday!* he thought.

"Excuse me, ma'am!" he called, hurrying over. "Do you need any help?"

She looked at him suspiciously. "Sure," she said at last, extending a frail arm. "Why not?"

"You can never be too careful," Sam told her as he looked both ways.

"Especially you," she replied meaningfully. "If I were a child, I would be afraid to walk to school."

"Right," Sam replied. He had no idea what she was talking about.

He dropped her off on the sidewalk, and she turned to him. "Don't talk to any more strangers today, understand? It's not safe." She leaned in, lowering her voice. "And lock your windows. Some have been taken right out of their bedrooms!"

"Okay," Sam murmured, backing away. She was starting to scare him. "Bye, now."

Sam hurried on his way, disturbed by the old woman's warning. He stayed well clear of an old gray van parked by the curb and turned onto another road. But soon, he had forgotten all about the woman's strange words and was instead thinking about how heroic it had been to help her cross the street. If only the kids at school had seen that.

As he turned the next corner, Sam felt a strange sensation at the back of his head. He slowed down and scratched it. Deciding it was nothing, he picked up his step again. Then he heard a quiet voice.

Slow down, it was saying. *Go to sleep.*

"I can't miss school," Sam said out loud without thinking. "What if there's a pop quiz?"

The voice grew louder, though it seemed like it was coming from far away. *Slow down,* it said again. *Go to sleep.* It was almost as if they were his own thoughts now, and his eyelids were becoming increasingly heavy.

Sam's pace slowed again, until he was barely shuffling along the sidewalk. *How strange to get so tired,* Sam thought. As soon as he broke the repeating message, a slight burst of energy flooded his limbs. But then the voice got even louder, and Sam slowed almost to a halt, his eyes barely open.

He looked around and saw a comfortable-looking patch of grass. So he walked over to it, lay down, and curled into a ball. People stared as they drove by.

That's okay, he thought. *They won't mind if I sleep for a bit.* Or maybe it was the voice speaking. He couldn't tell which was which anymore.

Just as Sam closed his eyes, he heard a vehicle screech to a stop and felt large, powerful hands lift him. *Maybe it's Mom,* he thought happily. But her hands seemed rather big, and she smelled kind of bad today. *Oh well,* Sam mused. Then he fell fast asleep.

JAMES BLINKED, STRAINING TO OPEN HIS HEAVY EYELIDS.
He saw a flash of crimson and then closed them again,
confused. He had never felt so groggy in his life and
wondered how long he'd been asleep. Only then did he
remember how he had gone to sleep in the first place.

The giant punched me! James thought. It had been like
getting hit in the face with a truck.

His mind began to clear, and James realized that he was
lying flat on his back. As he sat up, he saw that he was in a
bedroom furnished with very expensive-looking furniture.
A large mahogany dresser stood beside the queen-sized
bed he was lying in, along with a matching night table and
a small chair. The walls and ceiling were painted a deep
crimson.

He got up and quietly snuck toward the door, afraid of
alerting his captors. He didn't know why he'd been abducted,

but it obviously wasn't random. The giant had used his name.

He eased the handle of the bedroom door open and gingerly poked his head out, terrified of finding the enormous man standing guard. The bedroom was in the middle of a short hallway, finished in the same dark red color as the room he woke up in. To his right was a bare wall, but to his left, the hallway opened into a larger room, and there were two more identical black doors along the way. It was completely silent.

James crept along the wall, subconsciously hunching as he went. He stopped at the first door, turned the knob, and peeked inside.

It was another bedroom, and a boy was lying there, blinking at the ceiling. Before James could say anything, the boy stretched and sat up.

"This isn't my room," he said pleasantly, as if discussing the news.

The boy looked tall, even sitting on the bed, and he was handsome, with blue eyes, high cheekbones, and brown hair that looked almost purposefully messy. The only thing he was wearing was a pair of gray boxers that were well past their prime.

"Very strange," the boy continued, looking thoughtful. "It's coming back to me now. I was drugged by a hot blonde who wanted me to move her TV. I remember it all perfectly, actually. I wonder what they used."

He didn't seem overly concerned about the fact that he had been drugged and kidnapped.

The boy perched himself on the edge of the bed. "Hayden, by the way. Look at me, rambling on without even asking your name. You look like a Eugene. Close?"

James raised his eyebrows. "James. Back up a second. You got drugged by a blond woman?"

"Yeah. I assumed she was a cop, but I don't think it's standard practice to drug someone when you arrest them," he said, looking around the bedroom. "That, and the fact that this would be the nicest prison I've ever seen. Did she get you too?"

James shook his head. "No, two men. One of them punched me in the face."

"That's rough," Hayden said, climbing to his feet. "And now here we are. Speaking of which, where are we?"

"I don't know," James replied. "It looks like a weird house or something, but I'm not sure."

"Well, let's find out," Hayden said simply, and walked out into the hallway.

"We should be a little quieter," James whispered, rubbing his eye. It felt swollen, but not nearly as bad as he thought it would be. And his wrist seemed to be almost completely healed, which was just as strange.

Hayden opened the door across the hall and looked inside. "Here's another one!"

James hurried over. A girl was lying on the bed, her pale face framed by a tangle of black hair. She was still asleep.

Hayden walked right over to the bed and shook her. "Wake up!"

Immediately, the girl's eyes shot open, and she grabbed Hayden's wrist. "Are you with the elf woman?" she asked in a low voice.

Hayden glanced at James. "The elf woman?"

"Yes," she continued, still clutching Hayden's arm. "The one who abducted me. She was with a small man wearing a visor."

"This is getting weird," James muttered.

"Are you abductors or abductees?" she asked sharply.

"Abductees," Hayden assured her, wincing as her fingernails dug into his skin.

The girl released him. "Oh, sorry." She climbed to her feet and scanned James. He felt uncomfortable under her intense gaze.

"We should keep moving," Hayden said slowly, starting for the door. "You want to come . . . ?"

"Emily," she said.

James and Emily followed him down the hall, and together they walked out into a huge, rectangular sitting area. It was as big as the entire main floor of James's house, and the ceiling was at least two stories high. But despite its size, the room was sparsely furnished.

Four black leather couches ringed a wooden coffee table, while another two recliners sat off to the side. A second table stood between the recliners, set up with a white and black marble chessboard. The walls were bare, except for the one opposite the hallway they'd emerged from, which was almost entirely covered by a floor-to-ceiling mirror.

James spotted another hallway running parallel to theirs across the room, but as he started to walk that way, something else caught his attention. A massive, black stone fireplace stood between the two hallways, and above it, some sort of symbol had been painted onto the wall. It was a black, inverted triangle with six silhouettes in the middle.

It reminded James of the League of Heroes's crest, except with two added figures, and black instead of gold. *Where are we?* he thought.

"Nice," Hayden commented, staring at the fireplace. "This is the best kidnapping I've had in a while."

James spun around to face him, and Hayden grinned. "Just joking. First kidnapping."

James stared at him in disbelief and then continued on to the second hallway with Emily close behind. Once again, there were three doors. James opened the first one and found another identical bedroom. This time, it contained a small, skinny boy in a weird shirt.

Hayden opened the next door. "This kidnapping keeps getting better!" he said.

James glanced at Emily and then went to join Hayden. "Can you wake that kid up?" he called to her over his shoulder.

James followed Hayden through the door, where they found a blond girl lying on the bed, fast asleep.

"Cute, right?" Hayden said knowingly. He clapped his hands right next to her ear. "Wake up!"

The girl jumped and instinctively kicked Hayden in the stomach. He toppled to the floor.

"Ow," Hayden wheezed as James took a big step away from the bed.

"Where am I?" the girl asked, sounding close to hysteria. "Who are you?" She backed against the headboard. "Where am I?" she shouted.

"It's okay," James said, holding up his hands. "We won't hurt you."

"Answer the question!" she demanded.

"We don't know," Hayden mumbled, getting up again. "Do you play soccer or something?"

"Listen, we just woke up here too," James said soothingly. "We're trying to find a way out."

"A way out?" She looked past him at the door. "Are we being held captive?"

"Well, we could go ask whoever's behind that one-way mirror in the other room," Hayden suggested.

James hadn't thought of that. "You think they're spying on us?"

"Probably," Hayden said, heading back into the hallway. "There's only one way to find out. But first . . ." He opened the last door. "It's a bathroom," he told them. "Black tiles, very nice."

Hayden hurried back just as Emily and the skinny boy emerged from the other bedroom. The blond girl tentatively stepped out behind James, and for a moment, they all just looked at each other.

"So," Hayden said to the two newest members of the group. "What are your names? I'm Hayden, that's Emily, and this is James."

"I'm Sam," the boy said, looking terrified.

"Lana," the blond girl replied. "So no one knows why we're here?"

"Nope," Hayden said, "but let's find out." He walked up to the mirror and stood with his hands on his hips. "All right! What's the deal? We're a little confused in here!"

Nothing happened.

"Well, you talk it over," Hayden said.

"How do you know someone's behind there?" Sam whispered.

Hayden glanced at him. "Of course someone's there. Don't you watch movies?"

"Yes," Sam responded uncertainly.

They waited in silence for a minute, and then Hayden turned back to them with a guilty expression. "Or I'm wrong . . ."

As soon as he said it, they heard a click, and a door swung open out of the mirror. They all took a step backward, except for Hayden.

"See?" he said, grinning smugly.

James's enormous abductor walked out, and five others followed him. There was a short man with a visor, a beautiful woman in a red bodysuit, the handsome guy who had hit James with the club, a pale man with shoulder-length hair wearing a long cape, and finally, an older man with piercing blue eyes and a goatee.

They lined up in front of the younger group, examining them. James noticed that the giant was staring right at him, so he hastily averted his eyes.

"Welcome," the older man said. "You are awake at last. Now we can finally begin."

LANA FOUGHT THE URGE MAKE A BREAK FOR THE EXIT. SHE had a sneaking suspicion she wouldn't get very far. Worse still, the woman was staring at her with an absolutely terrifying intensity. Lana could almost *feel* the woman's displeasure.

"You obviously have questions," the older man continued. "I will answer the most pressing first. You have been taken for a specific reason, and you are being offered a special gift. These," he said, gesturing toward his companions, "are your mentors. Each has selected one of you, and you will function as their protégé. You will all live here together. At selected times, you will train one-on-one with your mentors or in larger sessions as a group. You will not be allowed to leave until your training is complete."

"What exactly are we training to *be*?" Hayden asked.

"Somehow I don't think this is an apprenticeship program. Unless it's for a weird fashion school, in which case, I'm loving the cape," he said to the long-haired man.

The older man turned to him. "Don't you recognize any of us?"

Hayden shook his head. "Nope, and I have to say, I'd probably remember if I'd seen you before."

"I do," Emily said quietly, and everyone looked at her in surprise. She nodded at the giant. "You abducted Nighthawk."

The older man raised his eyebrows. "I thought the League was hiding that information. In any case, you are correct, my dear. Allow me to introduce you." He turned to the big man. "This is the Torturer. Beside him is our youngest member, Sliver. Then we have Rono," he said, and the short man nodded. "Avaria, and finally, Leni."

The caped man just stared at them darkly.

"And I am the Baron," he finished, turning back. "We are the enemies of your famed League of Heroes. We are the shadows they are fighting against."

"You're the *Villains*?" James asked quickly, and then bit his lip, as if terrified that he'd spoken.

The Baron nodded, his gaze drifting to the symbol on the wall. "That is what they call us, yes. Rather uncreative, I think. We prefer to go by the Vindico."

"Sounds serious," Hayden said. "What does it mean?"

The Baron smiled. *"Vengeance."*

Lana's hands began to tremble. She was standing a few

feet away from the most dangerous people on the planet. "What do you need us for?" she asked.

He met her eyes. "You're to be the next generation, of course."

Lana looked at the other teens and saw the same bewilderment on their faces. Everyone, that is, but Emily's. She just nodded and raised her hand.

"Hi, I'm Emily," she said in a formal tone. "Nice to meet you all."

The Baron frowned at her, but she continued unabashedly.

"I have a few questions. First, I wouldn't mind knowing who each of you has selected as their protégé. I've been trying to guess, and I want to see if I'm right."

"Yeah," Hayden agreed. "No one here picked me. I was abducted by a blond woman."

"Kayla works for me," Leni said, clasping his gloved hands behind his back. "You will be my protégé."

"Oh . . . sweet," Hayden muttered.

"I've selected James," the Torturer said, and James's eyes widened.

"Sam will work with me," Sliver remarked. He wore a look of contempt, and Lana felt a pang of sympathy for Sam, whose lip was quivering.

"Emily," Rono said gruffly.

"Leaving Lana as my choice," Avaria finished, threat evident in her voice. Lana stole a quick glance at her supposed mentor. She remembered the languid, deadly shadow in the forest and her lightning-fast attack on Kyle.

Should I thank her? she thought. *Or run as fast as I can the other way?*

"Now you know," the Baron said. "As for me, I will be providing oversight for all your training, and so I have not taken a protégé for myself."

Emily nodded. "I see. But I must ask: what if we don't want to be your protégés? What if we don't want to fight the League? They are *superheroes,* you know; good and just and all that."

For the first time, Lana saw anger in the Baron's blue eyes. "I'm afraid you have no choice in the matter," he replied coolly. "You have been selected, and you will follow through with your training. Those of you who do not"—he paused, and looked at each of them in turn—"will be disposed of."

"I suspected as much," Emily said, "you being villains and all. Still, I'm sure some of our families are probably concerned. A police search might be under way."

Lana thought about her parents and wondered what they were doing. They would know by now that she hadn't gone to the movies. They must be searching the forest for her. Did they find Kyle's unconscious body? What had he told them? Lana remembered how terrified she was as he stood over her, wearing that arrogant grin. She never wanted to feel so helpless again.

The Baron laughed. "I assure you, they won't find you here. But don't look so forlorn. You are being offered a *gift*. Powers beyond your comprehension. The ability to strike back at a world that has been cruel to you."

He gestured at the group around him.

"My companions and I are prepared to grant you the power to do anything you want. We are willing to accept you as one of our own. From billions, you have been given this opportunity. Do not spurn it. You will see your family and friends again. But you will return to them as entirely new people. Someone strong, someone to be *respected*."

Lana saw that the other kids were now hanging on his every word. James almost looked hypnotized.

"But how can you give us superpowers?" Hayden asked. "I thought you had to be born with them."

"That," he said, "is the single most important lie the League of Heroes is built upon. It's a lie they have killed to protect. And it is also the reason the Vindico exists."

"But Courage said that—" James started.

The Baron cut him off. "You will come to learn that many things the League has told you are fabrications. When you learn the truth, you will see who the *true* villains are. But that's enough for now. Today you will have a chance to acquaint yourselves with one another. Some of you might be taken out for a quick interview with your mentor, but the real lessons won't begin until tomorrow."

He pointed at the wall to the right of the mirror.

"There is a panel on that wall that will open three times a day with food and drink. I will send some along shortly. We will announce who is to come for an interview later. Until then, I leave you with this thought: are any of you truly *happy* with the way you are now?"

He strode back through the door, and the rest of the Villains slowly followed, some taking one last look before they went. The door clicked shut, and the teens were left standing alone in front of the mirror, their reflections staring back at them.

"WELL, IT'S SETTLED," HAYDEN SAID AFTER A MOMENT, turning his head in both directions as he looked at his reflection in the mirror. "I am breathtakingly gorgeous."

He turned to Lana, who was still studying her reflection. "I don't want to alarm you," he whispered, "but I think that cute blond girl is checking you out."

Lana scowled and looked away.

"Can we talk about what's going on?" James asked incredulously. "We've been kidnapped by the *Villains!*" He gestured at the now-closed mirror door. "These people are responsible for the murders of eleven League members; possibly twelve if Nighthawk is dead. Not to mention all the civilians!" He lowered his voice. "The League will figure out that we've been kidnapped soon and come for us. Emily, how did you know that big guy abducted Nighthawk?"

"There's footage," she said. "I saw it. The League knows who it was."

"So they'll track these people down," James said. "I think we should—"

"My mentor guesses were off," Hayden interrupted, glancing at Emily. "What about yours?"

"I was largely correct," she replied. "Except for my own. I thought the elf woman had selected me."

"You're talking about the *selections*?" Lana asked, looking between the two of them in disgust. "Doesn't it bother either of you that we're being imprisoned?"

"To be fair, it's a nice prison," Hayden responded.

"It's still a prison," Lana argued, "and they have no right to hold us here."

"Exactly," James said. "Though I wouldn't mind learning more about these powers. If we had powers, we could break out of here, no problem. The League might even let us join and . . ." Lana shot James a dirty look, and his cheeks flushed. "But still, not cool," he added.

"My mom is going to be worried sick," Sam mumbled. "One time she almost called the police when I came home ten minutes late from school."

Hayden choked back a laugh. When everyone looked at him, he just smiled at Sam reassuringly. "Don't worry, I'm sure they'll let you send a message or something."

Sam shook his head. "I don't know why they picked me. I don't even like movies with bad guys."

"You *are* a strange selection," Hayden agreed. "I'm kind of a jerk, so I can see why they picked me."

"Do you think they chose us because they think we're bad people?" Sam breathed, as if that idea alarmed him more than anything else.

"I suspect it has more to do with our *potential* to be bad people," Emily replied. "He said that the world has been cruel to all of us in some way, remember?" She ran her fingers along the corner of the mirror, as if testing for structural weaknesses.

"What do we do now?" Sam asked.

"We'll have to wait," Hayden replied. "What else can we do?" He turned back to the mirror. "Can you send in some nachos?" he shouted, and then smiled at Lana. "I figure some communal food will help break the ice."

"What is wrong with you?" she snapped. "We've been kidnapped! They're going to kill us if we leave! Aren't you worried about your family?"

Hayden shrugged. "Well, Steve and Dan are probably wondering where I am, but they'll just assume I'm on a sleep bender. It happens. And my mom doesn't come by the house anymore, so I'm good there."

Lana frowned. "You don't live with your parents?"

"Nope. Got my own pad."

"That explains a lot," she muttered under her breath. "James, you seem normal enough. What do you think we should do?"

"I really don't know," he said. "For now at least, I guess we have to wait and see what happens."

"What about your parents?" Lana persisted. "Your friends?"

James shifted a little. "Truthfully, everyone probably expected me to skip school today. I doubt they've even called the police yet."

Lana turned to Sam, who was still staring at the closed door. "*You* at least have parents who are going to worry?"

Sam nodded, and his eyes started to water. "Yes. My mom must be so upset. I need to talk to her. I don't even know how long it's been!" A tear ran down his cheek, and he quickly wiped it with the back of his hand.

"Not too long," Emily said from across the room, where she was inspecting the inside of the stone fireplace.

"How do you know?" Lana asked.

Emily peered up the chimney. "Well, we could only go so long without food or water." She looked back. "But judging from the amount of hair on my legs, it's possible that we were asleep for two or three days."

Lana knelt down and felt her leg. "She's right. I shaved right before I went out, and it usually takes a couple days to grow back."

"A couple days?" Sam whispered.

"Ah, the science of leg hair," Hayden said. "Well, this is all pretty fascinating, but I have to use the bathroom."

When he came back to the common room, Emily was still wandering around, running her hands along the wall where the food panel was supposed to be. Lana was attempting to calm Sam down on one of the couches, while James sat opposite them staring thoughtfully at the black symbol over the fireplace.

Hayden sat down next to him. "So, James, why was everyone expecting you to skip school?" Hayden asked him as he plopped his feet up on the coffee table.

"I don't want to get into it."

Hayden nodded. "That bad, huh? Girl problems?"

"More or less," James muttered, rubbing his swollen eye.

"I see," Hayden said. "Shotgun Lana, by the way."

James quickly glanced at Lana, but she seemed not to have heard him. "Lana is sitting like six feet away from us," he whispered. "And you can't shotgun people."

"Sure you can. Now there won't be any future misunderstandings."

"Are you even a little concerned about this situation?"

"They said they just want to train us," Hayden said. "What's so scary about that? I wasn't learning much in English class anyway. Well, I assume I wouldn't have been had I been there."

"But they're going to teach us to be supervillains," James pointed out. "Super. . . . villains," he repeated slowly, as if speaking to a child.

"And your point is . . ." Hayden replied.

A whooshing noise made them both look up, followed by a thump. A section of the wall had slid open to reveal five plates of steaming pasta and a pitcher each of milk and water. In front of it, Emily was picking herself up off the floor.

"No nachos," Hayden said, disappointment evident in his voice.

James jumped to his feet. "Who cares what it is. I'm starving."

Soon the five of them were digging in hungrily.

"I'm going to eat way better here than I did at home," Hayden remarked, patting his bare stomach. "I hope we get a treadmill."

James turned to the mirror. "Can you please send him some clothes?"

"So, our plan has finally begun," the Baron said, folding his wrinkled hands on the table.

The Vindico were gathered in the Baron's meeting room, seated at a massive, elaborately carved wooden table depicting villagers fleeing from a dragon. The walls were black and adorned with bloodred tapestries of the Vindico's crest.

All were present except Avaria, who had decided to skip the meeting.

"So it has," Leni agreed from the far end of the table. He was absently tracing a gloved finger against his cheek. "But whether it will be worth our time is still up for debate."

"I agree," Rono said. He had removed his trench coat, revealing the metallic apparatus that covered his right shoulder. "And I still think murdering Nighthawk was a mistake. We've awoken the League to our return. How can that possibly help?"

The Baron turned to him. "That murder was a necessary part of the plan. The League is nervous now. They cannot venture out to investigate the disappearance of these children for fear that they will be picked off next."

"And while they cower in their headquarters, we'll be training our protégés," the Torturer said. He rubbed his massive hands together. "It's perfect."

"The League will find us eventually," Leni argued. "And we're all sitting ducks in this place when they do."

The Baron shook his head. "By the time they find us here, it will be too late. Our newest members will turn the tide of this war. We will finally have our revenge."

"And what if we can't get these kids to cooperate? What if they turn against us?" Sliver asked.

"Then we kill them," the Baron replied simply. "But to ensure that doesn't happen, we will coincide the training with a psychological program. Step one is to emotionally separate them from their friends and families. When they are adrift in their own self-pity, they will seek guidance, purpose, and power. That's where we come in. And to begin that isolation, we will use the announcements."

The Torturer grinned. He'd been looking forward to these. "Who's first?"

AVARIA SAT ALONE IN ONE OF THE BARON'S GUEST ROOMS WITH the heavy curtains drawn shut. Just enough light snuck in to illuminate the crumpled photograph she held in her hands. It was worn from travel, and the corners had begun to pull apart. But it was the only one she had, and Avaria took it everywhere.

An attractive young couple smiled out of the photo, sitting on a park bench in fall. One was a woman she didn't know, and the other a man she had desperately loved. They were both dead now.

"I'm trying," she whispered. "I can't find him."

There was a booming knock at the door. Avaria tucked the photo into the bottom of a drawer and composed herself in the mirror. She never showed any sign of weakness to the others.

The door rattled again, and Avaria answered it. The

Torturer stood there, his pronounced, Neanderthal features twisted into a smile. Avaria glared at him. "Yes?"

"We're going to do the first announcement," he said, "and we were hoping to start with Lana. We think she'll be the easiest to crack."

Avaria considered this. She had been hesitant about the personal announcements when the Baron first proposed them, but he was confident that the added emotional turmoil would push the kids toward their mentors.

"Very well," Avaria said. "I'll come to see her reaction."

Avaria followed the Torturer down the left wing of the Baron's manor. The enormous, redbrick mansion stood three stories high with an additional two levels beneath the ground. It also stretched the length of a football field, flanked on either end by two towers, and contained over a hundred rooms. The sprawling property was nestled in a forest some three hours from the closest town and kept well manicured by the Baron's servants.

"So," the Torturer said as they started down a flight of winding stairs, "did you hear? The League has been gathering at their headquarters."

Avaria studied the paintings lining the walls. "The Baron mentioned that, yes. It is to be expected with Nighthawk's murder. They will be afraid to travel individually."

"And now five kids go missing within a week," he added. "Did you see the paper today? It's on the front page. The whole country is in a panic."

Avaria sneered. "Good. They'll begin to wonder if their precious League can still protect them."

They reached the main floor and walked into an opulent hallway with ceilings twice as high as the Torturer. Real gold trim ran along the walls, while black statues of mythical creatures, knights, and the Baron's ancestors stood between every doorway.

They turned into the narrow control room, where the protégés' common area could be seen through a one-way mirror. Sliver and Rono were already waiting there.

"I just think we need to speed up the process," the Torturer continued, settling into a chair. It groaned under his weight. "If the League gets the drop on us here, we could all be wiped out at once."

"Let them come," Avaria said softly. "It's been too long since I've killed a League member." The three men looked at each other uneasily. "But I don't think they'll find us for a while," she continued. "The Baron has this mansion well hidden."

She watched as Lana leaned forward on the couch, listening to James tell a story.

"Give her the announcement," Avaria said coolly. "Let's see how she takes it."

"There were four League members in the house," James told them. "Phoenix, Dane, Falcon, and Mind. Those four were close friends and had moved in together a couple months before. None of the members lived alone; figured they were safer in groups, I guess. Well, it was four in the morning, so everyone was asleep. There hadn't been an attack in over a year, so maybe everyone just let their guard down."

James glanced pointedly at the mirror.

"That's when *they* showed up. No one knows how many exactly; the only witness reported seeing a large man crossing under a streetlight nearby and three others in the shadows. Anyway, they must have gotten in real quietly because the League report says that Phoenix was killed in her sleep. Someone broke her neck."

The other teens were silent, intently listening to James's story. They'd started talking about the history of the Vindico's war with the League, and James was now recounting their most famous attack, the Night of Ashes.

"They suspect that Mind woke up when Phoenix was killed; he might have felt the loss of her consciousness. Obviously, at that point he would have sensed the Villains and called for the others to wake up." James shook his head. "They never really had a chance. Dane never made it out of his room, and Falcon was killed as soon as he came through the door. Mind just had time to contact Thunderbolt before they killed him too."

"Terrible," Lana murmured.

"Yeah. And then, I guess to cover up their tracks, they set the place on fire before they left. It spread to two other houses next door and killed seven civilians. That's partly why they call it the Night of Ashes, but more so, it's because of Phoenix. People kept hoping they were going to find her alive in there, I guess, like the bird. After that, Thunderbolt was the only Founder left, and the League went into disarray. Some people thought the Villains had won the war. But against all odds, Thunderbolt managed to rally the League, and they started a ruthless hunt for the killers. The Villains went into hiding, and they haven't been heard from since."

"Until now," Emily finished thoughtfully.

Hayden stretched his arms over his head. "This is all too depressing for me. Let's change the subject."

"To what?" James said sourly.

"Hmm . . . does anyone have a significant other?" Hayden asked, looking around.

James scowled. "Is that really important right now?"

"Just answer the question," he said. "It will help us get to know each other. Sam?"

"No," Sam replied, his cheeks flushing.

"No," James said.

"Negative," Emily added.

Hayden glanced at Lana. "And yourself?"

She shook her head.

"A good-looking girl like you?" Hayden scoffed. "You must have a terrible personality."

Lana gave him a dirty look.

"I really need to go home," Sam said. He was tightly hugging his legs to his chest and had been since James started the story. "I keep thinking of my mom."

"Me too," Lana agreed. "First chance, I'm gone."

"I don't think that's a good idea," Hayden pointed out. "Getting disposed of sounds bad."

Emily nodded. "We should ask if we can send messages home. I need to tell my grandpa I'm okay."

"Yeah, I'm sure they'll be very understanding," James muttered. "They seem so pleasant, after all."

"What do you think—" Lana began, but was cut off as a voice materialized out of nowhere.

"Attention." James recognized the deep voice of the Torturer. "James and Sam, you will have the first interviews. And we also have an announcement concerning Lana." It sounded like he could barely contain his amusement.

Lana perked up, looking wary.

"While conducting their surveillance, Avaria and Rono discovered something very interesting. It turns out Lana's father, whom she is so concerned about getting back to, is not the family man she thinks he is. Every Tuesday night, when her father says he is going to his friend Dale's house for poker and drinks, he is actually meeting a younger woman from his office named Clara Getter. They also rendezvous over long lunch breaks, sometimes at Lana's house. Her mother is suspicious but as yet can't prove anything. She has tried so very hard to keep the strain of their marriage from Lana and her brother. And guess what: today just happens to be a Tuesday."

With that, the announcement ended, and everyone turned to Lana. Her eyes filled with tears, and she hurried out of the room.

"That was mean," Hayden said in a low voice.

The door swung open, and James's mentor leaned into the room. He gestured with a massive hand. "James, Sam, come with me."

JAMES AND SAM EXCHANGED NERVOUS LOOKS AS THEY WALKED toward the door.

They stepped into a dark, narrow room that looked out on their common area. Hayden had been right: it *was* a one-way mirror. A control panel was positioned against the bottom half of the glass and lined with six chairs.

Lana's mentor was just leaving, her shoes clacking off the tiled floor. Sam's mentor sat in one of the chairs, and he stared condescendingly at his protégé.

"James, come with me," the Torturer said. "Sliver is going to speak with Sam in here."

The big man marched out of the room, and after sharing one last terrified look with Sam, James hurried to catch up with his mentor's long stride. They walked down a lavishly decorated hallway, adorned as if it were a museum. An endless row of paintings hung on the walls, and the carpeting was thick and purple. Strange black statues stared at James as he walked by.

The Torturer came to a halt in front of a towering wooden door. "In," he ordered, pushing it open.

James took a few cautious steps into the room. It was a circular library, with dusty, book-filled shelves covering every inch of the walls. The shelves were tall enough to need a pair of rolling ladders that stood off to the side. James stopped and glanced back at his mentor. He was so scared that he felt like he was going to be sick.

"Sit, sit," the Torturer said, pointing to the reading area in the center of the library. He walked over and plunked himself into a brown leather recliner. "Take a load off."

"Okay," James replied hesitantly, settling into another chair.

"First things first, just call me the Torturer. No nicknames, please."

James wanted to ask what possible nickname could come from that, but he restrained himself. *Whatever you do, don't make him angry,* he thought grimly. This man was likely the one responsible not just for the Night of Ashes, but also the Portersfield Incident. James was sitting five feet away from a murderer.

"Now, I know quite a bit about you already," the Torturer went on. "I was watching you for a couple days before your fight with Mark. You had it pretty rough. That Sara girl; she really burned you."

"Yep," James said quietly. He glanced at the big man. "You saw me fight Mark?"

He laughed. "Wouldn't call that a fight. You got dropped like . . ."

"Right, potatoes," James muttered. "I remember."

"Don't worry about that, trust me." The Torturer made a fist the size of a volleyball. "Things are going to go a lot differently next time. Tell me, how much do you hate that kid Mark?"

James thought about that for a moment. "A lot."

The Torturer bared his yellowed teeth. "We're going to pay him a visit in a few days. To teach him, and you, a lesson." There was no mistaking the glee on his face.

James ran through a list of possible scenarios in his mind. The Torturer beating up Mark was a prominent one, and he found it deeply satisfying. *But this is the enemy,* he reminded himself, picturing Thunderbolt and his disapproving glare from the poster on his bedroom wall. *Ingratiate for survival, but don't get brainwashed.*

"So, how are you going to, well . . . train me, or . . . what is it you're going to do?"

The Torturer leaned forward. "How would you like to be huge?"

"Like . . . muscular?"

"Exactly. Bigger, stronger. Strong enough to crush Mark without breaking a sweat."

James shrugged. "That would be sweet."

The Torturer sat back, nodding his approval. "That's what I thought you'd say. I'm going to give you a special chemical to take, nothing you've ever heard of. I call it Genome AP."

James wrung his hands together nervously. He didn't like the sound of *special chemical*. "Is it safe?" he asked.

"Oh yeah, I've already used it. I've packed on a few pounds since then," the Torturer added, glancing regretfully at his stomach, "but I was cut, let me tell you."

"So . . . like steroids?" James asked, frowning.

"Not even close. Steroids are crude muscle supplements. Genome AP accelerates the development of your actual DNA. It's about a hundred times more effective."

James considered this. He'd pictured himself just about every day of his life as a muscle-bound League member, fighting for liberty and justice. He thought about picking up Mark and punting him through the football posts. That sounded pretty good too.

"Any side effects?" James asked.

"Well, it might be different for everyone, but I was fairly unaffected."

"Fairly?"

"Don't worry about it, you'll be fine. And a chick magnet."

James smiled. "Excellent."

"Now, I have to tell you, I've never taught anybody anything, so I don't know how to approach it. But I want you to turn out to be the strongest of these kids, got that? You have to respect me."

"You could eat me. I'm terrified of you."

"Good," the Torturer said. "We'll get along fine."

You're already going along with his plans! James thought

suddenly. *You can't betray the League!* He summoned his courage and then met the Torturer's eyes. "Can I ask you something?"

"Sure."

"Did you kill Phoenix and the others?"

"Leni killed Phoenix, actually. He hated her. Thunderbolt is the one I want."

"Why?"

"You'll learn everything in time. For now, focus on your training." The Torturer stood up, partially blotting out the light. "I'll have your first supplements ready tomorrow. You'll have a group session with Leni then too, so don't mess with him."

"Why did you pick me?" James asked.

The Torturer looked down at him. "Because you remind me of myself at your age," he replied simply. "Now, let's get you back. Sam might well be dead already."

James shot him an alarmed look, but the Torturer didn't seem to notice. James followed him back to the control room and hurried through the mirror door, which promptly shut behind him. Hayden and Emily glanced up from where they were sitting on the couches.

"Where's Sam?" James asked immediately.

"In the bathroom," Hayden replied. "Why?"

James relaxed a little. "Oh, okay. Did he say what happened to him?"

"Just that his mentor, Sliver or something, talked to him in his mind. I know, messed up, but then he said Sliver got really frustrated and sent him back in here. Sam didn't know what he did wrong," Hayden explained, looking James over at the same time. "What happened to you?"

"Just talked about my training; nothing really," James said, glancing back at the mirror. He didn't want to say too much, just in case the Torturer was listening. "Apparently he wants to give me superstrength."

"Sweet," Hayden mused. "I hope I get superstrength. I wonder what my interview will be like. Probably bad. My guy didn't seem pleasant."

"Yeah, I would be *really* polite," James said, remembering the Torturer's warning.

He sat down next to Emily and quietly told them about the rest of his discussion with the Torturer, including the murders.

"Oh, great," Hayden said when James told him about Leni being Phoenix's killer.

Sam returned soon after and told them about the strange voice in his head. Lana never came out of her room. Eventually, they all shuffled to bed, and James lay down, staring up at the ceiling in the same bedroom he'd woken up in earlier.

What if I take the superpowers and then just leave? he thought. *I can join the League and be the hero that ends the war.*

James suddenly realized how surreal this all was. Just a few days ago, he was the laughingstock of his entire school. Even his little sisters were taking shots at him. Today, he'd been offered the chance to have *superpowers*. His entire life was about to change.

James pictured himself wearing the famous navy-blue uniform of the League of Heroes, the golden symbol emblazoned on his chest. James Renwick: *Superhero*.

He fell asleep with a smile on his face.

SAM WOKE THAT NIGHT TO THE SOUND OF CRYING. HE BLINKED a few times, trying to remember where he was. It all came rushing back, and he fearfully pulled the blanket up to his chin. The shadows in the room seemed to darken.

Right before falling asleep, Sam had desperately wished that he would wake up at home. This entire experience would be nothing more than a bad dream, and today, he would eat breakfast, give his mother a hug, and go to school. Instead, here he was, lying in the darkness, and only Sliver was waiting for him.

Another muffled sob cut through the air. Despite his better judgment, Sam couldn't leave someone crying by themselves. It was his duty to see if they needed help.

He slid out from under the covers and pulled his jeans on. The air was cool, and he felt goose bumps trail up his skin.

Sam gently opened his bedroom door and stepped into

the hallway. He noticed light peering out from under one of the other bedroom doors. Lana's. *Poor girl,* Sam thought. He couldn't imagine how he would have felt receiving the same news.

Sam lightly knocked on her door. "Lana," he whispered. "It's Sam. Can I come in?"

The sobs choked off a little. "No. Sorry if I woke you."

"I can't sleep," Sam said. "I'm coming in."

He heard Lana sniffle and took that as an okay. Sam pushed open the door and found her sitting against the headboard, arms wrapped around her legs.

"Hey," Sam said, closing the door behind him.

"Hey." She wiped her eyes and rubbed the tears off on her pant leg. "I'm a mess."

Sam shook his head. "No, you're not," he assured her, and sat down on the end of the bed. "Are you okay?"

Her eyes started to water again, and she looked away.

"Not really. It's just . . . I just don't know what to believe. Is my dad really having an affair? I mean, why would they tell me that? My mom, she doesn't deserve that. And what if they're just lying to make me mad or something? But the thing is, I somehow could picture him doing it . . ."

She choked out another sob and hugged herself even tighter.

Sam looked at her for a moment, trying to choose the right words. "You shouldn't believe it," he said at last. "Because they could have lied, and you won't be able to know until you get out of here anyway. So you'll just beat yourself up over it."

That sounded pretty good, Sam thought. He sometimes watched Saturday morning talk shows with his mother.

"I know," Lana mumbled, tears streaming down her cheeks. "I shouldn't jump to conclusions. But why would they lie? To make me stay up all night crying? These people, they're sick. You heard how much he enjoyed telling me."

Sam thought back to his meeting with Sliver. The first thing Sam had asked was why Sliver had chosen him, to which his mentor harshly replied, "I had no choice."

Then a little voice began to prod around in his head, whispering half-formed words and merging with Sam's own thoughts. Sam didn't understand what was happening at first, but it had suddenly felt normal to have a discussion with only his mind, and he'd told the voice to leave him alone. At that point Sliver had given him a furious glare and told him to go back to the common room.

"They are very strange," Sam agreed, frowning.

Lana wiped her eyes again. "How long do you think we'll be here?"

"I don't know . . . hopefully not much longer. Sliver wouldn't really tell me anything."

"When I get out, I'm going to have a talk with my dad," Lana whispered. Sam noticed the deep-seated anger in her eyes, and it struck him that maybe the Villains had given her the announcement for exactly that reason. They wanted her angry.

"Lana, can we be friends in here?" Sam asked. "I like having someone to talk to."

She smiled. "I'd like that. And thanks."

"No problem. Let me know if you need anything."

Sam went back to his room, feeling much better himself. He already had one more friend in here than he did at home.

"I really hate that kid," Sliver muttered to himself from inside the control room, where he had been listening in on Sam and Lana's discussion.

He'd been sitting there for a few hours now, thinking about his first interview with his protégé. The boy was strangely adept, even more than Sliver had gathered from the stolen League file. With proper training, he would prove to be a valuable ally. But how could he best use Sam's abilities? Could the boy help him deal with the others?

It annoyed Sliver that he had to deal with such things.

In the two years since the Night of Ashes, he had been living a life of leisure.

A few weeks after the murders, Sliver had walked into a bank and mentally coerced a high-level executive to transfer twenty million dollars into his account. With it, he'd bought himself a massive yacht and spent the past two years in the lower Caribbean, using his powers to erase the memories of everyone he met. He was like a ghost, and he'd loved every second of it.

But his time away had become a source of heated contention between him and his former mentor, Leni, who'd spent those years plotting against the League and building up his private organization. He wanted Sliver to spend every waking moment pursuing the League's destruction.

Sliver was tired of Leni's lectures, tired of this whole war. Soon, things would change. Leni wanted more ambition from him, and he would get it.

Rono wandered into the room, interrupting Sliver's thoughts. He started inspecting the control panels.

"We literally control *everything* from here," Rono said, testing a switch. "Each room's temperature, how hard the bed is, the lights, you can even start water dripping from the ceiling. The Torturer is going to do cartwheels when we show him this."

The control room was the second step of the Baron's psychological program. The announcements would attack them emotionally, while their rooms wore them down physically, until they became weak and malleable. Sleep deprivation was an important part of the plan. They were supposed to let the kids have the first night as a reprieve, just to give them a false sense of security, and then the torture would begin.

Sliver glanced at Rono. "Let's test it out. Turn James's heat up."

"Done." Rono turned two dials, his eyes tracking a small readout. A sleeping James was visible on the camera feed in front of them.

"How long until he wakes up, you think?" Sliver asked, watching the feed.

"Five minutes. Shall we have a bet?"

"Definitely. I say ten minutes. Closest wins."

They both eagerly watched the screen.

"How about if we . . ." Sliver started. "Crap!"

On-screen, James had already begun to toss and turn. "How hot did you make it?"

Rono gave him a sly smile. "I turned it up by about twenty degrees."

"Well, I didn't know you were going to melt the kid," Sliver complained.

"Should have verified the conditions."

James was fully rolling around now, and he kicked the blanket right off the bed.

"Heats up fast," Sliver said. "This is gonna be fun."

They both chuckled and leaned back in their chairs. Sliver liked Rono, but he doubted he could save him. If he was going to get a pardon from the League, he had to deal with the entire group. No exceptions. And Sliver couldn't risk having them imprisoned. If they ever broke out, they would come for him first.

There was only one way to end this war: the Vindico had to die. The kids would just have to hope they weren't members before it happened.

A SHRILL BEEPING SPLIT THROUGH THE AIR, AND EMILY JOLTED
awake. Jumping out of bed, she threw on her clothes and
hurried into the common area. James was laying facedown
on the couch, wearing only his red boxers. His pale skin
contrasted sharply with the couch's dark leather.

"Stop the noise," he moaned. "Please stop the noise."

"I think it's a wake-up call," Emily said. "Speaking of
which, why are you sleeping naked in the living room?"

"I'm not naked," he muttered. "It was too hot in my
room. I don't know how any of you slept."

Emily frowned. "My room wasn't hot."

"Neither was mine," Hayden said, strolling past them
on his way to the bathroom. "I had a great sleep."

"What?" James said, looking up. There were heavy bags
under his eyes. "So I got stuck with the crap room?"

"I think they're all the same," Emily said. "Maybe you
have a fever?"

"That makes me feel better," James replied, shuffling toward his room. He had just rounded the corner when the alarm stopped. "Oh, *now* it stops."

"Attention," a low voice announced. "Breakfast will be served now. At its conclusion, you will have twenty minutes to be ready for our first group session. At that time the door will open, and I will lead you to the location of the session. You have approximately thirty-five minutes, starting now."

The panel on the far wall slid open, and Emily spotted plates full of eggs, bacon, and toast. Her stomach grumbled in anticipation, and she hurried over as the others filed into the common room.

"Do I smell bacon?" Hayden said as he came running from the bathroom.

Beside one of the plates, they found a folded white T-shirt, a pair of jeans, and some socks.

"I think these are for you," Lana said to Hayden.

"No thanks," he said. "I'm liking this no clothes thing. I was debating even wearing these boxers today." Everyone just stared at him, and he sighed. "Fine."

He reluctantly pulled them on and sat down.

"What do you think we're gonna do today?" Sam asked, pausing between bites.

"No idea," Hayden said. "Judging by my mentor . . . probably get beaten with a strip of leather."

Sam lowered his fork. "You think?"

"No," Lana said, shooting Hayden a dirty look. Her eyes were slightly swollen from crying all night. She finished her breakfast and put the empty plate on the table. "How are we all supposed to shower in twenty minutes?"

"We better pair up," Hayden suggested. "Should we draw straws to see who goes with me?"

James glared at him.

"Really, though, who wants one before we go?" Lana asked. "They do at least have shampoo and deodorant and everything else."

"James looks like he could use a shower," Emily said.

"Yeah," Lana remarked. "And I'd like one too. James, you can go first."

Hayden leaned forward. "You know, if you went at the same time, you could have twice as long a shower."

"Shut up," Lana and James both said at once.

Hayden shrugged. "Just doing the math. I tried, James."

James shook his head and started for the bathroom.

Exactly thirty-five minutes after the announcement about breakfast, the mirror door swung open. Emily led them through the doorway, stopping short in front of the caped man on the other side. The room was dark, and he looked like a living shadow.

"Today is your first group session," he told them, "which will supplement your individual training. You do not speak unless I ask you to. Not to me, not to each other. If you do, there will be consequences. I am not a patient man." He let the threat of his words hang in the air. "Follow me."

With that, Leni strode into the hallway, his cape billowing

behind him. He led them into a small classroom and gestured at five desks that had been laid out.

"Sit," he commanded, and walked to the front of the room. A blank chalkboard hung behind him, but the rest of the walls were bare, and there were no pens or paper on the desks.

The protégés quickly found a seat.

"Today's lesson will be a short one," Leni said, beginning to pace. "You will listen carefully and then proceed back to your quarters. I won't get into the history of this society, nor the full reasons behind our war with the League. The Baron is the historian, and he will explain all of that when the time comes. But for now, know this: the Vindico was created *by* the League of Heroes."

Lana and Sam exchanged confused glances. James looked openly dubious.

"I will speak to you of one important point of contention: the source of supernatural abilities."

He extended one of his gloved hands, and their chairs suddenly floated upward. Hayden watched in amazement as his feet left the ground and saw that the others were grabbing at their seats, trying to hold on.

"There are three competing theories to explain how and why these abilities naturally manifest themselves. The first is called the environmental mutation theorem, which speculates that human-made changes to the atmosphere, specifically radiation, are altering genomes. The second is the evolution theorem, which cites that humans were always meant to develop these 'superpowers' and that in time, all humans will possess them. But it is the last theory that is the greatest cause of debate, the one held by the League of Heroes. Their belief is that supernatural abilities are not chosen at random, but rather, that they were purposefully selected by *destiny* to become members. It is their sacred mantra: the choice of fate."

Their chairs dropped back to the ground.

"Of course," Leni continued, pacing again, "this means that the artificial granting of superpowers cannot exist. And for thirty-five years, the League has fought desperately to hide the truth. They have murdered, lied, and covered up any evidence disproving their theory. And it is for that reason they've worked so hard to hide the identities of the Vindico. Why? First, because some of us are living proof that artificial superpowers do exist. Second, because each of us represents a hidden secret from the League's past. And third, because some of us are former members."

James raised his hand. "If you were members of the League, why have we never heard of you?" James asked. "And why don't they want people to know about artificial superpowers?"

"You've never heard of us because we served the League under different names," Leni replied simply. "Any photos have long been wiped from the records. And they don't want you to know about artificial superpowers because they don't want to share their influence. If people think they were 'chosen by fate,' then they will have the sole right to determine justice in the world. The problem is that their organization is corrupt, arrogant, and ineffective. They spend more time consolidating and protecting their power than helping those in need."

He stopped pacing and pointed a gloved finger at Hayden, whose chair began to shake.

"They don't want you to have these abilities. When they find out you have them, they will sentence you to life on the Perch or death," he said, walking toward Hayden. "I have been to that barren, snow-blasted island; I have seen the metal prison perched atop its cliffs. I assure you, death would be better. But the Vindico believes that you deserve a different life: one of purpose. We believe that the League of Heroes must be replaced and that we, along with our protégés, should be the ones to do it. You have a simple choice in front of you. Do you want to live a normal life, or do you want to be something *special*?"

Hayden's chair abruptly stopped shaking.

"That will be all for today. Go back to your quarters," Leni said. "Hayden, stay behind. And if any of you are thinking about veering from the course, I don't recommend it. You don't want me to have to come fetch you."

Everyone hastily filed out, and he looked down at his protégé. Hayden fidgeted nervously under Leni's gaze.

"Tonight we will have our first one-on-one session," Leni said. "You will pay attention to everything I say. You will hang on my every word, or I will replace you without a thought. I do not like to repeat warnings."

"Okay," Hayden mumbled, feeling like every muscle in his body had frozen.

"Good. Now go."

Hayden hurried out of the classroom and leaned against the wall, shaken by Leni's words. He jumped when he saw a tall, black marble statue of a dragon standing beside him, its mouth opened wide, as if preparing to bite. Hayden stared at its razor-sharp fangs and considered his options. Right now, there were only two: stay here or escape.

The latter was dangerous, but Hayden didn't like being threatened, and he had a sneaking suspicion that Leni might actually kill him before the training was over. It was time to get out of here. He felt guilty about leaving the others, but if he escaped, he could always send the League back for them.

Taking a last look down the hallway, where his fellow protégés had already gone through the control room door, Hayden turned and started running in the opposite direction. His eyes darted from one closed doorway to the next; he expected someone to burst forth at any moment. Even the statues seemed poised to attack. But he made it down the hallway without incident and emerged into a magnificent lobby.

A massive chandelier hung from the domed, golden ceiling, and winding staircases curled around both walls, leading to second and third levels. White marble tiles covered the floor, gleaming in the sunlight that poured in from a pair of three-story windows. Hayden spotted the front entrance between them and sprinted out the door.

He found himself on a half-circle stone patio looking out

onto a seemingly endless front yard. A driveway looped in front of the patio, but it trailed off into the distance, and he couldn't see its end. Even worse, a thick wall of trees wrapped around the entire property.

"Crap," he muttered.

Hayden took off along the mansion wall, aiming for the forest. He saw someone hunched over a flower bed, gardening, so he ducked behind a line of sculpted hedges and kept running.

Hayden was already tired by the time he reached the edge of the mansion, but he knew he couldn't slow down. He ran across the last stretch of property and plunged into the forest. The trees were dense, and Hayden weaved around them, slapping the branches out of his face as he went. He missed one and felt it slice across his cheek.

The shadows thickened as he ran deeper into the woods, and soon it became dark under the overlapping canopy. Spotting a shaft of light, he stumbled into a clearing, bordered on all sides by the watchful forest. There was an opening between two trees on the far side, and Hayden started for it.

With an earsplitting crack, both trees snapped in half and fell toward each other. They stopped a few feet from the ground and then hovered there, barring his way. Hayden stepped back. *What is this?* he thought fearfully. *A magic forest? They could have mentioned that in our orientation!*

He spun around, ready to flee in the other direction, but froze.

The branches on the far side of the clearing bent aside, and Leni walked out of the shadows.

"Going somewhere?" he asked coldly.

"Uh, I got lost. Took a wrong turn on the way back to the common room. It's very confusing with—"

"The Baron and I both warned you not to attempt escape," Leni cut in. "It seems you have a problem listening."

Hayden heard rustling and glanced back to see the two fallen trees floating toward him, their leaves brushing against the grass. They were spinning in midair, exposing the shards of wood at the bottom where they'd been snapped off.

He turned back to Leni. "I'll listen! No more escaping! From here on, I'm good."

Leni narrowed his eyes. "Is that so?"

Hayden felt an invisible force grip him, and his arms were squeezed against his sides. Then his entire body floated off the ground.

"Just give me another chance," Hayden pleaded.

Leni smiled. "I'm not going to kill you . . . for now. But we can't allow this to go unpunished. Perhaps this will be useful. You can serve as a lesson to the others."

"A lesson?" Hayden asked nervously.

"Indeed." Leni lifted a hand. "A lesson—and a warning."

Hayden felt the pressure on his body increase, as if he was stuck in a vise. Out of the corner of his eye, he saw the trees rotate again, pointing the jagged edges away from him. They hovered there for a moment, and Hayden realized what was coming.

This is going to hurt, he thought.

Then the trees flew toward him.

"I JUST WANT TO KNOW WHY THEY CHOSE US," LANA SAID, twisting a strand of blond hair between her fingers. She was sitting with James and Sam in the common area, where they'd been since Leni's disturbing group session. Emily was taking a nap in her room.

"At least your mentors actually talked to you guys," Lana continued sourly, glancing at the mirror. "Mine still hasn't said a word to me since I've been here. But as soon as she does, I'm going to thank her and then tell her to pick someone else. I'm going home."

"Thank her?" James asked. He propped himself up on his elbow. "What for?"

Lana hesitated. "She saved me from something. I don't really want to talk about it," she said before James could ask. "Sorry."

She looked away, and there was a moment of awkward silence.

"I wonder what Hayden's doing," Sam said, quickly changing the subject. "He's been gone for a while now, and Leni didn't sound happy when we left."

James rolled onto his back and stared at the crimson ceiling. Six round light fixtures cast an orange glow over the common area, and there was a large vent above each wall. "You have to admit," he said, "Leni made some good points."

"You're going to believe that maniac?" Lana asked.

James held his hands up. "I'm just saying some parts made sense. Don't get me wrong, I'm a huge fan of the League. But every day, I thought for sure I was going to wake up with powers. *Every day.* I know it's possible to get them until seventeen, but for some reason, I was sure I was going to get them when I turned twelve, just like Thunderbolt did. And when I woke up that morning without them, it was like I realized I was never going to be a League member. I was miserable. And now I find out that you can actually get superpowers without developing them naturally? Why shouldn't we be able to have powers too? Why should the League get to decide?"

Lana rolled her eyes. "Yeah, 'cause look how good these guys turned out. The people telling you this are *evil*, James; that's the point. Can you blame the League for not wanting everyone to have powers?"

"Well, we're not going to be evil," James pointed out.

"What do you think they're trying to do?" Lana asked, raising her voice. "You're just so excited to get powers you're not listening to the other part."

"Listen," James said, "if they think they're going to turn us into villains by giving us speeches in a dark classroom, they've got something else coming. They're going to have to do a lot better than that. I mean, just because he says—"

The mirror door swung open, cutting him off. They turned toward it, but for a moment, nothing happened.

Then a silhouette became visible in the darkness. Hayden floated limply into the room, as if he was strung up on invisible lines. His face was mottled with black and purple bruises, and a huge, stitched-up cut ran through one of his eyebrows and down his cheek. His white T-shirt was stained with blood.

James slowly stood up. "What the . . ." he whispered.

Without warning, the door slammed shut again, and Hayden dropped to the ground. The three of them stared at his crumpled form, too stunned to react.

"Ow," Hayden muttered.

"Are you all right?" James asked, snapping out of it. He hurried to Hayden's side.

"I've been better," Hayden replied weakly.

James knelt down and grabbed one of Hayden's arms, trying to lift him. He glanced back at Lana and Sam, who were still sitting on the couch, staring. "Help me!"

Lana scrambled over and took Hayden's other arm. Together, they managed to lift him back onto his feet, and he leaned heavily on James's shoulder.

They half-dragged him to one of the couches and gingerly laid him down.

He smiled. "Much better."

"What happened?" Lana asked, her hand over her mouth.

Sam still hadn't moved. He looked like he was going to cry.

"Leni doesn't like when you try to escape," Hayden said.

"You tried to escape?" James asked in disbelief.

"Yeah. I wouldn't recommend it."

Lana tentatively lifted the bottom of Hayden's T-shirt. His entire midsection was wrapped with thick white bandages. "What is this?" she breathed.

"I think she mentioned broken ribs," Hayden replied faintly. "Like, all of them. A nice old lady patched me up. She gave me some meds, so I feel nice." He smiled again. "She said I would be screaming otherwise."

"These people are terrible." Lana shook her head. "They could have killed you."

"How far did you get?" James asked. He glanced up at the mirror, wondering if anyone was behind the glass. It might have been his imagination, but he could almost feel them watching.

"The woods. Then the trees beat me up," Hayden said.

"They must have really drugged him," James whispered to Lana.

"Attention." They all flinched as the Torturer's booming voice sounded over the speakers. "Emily and Lana are to come to the door for their sessions. I also have an announcement regarding James."

"Oh, great," James said.

Hayden turned to Lana, looking deeply saddened. "What

they said to you was mean. They never should have hurt your feelings."

James frowned; that was the most sincere thing he'd heard Hayden say since they'd gotten here. *The drugs must really be affecting him,* he thought.

"Uh . . . thanks," Lana replied, flushing.

Emily walked into the common room but stopped short when she saw Hayden. Her eyes widened. "What happened?"

"He got caught by—" James started to explain, but he was cut off by his mentor's voice.

"We picked James up a few days after he found his girlfriend of two years, Sara, cheating on him with his former best friend, at his own party."

"That's why you were so sad," Hayden said sympathetically.

"It may sound bad," the Torturer continued, "but it's even worse than he thinks. Let me tell you a love story."

James sat down on the edge of the couch, feeling miserable.

"James has been in love with Sara since he was ten years old, but it wasn't until he was twelve that he got the confidence to approach her. One day, James gave her a note asking her out."

"How does he know that?" James muttered.

"She said yes. After years of waiting, Sara was finally his girlfriend. They spent two happy years together before this latest development. But unfortunately, there's more to this story than James is aware of."

What is he talking about? James thought warily.

"It turns out Sara had already been cheating on James for months before he caught her. With Mark several times, as well as Nicholas, Johnny, and Pat. Worse still, everyone in the school knew, including his best friend, Dennis. Everyone but James. Right now, the rumor going around is that James is just too embarrassed to come to school. Even the teachers believe it. And Mark? Well, he's dating Sara now, and they're very happy together. That is all. Emily, Lana, come to the door."

"Wow," Hayden mumbled. "Sara is a jerk."

James felt tears forming in the corner of his eyes. He blinked, trying to fight them back. He was already embarrassed enough.

"It might not be true," Lana said.

"Oh, I believe it," James whispered.

She squeezed his shoulder and then followed Emily through the mirror door.

14

"CAN I HANG OUT HERE MORE?" EMILY ASKED RONO, BARELY
containing her excitement as she wandered around his
computer lab. Her eyes scanned the sophisticated equipment. Fifteen different computer screens portrayed riots
of code, surveillance videos, and sensor readings.

"Of course," Rono replied. He was standing by the doorway, wearing the same brown trench coat and silver visor
he'd had on the night of Emily's abduction. He seemed
pleased with her reaction. "We will do most of your training here."

"It's the best setup I've ever seen," Emily commented,
running her fingers along a massive screen. "You could
hack anything from here and do it undetected, I bet."

He smiled. "Yes, as you will see."

Emily continued to inspect the lab for a few more minutes, scrutinizing every button and blinking light. There
was a large rifle lying on the end of the table, and her eyes

lingered on it for a moment. She heard Rono shifting uncomfortably behind her. He must have forgotten to put the rifle away. Emily let him sweat it out for a few more seconds and then turned to face him.

Rono quickly gestured to a seat. "Sit, please. We have a few things to discuss."

She sat down and felt the leather chair automatically adjust itself to match her posture. *Very impressive,* she thought, already feeling right at home.

Rono rolled his chair slightly to the left, putting himself between Emily and the rifle, and then sat as well. He'd removed the trench coat, and she noticed a metal apparatus that ran over his shoulder and across the upper left side of his chest.

"Now," he said slowly, as if carefully choosing his words, "to begin with, I chose you for a few reasons."

Emily leaned forward and brushed a loose bang out of her eyes. She had been waiting to hear this.

"First, and most importantly, your inherent aptitude for technology. I was very impressed by your coding and hacking abilities. I tracked you down through your online persona; the Black Arrow is infamous for her ability to break into anything."

"Including the League network," Emily boasted. She glanced at his computer equipment again. From here, she could probably crack the network in a couple of hours.

"Yes," Rono agreed, following her gaze. "I monitor their network for information, and I detected your early attempts to break in. From there I found out all I could about you: your age, where you lived and went to school, and everything that was on your computer."

Her eyes widened. "You *are* good."

"That is what initially led me to you, but it was your personality that settled my decision. You are strangely detached and observant, perhaps even calculating. In that way, you are like me. But you also can have a fiery temper, and you are very forward. Those might be welcome additions to my own traits." He met her eyes. "However, there are some aspects of your character I am still uncertain of."

"Like what?"

Rono hesitated. "I'm not sure of your mental stability . . . in that, I do not fully understand the way your mind works."

"How so?" Emily asked.

She wasn't insulted; just about every teacher she'd ever had mentioned something of the sort. They usually preceded the talk by telling Emily that she was categorically brilliant, after which they would question her home life. Her parents had never been to a parent-teacher conference, even when she was in kindergarten, so it was up to Emily to explain her relationship with them. At those times, she just used the word *normal*. It was never a lie since the definition of normal depends on the person using it.

Rono scratched his forehead, frowning. "What I mean is that you are detached, but possibly a little too tenuously. If I train you and give you the technology to accomplish our goals, I am unsure of whether you would use it in the correct way."

"What is the correct way?" she asked suspiciously.

"In whatever way we decide is best."

Emily leaned back, the chair's motor whirring as it readjusted to the new position. "So you wonder if I will follow orders?"

"Essentially, yes."

"Hmm . . . I see your problem. For one, I already attacked you. I showed no fear of you and haven't since. So you think that if I have no fear now, why should I when I am more powerful? Such is the age-old quandary confronting the master-apprentice relationship. If the master makes the apprentice too strong, then they have no need for the master, specifically in the evil realm, where they cannot be expected to uphold morals, when morals are what they are being taught to ignore. Yes, I see your problem."

Rono stared at her, and then sighed. "Well, I've chosen you now, so we might as well try. I intend to make you strong indeed, but I warn you, if you decide to rebel, the Vindico will swiftly cut you down. You are smart, though, very smart, and you know that. We will proceed as planned."

"Can I send a message to my grandpa now?" she asked.

"Not yet," he replied. "Don't worry; in a few days, I'll send him an anonymous message. We need to keep things secret for as long as we can. The League knows of your disappearances. The entire country is in a panic: parents are keeping their children home from school; no one is venturing outside after dark; the sales of alarm systems have skyrocketed. The League is completely overwhelmed with thousands of panicked sightings and the swarming reporters that follow them. We need to let the fear fester for a bit longer. Anything else?"

"When can we start?" Emily asked eagerly.

Rono smiled and gestured to a keyboard. "Now."

"Sit," Avaria ordered Lana, pointing to a small wooden bench.

They were in a large, gray-tiled room illuminated by phosphorous lights. Punching bags were hung throughout the space, as well as several human-shaped dummies and a substantial weapons rack. Lana stared apprehensively at the gleaming swords and rifles.

Avaria paced back and forth like a cat stalking its prey.

"I will tell you now, I was not impressed by your wake-up," she said, and Lana instinctively looked down at her feet. "Look at me," Avaria snapped.

Lana met Avaria's eyes and felt a stirring of injured pride. *Who is this woman to judge me?* she thought. She held her mentor's cold gaze, and Avaria finally nodded.

"Better. You recovered somewhat, enough to grow angry about your imprisonment. Then you received news of your father, at which point you broke down again."

"Was that true?" Lana asked quickly. "Is he really cheating on my mom?"

"Yes. I had audio and camera feeds in your house. I saw him and the other woman in the recordings and then figured out the details from there. If you don't believe me, I still have the tapes."

How could he? Lana thought numbly. *How could he have done that to us?* Her parents fought sometimes, but Lana had always assumed it was normal. *He doesn't even love her,* Lana realized, thinking of her mother, crying at home. *If he doesn't love her, maybe he doesn't love me.* She suddenly felt more bitter than sad, and it must have shown on her face.

"You *should* be angry," Avaria said, coming to a stop. "That was the correct reaction in the first place. Doesn't it feel better than moping about? Tears solve nothing."

Lana glared at her. "My dad is cheating, and you expect me not to cry?"

"Yes. I expect you to feel rage, righteous anger. It will cleanse your weakness. Your father is ruining your family. What are you going to do about it?"

Lana hesitated, then shook her head. "I don't know."

"You don't *know*?" Avaria asked mockingly. "Do you want to know what I would do?"

In a single, incredibly smooth motion, Avaria did a one-handed back handspring and roundhouse kicked one of the punching bags right where a human face would be. The noise was like a thunderclap, and the reinforced bag skidded ten feet backward.

She turned to Lana. "Lesson learned."

"So, kill my dad?" Lana asked sarcastically. "That's your answer?"

"Justice. That is my answer."

Lana shook her head again, not wanting to be baited. "I'll tell my mom so she can move on with her life. That's justice enough."

"That's justice? He doesn't love her. He obviously doesn't love any of you if he would tear apart your family on a whim. So your answer is to give him an easy out?"

Lana stood up from the bench, shaking. She could think those things about her dad, but it was different coming from this complete stranger.

"You don't know him," she growled.

"It appears I know more about him than you do. I am not blinded by adoration. Your father is swine."

The comment sent Lana's bubbling anger over the top, and without thinking, she charged. Lana pulled back her right hand, ready to punch the woman squarely in the face. That was her plan, anyway.

Avaria smiled and then dodged the punch with unnatural speed, moving in a blur. She spun behind Lana, grabbed her outstretched wrist, and twisted it behind her. Lana gasped as pain lanced up her arm and shoulder.

Avaria clutched Lana's throat with her free hand. "Wouldn't that have been satisfying to send me flying across the room?" she whispered.

Lana struggled to free herself, but Avaria's grip was like iron. *Helpless again,* she thought. She remembered Kyle standing over her in the forest, wearing an arrogant smile.

"You don't have a chance against me," Avaria said softly. "Next time, I will make you suffer. But if you listen to me, I will give you the power to have your revenge. On your father, on *Kyle*"—she hissed his name—"and on all the others who have hurt you."

White spots began to appear in Lana's vision, and she stopped struggling.

"This session is over. I will take you back now."

Avaria released her, and Lana gasped again as the strain on her throat eased. She turned to face her mentor, but she wasn't going to try anything. She'd learned that lesson.

Avaria led her back to the control room and pushed open the door. Without a word, Lana hurried past and went straight to her bedroom, ignoring the boys on the couch. She dropped face-first onto the bed.

How could he do that? she thought.

The last night she'd been home, her father had been making jokes around the dinner table. Everything had seemed perfectly normal. The thought made her even angrier for some reason, and despite herself, Lana began to wonder what it would be like to have Avaria's supernatural strength. If Lana had the same power, she would never be helpless again.

When she finally fell asleep, she dreamed that Kyle was standing over her in the forest again. But this time, Lana stood up, and Kyle was no longer smiling.

15

JAMES WAS SITTING ON ONE OF THE RECLINERS, MOPING.
He hadn't said a word since he received his announcement.

"You need to stop dwelling on Sara," Hayden said. He
was still sprawled out on the couch James and Lana had
placed him on earlier. "Who cares what she's doing?"

"Did you even hear that story?" James asked. "I was in
love with her for years! She was cheating on me for like
half the time we were dating! And it's even worse that everyone thinks I'm too much of a coward to come to school."

"Oh yeah," Hayden said. "I forgot that part."

James scowled at him. The drugs were obviously wearing off.

"Won't your parents tell the school you're missing?"
Sam said, trying to cheer him up. "Someone must have
called to see where you are."

"I'm sure they did, but that won't stop the rumors," James muttered. "All I know is I can't wait to push open the front doors and walk down that hallway with muscles bursting through my shirt. Then Mark will be sorry," he added darkly.

"Wow, you were easy," Hayden said. "Leni is at least going to have to ask nicely if he wants me to be a murdering supervillain. I still don't even know what he's going to do to me, besides beat me with tree trunks. Speaking of which, can someone adjust my rib bandages? They're bunched."

Sam hurried over. "Sorry I didn't help before," he said, sounding embarrassed. "I was in shock, I think." He pulled on the bandages, and Hayden gasped, his face contorting in agony.

"Sorry, sorry!" Sam yelped.

"Just joking," Hayden said. "Actually, it doesn't hurt nearly as bad as it should. I think they gave me some crazy stuff to speed up the healing. That old lady said I should be ready to go in a day or two, which makes no sense. Leni is a jerk, let me tell you."

"We should be careful what we say," Sam whispered, gesturing toward the mirror.

Hayden smirked. "What? You think they're really sitting there watching us all day like a reality TV marathon? Today on *Becoming a Villain*, teens mope about heartbreak and high school gossip, and James gives several brooding looks!"

As soon as he finished speaking, the mirror door swung open. "Hayden, come with me."

"Crap," Hayden whispered.

Hayden floated after Leni as he made his way through the enormous lobby. Leni had grown impatient with his limping and mentally yanked him off his feet.

They continued into the right wing hallway, and Leni finally stopped in front of a black door framed on either side by statues of grim-faced men with swords. Leni closed his eyes, and after an elaborate series of clicks, the door eased open.

Inside was the strangest room Hayden had ever seen. It was the size of their common area, and the air was very cool. The only light came from a few orange-hued lanterns scattered along the walls. But it was the contents of the room that were the most peculiar. There was a pile of black stones, four full-sized human dummies, a rack of pole-like weapons with gleaming blades, a heap of black sand, and a fire pit. The only other object was some sort of large computer with a seat in front of it.

"Could use a plant," Hayden said, still hanging in midair. "Maybe a fern."

"Silence," Leni commanded as he strode toward the computer.

"Okay."

Hayden had always had the very unfortunate habit of rambling when he was uncomfortable, and it often got him into trouble. *Stop speaking,* he told himself firmly as he floated after his mentor. *This man will actually kill you.*

"This is my training room," Leni said. "There is another combat room the others use, but this room is specialized for my specific needs. Here you will learn to use your abilities. Only when you have mastered every task that I have prepared will I deem you fit to join this society."

"I never did well in school," Hayden pointed out. "I find the grading system an unfair way of—"

Leni's eyes flashed. "You're speaking."

"Right." *Shut up,* Hayden thought urgently.

"As I was saying, you will still have your group sessions, but I care little what you do there. Your time with me is what's important, and you will utilize it fully. If you do not sharpen your mind, you will fail. If you fail, then you die."

Hayden was about to respond but bit his lip at the last second.

"Let me give you a demonstration. Well, another one, I suppose," Leni added, glancing at Hayden's bloodied T-shirt with a hint of amusement.

With a flick of his finger, Leni turned Hayden in midair, until he was facing the middle of the room.

The pile of black sand began to swirl. It rose off the ground like a school of fish, twisting and weaving in complex patterns. Hayden's eyes widened as the black cloud formed into one of the long weapons he'd noticed on the rack. The blade pointed at Hayden and then suddenly flew toward his head.

Hayden shouted in panic, but the weapon stopped just in front of his nose. It hovered there for a moment and then dissolved back into a pile of sand on the floor.

"I think I just wet myself," Hayden murmured.

"What you saw takes a mastery that you may never know. We will see how deeply your talents run."

Hayden glanced at him. "You mean I have the power to do that?"

"Everyone has the potential for MPA, to some extent. In most, it's too limited to be realized. You have an aptitude for these abilities, a greater mental capacity than normal, doubtful as that may seem. That is why you were selected. I can assure you, it was not for your personality."

"I always did feel rather smart." He paused. "What is MPA?"

"Mental projection abilities," Leni said, lightly tapping his temple with his finger. "They can manifest in two forms: telekinesis, which you and I possess, or telepathy, like Sliver and Sam. The League possesses several of each, though they are not as strong as Sliver and I. We are the most feared of all the Vindico because we can kill without ever touching our victims."

He spun his finger, and Hayden's limp body turned again.

"But I didn't conduct your initial testing, and I don't rely on others for my information. So, why don't we see if you really have what it takes."

Hayden floated over to the computer and was lowered into the seat. He grimaced as a stab of pain raced up his back. A blank screen stood before him, and on top of that, a cylinder was pointing at his head.

"We will test to make sure the preliminary readings were correct. You better hope they were."

"I was never tested," Hayden said nervously. "You sure you have the right guy?"

"You wouldn't remember this test. It was conducted while you were sleeping."

Hayden frowned. "That's kind of creepy. When did—"

"Silence!"

Hayden anxiously stared at the screen. He had a feeling that if he didn't have this ability, Leni would kill him on the spot. His mentor closed his eyes, and the words INITIALIZING TESTING appeared on the screen, while incomprehensible numbers streamed across the bottom. All of a sudden a white light leapt out of the cylinder, focusing on Hayden's forehead. He closed his eyes under the intense glare.

It felt like something was pushing its way through his mind, looking under the layers of thoughts and emotions. It kept delving deeper, and Hayden was powerless to resist it. Then, just as abruptly as it had begun, the white light switched off, and Hayden opened his eyes. TESTING COMPLETE scrolled along the screen. He slumped, feeling strangely tired from the ordeal.

Leni was staring at him. *Uh-oh,* Hayden thought numbly.

"You pass," Leni said. "You are fortunate. I will train you." He paused. "You will never become as powerful as me, but I can still make you strong. Far stronger than your fellow protégés. Tomorrow we begin your training, here.

If you can move one speck of sand by the end of the day, I will consider it a success. Tomorrow you will walk, so heal quickly."

"Bet you I move five specks," Hayden said.

"We shall see."

Hayden floated off the seat again and followed Leni out of the room. He had never liked school, but for once, Hayden was going to *try*. He wanted Leni's abilities, and more importantly, he knew his life depended on just how powerful he became.

I'm going to prove Leni wrong, Hayden thought, *and then I'm going to kick his ass.*

"WE'RE TAKING *THIS?*" JAMES ASKED SKEPTICALLY, GLANCING up at his mentor.

They were standing in the middle of a massive concrete parking garage the morning after James's announcement, surrounded by expensive cars, limos, and motorcycles. There was even a strange futuristic-looking black vehicle in the corner that didn't have any wheels. But the Torturer had led him through all of those and stopped in front of an old gray van. Its paint was flaking off, exposing spots of rust.

"What did you expect?" the Torturer replied as he started around the hood.

"I don't know, like a cool jet or something." The garage was so big that James could hear his voice echoing off the walls.

The big man laughed. "I think that would kind of stand out in Cambilsford. We need to be more discreet."

"Yeah, I guess," James agreed, still not quite sure why they were making the trip in the first place. "How far of a drive is it?"

The Torturer climbed into the driver's side, and the whole van tilted a little to the left. "Not that far: five hours or so."

"The Vindico's headquarters are that close to my house?" James asked in amazement, settling in the passenger's seat. "I mean, I know Portersfield was only two hours from Cambilsford, but I didn't think—"

"What do you know about Portersfield?" the Torturer asked sharply, turning to James. He keyed the ignition at the same time, and a deep, grating rumble erupted from the engine.

"Uh," James said, startled by his mentor's reaction. "Just that an unidentified Villain—"

"Unidentified." The Torturer shook his head, glowering. "They do everything they can to hide the truth." He pressed a remote on the dash, and the garage door lifted smoothly into the ceiling, flooding the room with light. "Go on."

"Well, the news report said he robbed a bank and flipped some cop cars," James continued tentatively, sneaking glances at the huge man. He wished he hadn't brought it up. "And uh, well . . . he killed four cops. Then, when he was trying to escape, Firefly intercepted him."

James squinted as the Torturer steered the van out of the garage. He hadn't seen sunlight for days.

"And what then?" the Torturer asked, hitting the gas pedal. The tires screeched, fighting for traction, and then the van barreled down the driveway.

"He killed Firefly," James mumbled.

The Torturer turned to him, his eyes narrowed, and James shrank in his seat. *Please don't eat me,* he thought.

"Yes, he did," the Torturer said quietly. The big man suddenly broke out laughing and clapped James on the shoulder. The blow almost knocked him right through the passenger door.

"Look how scared you are," he guffawed. "*I* killed Firefly; it's no secret around here. But the League only told the public half that story, as usual. They somehow forgot to mention that Thunderbolt is the reason I robbed that bank."

James frowned. "Thunderbolt? Why would he—"

"It's a long story," the Torturer said as the driveway plunged into the forest. Tall trees formed a canopy overhead, creating a tunnel. "That's the Baron's department. And we have business to take care of. Before I forget, take this."

He dug into his pocket and withdrew a small glass vial. It was half-full of black liquid.

James stared at it apprehensively. "Is that . . ."

"Genome AP," he said. "As I said, it's much improved from what I took. I used to drink glasses of the stuff. And the main danger was always the muscle *expansion,* which is why I'm as big as I am. This stuff is still going to expand your muscles, but more so, it's going to make them *dense.* You won't get nearly as big as me, but you'll get just as strong and just as hard." He grinned. "You'll be able to take laser blasts without going down, and bullets will barely even break your skin."

The Torturer handed him the vial, and James unscrewed the top. *You're going to be a superhero,* he told himself as a pungent smell filled his nose. *You're going to be a superhero.* He drank the liquid, almost gagging as it crept down his throat. It felt like he was drinking crude oil.

"Only twenty more to go," the Torturer said, taking back the empty vial. "One a day. Tell you what, I'll send it with breakfast from now on."

"Thanks," James managed, fighting back nausea.

The Torturer nodded. "Now, to today's venture. The Baron thought it was too soon for us to leave the mansion, but I want to start off your training with a little demonstration of what you're going to become."

Five hours later, James felt someone nudging his shoulder, and he blearily opened his eyes. He'd tried to keep mental track of where the Vindico's headquarters were, but the winding route through the forest had left him hopelessly confused, and he'd fallen asleep instead. James always fell asleep on long car rides.

"Home sweet home," the Torturer said softly.

James stared out the window as they drove past the farmhouses that circled Cambilsford. It felt like he'd been gone for months.

"We need to intercept Mark somewhere," the Torturer continued. "Privately would be best, but as long as it's not around anyone you know, that should be fine. We want people to question if he *really* saw you. How does he get home from school?"

James frowned. "The town bus, I think. But how is that private?"

"It's not, but our options are limited. It should mostly be strangers, at least."

"What if Sara's with him?" James asked nervously.

"Don't worry," the Torturer replied. "We're going to make sure he's alone. If he is, we're going to get on the bus at a later stop, but we won't sit together. We'll let him talk to you, then as soon as he does or says anything, *pow*!"

He emphasized the *pow* by slamming his giant fist into his palm. It was so loud that the driver of the car next to them looked over.

James was still uneasy. "But all the people on the bus will see. Won't they call the police? What if they notify the League?"

"The League is on the other side of the country, investigating a sighting of some big guy they thought was me," he said, smiling. "They can only deal with one sighting at a time because they're too scared we're gonna pick them off if they split up. And the police will get a big surprise if they bother us. We'll leave quickly anyway. In and out, no problem. Trust me."

"All right," James said, his stomach clenching.

They parked a few blocks away from the school. At the Torturer's instruction, James quickly walked down the street and positioned a camera in a bush across from the school's bus stop. By the time he climbed back into the van, the camera feed showed Mark saying good-bye to Sara and a few of his friends. Several minutes later, the bus pulled up, and they watched him get on.

The Torturer pushed open the van door. "All right, he's alone. Let's go. It's time for our rendezvous."

They hurried to the bus stop closest to their parked van. The Torturer sat down on the bench, while James stood anxiously by the curb. He shivered as a cold wind picked up.

"Remember, just fold your arms to signal me whenever he says something particularly insulting," the Torturer reminded him. "Or if he punches you, that would obviously be my signal."

"Right," James said, peering down the road. He doubted Mark would walk up and punch him on a bus, but he would most definitely say something insulting.

After another couple of minutes, the bus rounded the corner. James fidgeted in nervous anticipation, clutching the fare the Torturer had given him. Trying to compose himself, he got on and deposited the change.

He scanned the bus and saw Mark sitting near the back. James met his eyes and then pointedly sat at the front. The Torturer traipsed past, his head barely clearing the ceiling, and James heard him plunk down somewhere in the middle. The driver was watching the Torturer suspiciously in his rearview mirror, but when he looked up at him, the driver hastily averted his eyes and hit the gas pedal.

As soon as the bus pulled away from the curb, Mark appeared beside James's seat.

"James? Where have you been?" he asked.

James was instantly reminded of how much he didn't like Mark. He was wearing a tight yellow T-shirt, his hair was gelled up perfectly, and his handsome features were twisted into something resembling concern.

"I've been away," James said coolly.

Mark frowned. "Away? Where? I mean, at first, people told me you were staying in your room, skipping school. And then I saw your picture on the front page, along with those other kids, and it said—"

"You what?" James cut in.

"I saw you on the front page." He raised his eyebrows. "You didn't know? It's on the news too; it's everywhere. They said you disappeared, along with those other four kids, all in one week. Some of you right out of your own houses." Mark shook his head. "Some people started saying it was the Villains; Thunderbolt was taking a lot of heat. And now here you are! You have to tell someone!"

James looked straight ahead, reeling. Their faces were all over the news? Was his family being swarmed by reporters? Did everyone think he was dead?

"Well, listen," Mark said, sounding uncomfortable, "either way, I want to apologize. When I thought you might . . . well, you know, I felt terrible. Getting with Sara, that was stupid. And I shouldn't have punched you back that morning. You had every right to be mad at me."

James glanced at him, surprised. This wasn't going as planned.

"No, you shouldn't have," James said. "And yes, getting with Sara was stupid. And you know what, ignoring me for the past couple years wasn't very nice either."

"I know," Mark agreed, leaning against one of the hand bars. "I got carried away trying to fit in with the team, you know? I mean, those guys . . . you know how it is."

James folded his arms sourly. "Not really," he muttered.

"Well, either way, I screwed up. Give me another chance?"

The bus came to a stop at a red light.

"What, now you're just going to be nice to me again?" James asked sarcastically.

Mark shrugged. "Yeah, I mean I think it's overdue . . ."

James heard heavy footsteps. *Uh-oh,* he thought. He'd forgotten about the signal. Mark's face blanched as two massive hands lifted him off the ground.

"Payback time," the Torturer growled in his ear.

James jumped to his feet. "Wait, maybe—"

But before he could finish, the Torturer spun around and tossed Mark right through the far window. The glass shattered, and terrified screams filled the bus.

The Torturer turned back, laughing uproariously, but stopped when he saw the look of horror on James's face. "What?"

"Did you kill him?" James shouted.

"No, no, he landed on another car," the Torturer said, pointing to the smashed window. "It broke his fall a little. See?"

James looked out the window and saw Mark lying on the hood of a green sedan, groaning. The driver was already out of the car, shrieking and looking up at the bus.

"We should leave," the Torturer suggested. "I'll signal the van."

James stared down at Mark, guilt roiling in his stomach. Guilt, and just the slightest bit of amusement. He bit down the thought, horrified with himself, and then the Torturer dragged him out of the bus. The terrified bus driver was hiding in the corner of his seat.

They sprinted to the next side street, and James saw the van speeding toward them with no driver at the wheel.

"How . . ." James began.

"Remote steering," the Torturer said. "That van has some tricks up its sleeve."

It screeched to a halt beside them, and they clambered inside. Then the Torturer hit the gas pedal, and they sped away just as the first sirens split through the air.

"STAND IN A GROUP RIGHT HERE," AVARIA ORDERED, AND
everyone hurried to get to the spot. No one wanted to make
her angry.

In fact, everyone looked absolutely terrified to be there,
apart from Emily. Ever since her initial defeat, Emily had
been eager for another encounter with Avaria. She'd always been fascinated with stories of powerful women, and
Avaria personified strength and confidence. She was like
all the great woman warriors Emily had ever read about.

In fact, aside from missing her grandpa, Emily couldn't
have been happier. Here, people paid attention to her and
even treated her like a friend. That was something new
to her. Emily's parents moved from China when she was
very young, and because she hadn't spoken much English, she'd never really made friends as a child. Instead,
she turned to her computer for companionship, and that
hadn't changed. In fact, Emily had never hung out with

any kids her whole life. Why would she want to go home?

Avaria began to pace. "You will not be receiving any verbal lessons from me. You have the Baron and Leni for that. I have decided you would be best suited to learn hand-to-hand combat, both as a practical means and for exercise."

Hayden nudged Sam and gave him a knowing look. "Treadmill time," he mouthed.

Hayden had recovered remarkably fast through the night, far quicker than seemed possible, and he could already stand and move around on his own. Even the vicious bruises lining his face had begun to fade. The only indication of the severity of his beating was his bloodstained T-shirt and the tightly wrapped bandages beneath it.

"You will all be getting specific powers or training of some kind, but each member of the Vindico is also very capable in simple combat. There are times when you must rely on your hands to dispatch your foe. Today, I will test your hand-to-hand abilities. Hayden, step forward."

Hayden glanced at the rest of them, looking uncertain.

"Now," Avaria commanded, and Hayden limped forward. "Have you ever fought before?"

Hayden seemed to consider the question. "Do video games count?"

"No. Have you ever *actually* fought anyone?"

"Well," he said thoughtfully, "not since the fifth grade, when Danny Rockwell came over and—"

"Silence," Avaria cut him off. "Let's see what your natural abilities are."

Hayden paled. "Please don't maim me."

"Attack."

"That's okay, I get it, you're going to beat me," Hayden said, putting his arms up in surrender. "Consider me beaten."

"Do it or I attack you," Avaria hissed.

Hayden sighed. Then he took a quick step to the right and raised his arm, preparing to strike.

He moves fast, Emily thought, *and very smooth, despite the fact that he is already hurt.* Either Hayden was lying about his fighting experience, or he was a natural.

Unfortunately for him, Avaria was much faster. She spun to her right, crouching, and Hayden's punch sailed over her head, passing through the edges of her long black hair. He made a wise move, and continued his motion in an attempt to get away from her. Then he pivoted, bringing his arm up to guard his face.

However, Avaria had already reversed, and she came at him low, underneath his guard. Her right leg lashed out, striking Hayden in the stomach, and he landed flat on his back almost ten feet away.

"Yep, you beat me," Hayden wheezed.

Avaria stood up straight, showing no signs of stress or fatigue. Emily stared at her in awe.

"You are better than expected," Avaria said to him. Hayden just lay there, motionless. "You may have promise yet." She turned back to the group. "Next?"

"Me!" Emily volunteered eagerly, stepping forward.

"Very well," she replied. "Attack!"

The fight lasted about three seconds. Avaria ducked and

swept out Emily's legs with a kick, sending her crashing to the floor.

I guess I need more training, she thought, crawling to join Hayden.

Avaria turned to Sam. "Now you," she instructed.

Sam looked like he might wet himself. He glanced at Lana and then took a few tentative steps forward. There was already sweat glistening on his forehead.

Avaria watched him like a cat ready to pounce. "Attack."

Sam smiled sheepishly. "I already know that I need a lot of work with fighting, more practice and all. So you can just count me as a full beginner and start from scratch."

"Attack or I do."

"I really don't want—"

Before he could finish, Avaria leapt at him. Sam just closed his eyes.

Avaria gripped either arm, spun him once, and then let go. Sam flew across the room and slammed into the tiles. He slid along for a few more feet and then didn't move. Emily put her hand over her mouth, horrified. Lana tried to get to him, but Avaria wheeled on her.

"He will get up on his own, and he will learn to defend himself. Now it's your turn."

Sam slowly began to push himself up.

"You could have killed him," Lana whispered vehemently.

Avaria smiled. "Could have."

"Does this make you feel good?" Lana asked, gesturing to the others. "Beating up on kids?"

"You want to make me pay, don't you?" Avaria said. She

began to pace again, her eyes focused on Lana.

Lana looked away. "I can't beat you."

"No, you can't," she agreed. "But I will teach you how."

"You lie. You wouldn't make me as strong as you."

"I would, and I will. But first, attack. Show me your anger."

"Fine!" Lana shouted, and ran at her.

Lana was obviously a fast learner. She changed direction at the last second, pivoting to her left foot and kicking with her right. At the same time, she swung her right arm at Avaria's midsection and put her left up to guard her face.

Avaria didn't even dodge. She just stepped forward with incredible speed and punched Lana right in the stomach. Lana bent over, gasping, and Avaria grabbed her hair and wrenched her head upward.

"Better," she said approvingly, and then shoved her to the floor.

Avaria turned to the rest of the group. "Now, everyone get to a bag. I know what you can do; now we'll see if we can make you better. You don't leave until you're dripping sweat, so work hard, or you stay here all night."

Hayden and Sam hurried off to the various punching bags scattered around the room, while Emily hobbled over to Lana.

"Are you okay?" Emily asked.

Lana stood up and shot Avaria a malevolent glare.

"Fine," she said, starting for a bag. "If Avaria wants me to get strong, then that's what I'll do," she snarled.

Lana began punching the bag, scowling. For the first

time since they'd been there, she wasn't thinking about how to get home. She was thinking about how to make Avaria pay. And of course, that was exactly what Avaria wanted.

Five long, slow hours after they'd fled the bus, the Torturer steered them back into the Baron's garage and parked the van.

James had been silent most of the way home. Somehow, seeing Mark on the hood of the car hadn't been what he had in mind. *If I don't even like hurting my nemesis, how am I supposed to be a supervillain?* he wondered.

Stepping out of the van, the Torturer groaned and stretched. "I'm beat. I'll take you back to your room."

James followed him into the mansion. "You think I could get the heat turned down a bit tonight?" he asked hopefully.

The Torturer seemed to consider that. "Yeah, I can turn it down."

When James walked into the common area, Hayden and Sam were lying on the couches.

"How was your day?" Hayden asked, looking up.

"Long," James mumbled. "Yours?"

"Painful," Sam said.

"I'll get the details tomorrow." James started for the bathroom but paused. "Oh yeah . . . our disappearance is front-page news."

"Sweet," Hayden said. "I hope they used a good picture of me. Did you see it?"

"Nah, just heard about it," James replied, heading down

the hallway toward the bathroom. "I've got to go to bed; I'm exhausted. Night." The shower was running, so he knocked on the door. "Can I just use the bathroom quickly?"

James heard some rummaging and then the door swung open. Steam rushed out, followed by a sopping-wet Lana, wrapped in a white towel. James stared at her for a moment, speechless.

"Go ahead," she said, gesturing behind her.

"Thanks." James stepped inside and shut the door. *Wow,* he thought.

"Thanks . . . again," he said on the way out.

Lana bunched up the towel a little more. "No problem. Did the trip go all right?"

"Long story. I'll tell you guys in the morning."

"See you in the morning, then." She smirked. "If we can sleep."

"Yeah, *if* being the operative word," James agreed. "Night."

James went to his room and stretched out across the mattress. Despite everything that had happened during the day, his mind went to Lana. He fell asleep thinking of her.

18

THE NEXT MORNING, THE PROTÉGÉS WERE SITTING ON THE COUCHES eating breakfast when the Torturer's now-familiar voice boomed over the speaker. They all lowered their forks in trepidation.

The night had been awful again. Lana had eventually given up on sleeping and wandered out to find that Sam, Emily, and Hayden were already lying on the couches. All of their bedrooms were simply too hot, their beds too hard, and Sam said that quiet voices had been haunting him. Only James had stayed in his room for the night.

"Today's group session will be conducted by Sliver and will begin in thirty minutes. There are also a few announcements. At Avaria's suggestion, we have decided that you will be going to the combat room to train every day before bed. Second, we will be providing you with new clothing first thing tomorrow."

"About time," Lana whispered to Sam, and he nodded.

"And last but not least." The Torturer's voice perked up. "We have an announcement pertaining to Hayden."

Hayden smiled and rested his chin on his hands. "Finally," he said. "Let's see what they got on me."

The Torturer began in a slow, dramatic voice.

"Hayden may have informed you that he lives in a house without his parents. Perhaps he has not yet told you why. Let me give you a little history. Hayden's mother ran away from home at seventeen: away from her abusive father, to be specific. Naturally, she went to the big city, where she became a housekeeper. It wasn't the best job, but she was getting by. The very next year, she met a wealthy client named Albert Hinnigan. They started dating, and little Hayden was conceived."

Lana glanced at Hayden, but so far the story seemed to have no effect on him. He was just listening intently.

"But, as is so often the case, the relationship didn't work out. Albert met someone else and moved on. Hayden's mother was absolutely crushed. But Albert is the good guy in this story. He left checks at regular intervals throughout Hayden's entire childhood, and his mother put a lot of money away. Eventually, it would be used to buy a house for her son. But why isn't Hayden living with his mother now, you ask?

"Well, three years ago, Hayden's mother met another man, Rob Toasley. She fell for him immediately. But he was very conservative, so at first, Hayden's mother didn't want to tell him she had a kid. They always met at his house, never hers. She managed to hide Hayden's existence for almost a year, which is pretty impressive, though a testament to her subpar parenting. Eventually, she realized she had to make a choice. And she chose Rob.

"She bought a house in the suburbs to move in with Hayden. That's what she told him, at least. She actually bought the house so she could leave fourteen-year-old Hayden to fend for himself. He saw her occasionally, on weekends sometimes. But she got pregnant again and began living with Rob permanently. Hayden doesn't know this, but he has a half sister named Lillian.

"Hayden hasn't seen his mother for over a year. And when someone finally tracked her down to tell her Hayden was missing, she never made a phone call, never made the drive. She didn't lose a night of sleep. That is all."

Lana was speechless.

Hayden still had his chin resting on his hands, looking pensive. Finally, he sighed and leaned back. "I always wondered how she could afford that house," he said. "Thank goodness for Albert."

Lana frowned. "Did you hear *any* of that?" she asked.

The story had been awful, much worse than hers. Her dad might be having an affair, but Hayden didn't even have a father in his life, and his mother had abandoned him to start a new family. That was beyond comprehension for her.

Hayden nodded. "Most of it, though I tend to fade out of long stories."

James started laughing, and Sam and Emily joined in.

"You're ridiculous," Lana muttered, but she couldn't hold back a grin. "Totally ridiculous."

"Thank you," Hayden replied seriously. "Now, anyone grabbing a shower? Want a partner?"

Half an hour later, the protégés filed into the same shadowy classroom Leni had brought them to a few days earlier. Sliver was casually sitting on a black chair at the front of the room, watching them come in. He almost looked bored.

"Sit down and close your eyes," he instructed, and they quickly settled into their chairs. "No one speaks, and until I tell you, no one opens their eyes. If you do, you will find out why they call me Sliver."

As soon as the word came out of his mouth, a weird, echoing voice repeated "Sliver" in the back of Sam's mind, and he shuddered.

Yesterday, before Avaria's group training, Sliver had taken Sam out for a second individual lesson. They'd spent hours working on perceiving the minds of others, and already, Sam's sensitivity had grown. He had yet to decipher any actual thoughts, but following Sliver's lead, he'd managed to find traces of emotions in the others around the mansion.

Sliver began his lesson. "The League has two telepaths of their own, and they will try to use their powers to locate you, read your thoughts, and control you. A true telepath can render an untrained opponent completely useless. As such, you must all learn to shield your minds. When you sense intrusion, you must locate your internal voice and follow that alone. It is not as easy as it sounds. For today's session, I will illustrate how it works."

Do you hear me, Sam? Sliver whispered into Sam's mind. It was like a voice talking from far away, but just loudly enough that Sam could hear it.

Yes, he replied, still slightly unnerved by the connection.

Good. While we will spend time training the others, they are mostly here for our own uses. Understand?

Sam frowned. *Not really.*

We are going to practice delving into their minds, so that you can feel what it's like to read their emotions and their most vivid thoughts. Once you can do that, you can control them.

That doesn't seem very nice . . . Sam started.

Silence! Sliver snapped, and Sam felt a rush of his mentor's impatience flood through him. *Let's start with Hayden.*

Sam opened his eyes and glanced at Hayden, who was smiling and twiddling his thumbs, though his eyes were still closed. *You want me to go in there?* Sam asked dubiously.

Yes. Focus, just like I told you, and then follow my lead.

All right, Sam said, and even in his head it sounded like a whimper.

Concentrating on the area around him, Sam closed his eyes again and felt the other four protégés as tumultuous clouds of mental energy. Sliver had explained that once a telepath actually spoke to someone, he could listen for that person's voice and associate it to their specific train of thought. So while a telepath couldn't identify strangers without digging into their subconscious, he could always identify those he already knew by simply *listening*.

Using this technique, Sam found Hayden's internal voice and focused on it, feeling the surge of emotions as his own. First, Sam sensed boredom, and then, as he went a bit deeper, delight at some hidden thought came to the forefront. Sam carefully reminded himself that it was Hayden's pleasure that he was experiencing, not his own, before he continued. It was a strange sensation, as if he was partially detached from his own mind and wandering around inside of Hayden's.

You've connected to his consciousness, Sliver said. *Good. Now, can you sense any distinct thoughts?*

Sam tried to quiet the influence of Hayden's emotions, as Sliver had instructed, and listened for any comprehensible words.

I wonder if they'll give her a uniform. A nice tight bodysuit, maybe.

Was that him? Sam said.

It was, Sliver replied, sounding amused. *I believe he's referring to Lana.*

What's that other feeling? Sam asked as he sifted through the changing emotions.

That would be arousal.

Ew, Sam said, making a face. *Can we move to someone else?*

First, you must learn to control him. He is untrained: it will be simple. Tell him to strip to his boxers.

Why would I—

Do it!

Shaking his head, Sam focused on Hayden's thoughts again and then projected his own voice into the current. Soft and understated, as Sliver had taught him.

Strip to your boxers, Sam whispered, feeling very awkward.

There was a moment of doubt in Hayden's mind as he questioned the origin of this new thought. Sliver's voice joined Sam's, repeating the same message. Sam felt Hayden weaken immediately and then break.

Opening his eyes again, Sam watched in amazement as Hayden pulled off his shirt and pants, all with his eyes still closed. He was now sitting only in his faded boxers.

Excellent, Sliver said, *we can leave him for a while. Now see if you can enter James's thoughts.*

Sam did as he was told and soon found James's voice at the desk behind him. His most direct and tangible emotion was not boredom or even fatigue. Something else was there. *What is that?*

Infatuation, Sliver replied. *It is a pungent emotion, so his thoughts should be easy to track. Who is he thinking about?*

It took Sam only a few seconds to figure it out. *Not Lana again,* he thought. Then he saw a fleeting image, as if he had briefly remembered something. *Did you see that?*

That, Sliver replied, barely containing his amusement

now, *was Lana in a towel. He was picturing it so strongly that even we could see it.*

Tell him to go run his fingers through her hair, Sliver ordered.

What? Sam asked. *I can't do that. That's—*

Now!

Sam sighed inwardly. *All right.* Focusing on James's train of thought, he injected the command. James's mind was already so absorbed with Lana that the instruction came naturally, and Sam didn't even need Sliver's help to break him. James opened his eyes and slowly rose out of his chair.

Sam turned around, catching a glimpse of Sliver's wide grin, and watched in horrified fascination as James shuffled toward Lana's desk. Coming to a halt beside her, he bent down and ran his fingers through her blond hair.

Lana reacted instantaneously. Her eyes shot open, and then she punched him right in the face.

Sliver erupted in laughter as James yelped and toppled backward to the floor. Hayden and Emily both opened their eyes as well, and Hayden hastily covered his bare chest with his hands.

"What the . . ." he said.

"Why are you naked?" Emily asked. She shifted her attention to James, who was now tenderly rubbing his eye on the ground. "James?"

"He scared the crap out of me!" Lana shouted, pointing at him.

"I didn't mean to," James protested. "That really hurt!"

Lana scowled. "What do you mean you didn't . . ."

She paused and then turned to the front of the room, where Sliver was still laughing. Her eyes shifted to Sam, and he felt his cheeks burning.

"Sorry," he murmured.

19

THAT NIGHT, HAYDEN STUMBLED OUT OF THE BEDROOM, HIS EYES half-closed. His hair was sticking up on one side, while the other half was plastered against his forehead with sweat. He cast himself face-first onto one of the couches.

"Why?" he moaned.

He was not alone. James was sprawled out on the couch next to him, while Lana and Emily were strewn across the other two.

"Why can't we just sleep?" Hayden mumbled. "It's not fair."

"Tonight was the worst by far," James agreed. His left eye was swollen again from where Lana had punched him.

"Definitely," Lana said. "What's the point of—"

A loud shriek split the air, and they all bolted upright. Sam came barreling down the hallway in his underwear. Without slowing, he jumped onto one of the recliners and curled into a ball, shaking.

"I want to go home," he said. "I want to go home."

"What happened?" Lana asked.

"I don't know," Sam whimpered. "All of a sudden my sheets pulled tight against me, and I couldn't move. The ceiling opened up, and a bright light shone on my face and said, 'You are being replaced, Samantha,' and then the sheets let go and the whole bed tipped over." He hugged himself even tighter, still trembling. "I thought I was done for."

Lana glared at the mirror. "They're probably in there having a big laugh."

"Most likely," Hayden agreed, rolling onto his back. "Well, it's not all bad. At least we can sleep out here. It's like a little slumber party."

As soon as the words left his mouth, the lights began to flicker. Wind howled in from the vents in the ceiling, sending everyone's hair flapping around them. Lana fought to hold on to her sheet, which was billowing into the air. Sam screamed and burrowed into the recliner, while Emily tried to protect her face. James just gave up and lay there.

I need to stop saying things like that, Hayden thought as he dug his head in between the cushions.

Emily awoke to the whoosh of the sliding panel. She slowly pulled her face from the couch and wiped the drool from the side of her mouth.

She looked around. Hayden's head was under the cushions, while Sam was blinking groggily from the recliner, where he was still huddled in a ball. On the couch next to Emily, Lana's windblown hair was completely covering her face. James was lying on his back, and one of his arms was draped over the side of the couch, his fingers curled up like a dead spider.

Emily pulled herself up and turned to the panel. Breakfast was there, and beside it were bundles of clothing. She hurried over. There were five piles and a piece of paper with a name on each. Emily found hers and noticed that it was entirely black, as she preferred.

"Wake up, everyone! Breakfast and clothes are here!"

Several loud groans answered her. Lana poked her head over the couch.

"We got clothes?" she mumbled.

"Yep. I'm going to go change."

Laying out the pile on her bed, Emily saw that she'd been given a black shirt and matching pants, both unmarked. Also included were new socks and underwear. She stripped down on the spot, casting off her dirty clothing with relish.

As she unfolded the pants, something fell out onto the ground. Emily bent down and picked up a gleaming, silver half visor. It was much sleeker and more stylish than Rono's, just wide enough on the end to cover her eye.

She gently placed it around the left side of her head, the same side Rono wore his, and as soon as the visor touched her skin, she felt the tiniest bit of suction as it attached itself. The end came across her left eye, so that she was looking through a screen.

"On," she instructed, hoping that it was voice-activated like most of Rono's devices.

She heard a little hum.

Suddenly, readings scrolled across the top and bottom of her vision. The visor began analyzing the size and positioning of all the contents of her room and then provided a careful readout of her own current physical condition.

"Awesome," she whispered, and then raced back to the common room to show everyone.

"She must be kidding me," Lana muttered.

She'd only been given one article of clothing: a scarlet, one-piece jumpsuit. Lana had been hoping for some sweatpants and a hoodie.

But the clothes she'd arrived in definitely needed to be washed, and she supposed she could get them back soon. *I guess it's a jumpsuit for me,* she thought bitterly, grabbing the outfit and crawling under her blanket to change.

After much cursing and wrangling, Lana emerged wearing the red one-piece, her other clothes cast about under the covers. She stood up, feeling very strange. The jumpsuit was reinforced in some areas with much harder material: around the ankles, wrists, and forearms and over her ribs and sternum. Yet it was very flexible and clung to her body like saran wrap. *A lot like Avaria's outfit,* Lana thought, and despite herself, she couldn't help but like it. It would at least absorb some of the more violent blows during sparring.

Scooping up her clothes from under the covers, she went back to the common room.

Everyone else was already there, admiring their new outfits. Breakfast sat forgotten in the panel. Hayden was spinning around, his new cape swirling behind him. He wore all black like his mentor, except that he had no gloves or boots on. Sam was wearing an elegant purple shirt, which contrasted with his mocha skin, and crisp dress pants. The expensive clothes made his mop of curly hair look very out of place.

James was watching the proceedings with a frown. He was wearing a forest-green shirt and brown pants that were both much too big, making him look twice as skinny.

Everyone turned to look at Lana as she came in. James flushed, and Hayden broke out in a lopsided grin.

"Well, hello," Hayden said.

"Shut up," she snarled, biting back a smile.

Lana hated to admit it, but she was starting to find Hayden more and more attractive. He was arrogant and insufferable, and because of that, she'd assumed at first that he was a spoiled rich kid. But when Lana had heard the story about his mother, she realized there was probably a lot more to Hayden than he let on. He was putting on a confident act, and who could blame him? He'd basically been abandoned since he was fourteen years old.

But Lana already had enough things to worry about in this place. Getting involved with someone was the last thing she needed.

She threw her old clothes next to the plates, where the others had already started a pile.

"I like the outfit," Hayden said. "It's very supervillain," he added, mocking a fashion commentator. "It just screams: I am full of rage, and I still look sexy."

Lana laughed and shook her head.

"And then we have James," Hayden went on, "who's bringing back the peasant look with aplomb." He snapped his fingers. "He may be plain, but he packs a wallop." He winked, and James became even redder.

Hayden turned to Sam. "And, of course, our eligible and tantalizing bachelor, Sam, who is reinventing elegance with a stylish new outfit courtesy of Villaineo Vivide. Get ready to take some cold showers, ladies."

He whirled to Emily, his cape spinning behind him. "And here we have our shadow lady: lithe, mysterious, and sporting a metal eye. While you're checking out her new clothes, she's looking right through yours."

Emily looked at James and opened her mouth in shock. "James, I had no idea how muscular you are!" she gasped, and James's face finally went as red as Lana's jumpsuit.

"And how about *your* outfit?" Lana asked with a raised eyebrow, looking Hayden up and down.

He strutted forward, swinging his hips. "This outfit makes a statement," he said in the same commentator voice, fingering his jet-black shirt with one hand and swinging his cape with the other. "It says, I hate you, your mother, puppies, rainbows, sunshine, fun, long walks on the beach, people who encourage others," he listed off on his hand, still strutting. He spun in front of Lana and posed with his hands on his hips.

"Well, aren't we the team now," Emily said. "We're starting to actually look like supervillains."

"I still don't feel like one," Sam muttered.

"Good morning," the Torturer's voice cut in. "I see you've all found your new clothes. You will have a group session with Rono this morning, and your individual sessions will follow. For some of you, today marks the beginning of new stages in your training. Now the real stuff begins. Rono will be at the door to pick you up in fifteen minutes, so eat your breakfast and be ready."

RONO ASSEMBLED THE PROTÉGÉS INTO A STRAIGHT LINE, FACING him. He wore his usual brown trench coat, but today he had a gun strapped to his leg and a vicious-looking rifle slung over his back. Sliver stood beside him, surveying their new attire.

James looked around the room they'd been brought to. It was long and rectangular, and the walls, floor, and ceiling were covered with gray plating. He spotted several weapons racks on the wall, all containing an assortment of handguns and rifles. He'd made sure to position himself beside Lana, and he nudged her and gestured at the weapons.

"I know," she mouthed, looking disturbed.

Lana had been somewhat distant with James since yesterday's hair-stroking incident; she'd barely looked at him during the evening workout. He wasn't sure why she was acting that way since Sam had already explained what happened. But James was determined to fix it somehow because no matter what he did, he couldn't stop thinking about her.

"Think he's compensating?" James asked quietly, and she smiled, the first positive reaction he'd gotten from her in a while. It was enough to set his skin tingling.

"No talking!" Rono barked.

As the little man scowled at them, Hayden glanced at James and shook his head.

"Remember the shotgun," he murmured.

"What shotgun?" Lana asked, looking between them.

James bit his lip. "I think he means on the wall—"

"Quiet!" Rono commanded, and Emily frowned at James.

This reminds me of school, James thought bitterly. *Everyone talks, and I get in trouble.*

"This room is specifically designed for weapons training," Rono began. "Regardless of the powers you receive, the ability to properly and accurately utilize a weapon will be invaluable to you. We have weapons here you have never seen or heard of as they are beyond the technology of even the top military capabilities. I know, because I invented them. And in case you get a funny idea that you can use these weapons to escape, I don't advise it. Sliver is here to monitor your thoughts, and he'll know what you're going to do before you ever pull the trigger. And even if you did manage to get by us, you will be detained and punished very severely—severely enough that you'll wish you were killed in the escape attempt."

"That's true," Hayden agreed. "The magic forest will attack you."

Lana smirked, and James glared at Hayden's back. Lana and Hayden had been talking more since Hayden's announcement, and last night they were laughing away as they did sit-ups together in the corner of the workout room.

"Ah, that's right," Rono said. "I forgot one of you already found that out. All the better, then. The rest of you won't be so stupid. Now, the first weapon you will learn to use is a plasma discharger." He slipped the gleaming black gun out of the holster on his leg and showed it to them. "This is one of our basic guns. When you become full members, you'll all receive one. Essentially, this side chamber here ionizes plasma, and then it bursts out of the nozzle as a red flash. If you want to merely stun your enemy, you switch this lever, and the flash will be blue."

He spun and fired across the room, releasing a red bolt. It hit the wall and erupted with a blinding flash.

"Cool," Hayden said.

Rono turned back to them. "I will have a series of targets cross the room, and you will take turns firing at them. Then we'll try out one more basic weapon today, just to introduce it." He gestured at the rifle slung over his back. "The repeating plasma rifle. Now," he said, raising his voice, "activate target one."

A hidden panel slid open in the wall about forty feet away. There was a whirring noise, and the floor in front of the open panel started to move like a conveyor belt.

"Who wants to shoot first?" Rono asked, hoisting the gun.

"Me!" Emily shouted.

She eagerly hurried over, and Rono handed her the plasma discharger. Behind him, something started to emerge from the panel.

They can't be serious, James thought. He tentatively put his hand up. "Um, is that a baby carriage?"

"Yes," Rono said. "I thought it would be a good place to start. You know, desensitize you right off the bat."

A baby's cry echoed across the room. Sam looked like he was about to faint.

"Go ahead, Emily," Rono said, taking a long step out of the way. "Hurry, it's almost three-quarters of the way across."

"Emily, you can't shoot a baby!" Lana protested.

"It's not a real baby, right?" Emily asked Rono.

Rono shrugged. When Emily continued to stare at him stone-faced, he finally waved a hand. "No, it's mechanical. Now blow the thing up."

Emily raised the discharger.

"Emily, maybe you should make sure . . ." James started.

Sighting her target with one eye, Emily aimed for the slow-moving carriage and fired. The red bolt struck it full-on, and the carriage exploded dramatically, spraying flaming pink lace and pieces of mechanical baby all across the room.

James felt something sharp digging into his arm and saw that Lana had grabbed him. When he met her eyes, she quickly let go.

"Sorry," Lana said, sounding embarrassed. "I thought she just blew up a baby."

"No problem," James replied. "Technically, she did."

She laughed nervously.

"Remember the shotgun . . ." a faint voice whispered, and James shot Hayden a dirty look.

"Why does he keep . . ." Lana started.

"Quiet!" Rono took the gun back from Emily. "All right, who's next?"

Leni stalked down the central corridor of his personal headquarters, his boots echoing off the black stone. It was mostly underground, stretching through the underside of a rolling green hill in northern Pennsylvania.

The only visible feature on the surface was a large, plain brick country house, surrounded by impenetrable hedges and scratching brambles. The locals thought that a wealthy old miser lived there and that the black vans constantly coming in and out of the driveway brought him paintings and sculptures to add to his enormous collection. They were half-right. Leni had killed the old man two years ago, when he first went into hiding after Phoenix's murder. Here, he'd rebuilt his fractured organization, tunneling these black corridors into the soil.

Reaching the end of the hall, he took a sharp right, passing through a black iron door that opened at a wave of his finger. Inside was a circular room, ringed with blinking red display panels that were manned by six of his operatives. In the center stood a raised platform with a single chair, and everyone in the room cowered as Leni marched up the steps and sat down. As soon as he did, the screens surrounding the seat thrummed to life.

"Report," he commanded.

Kayla, the blond operative who had lured Hayden out of his house, hurried to the base of the platform, clutching a data pad. "Project Nightfall is proceeding as planned. The shipment of stun panels arrived on schedule and can be taken back to the Baron's mansion on your return."

"Good." The near completion of Project Nightfall was the reason Leni had made the long trip back to his base. He couldn't risk mentioning the project in any transmissions from the mansion. It had to be kept an absolute secret from the other Vindico members. "Continue."

Kayla snuck a brief glimpse at the data pad. "The League is still largely gathered at their headquarters in New York, though we have reports that some detachments have begun to leave the premises. We think that members went to investigate the incident in Cambilsford, and it also seems they re-inspected the homes of both Hayden and Sam. My guess is they've confirmed the Vindico is behind the disappearances."

"That was to be expected eventually," Leni replied, but he knew the clock was ticking now. If the League knew the Vindico had taken the children, they might have guessed why.

"There's something else," Kayla continued quietly.

"Thunderbolt has left headquarters again." She hesitated. "But as before, we've lost track of him."

Leni considered this information. It was definitely troubling news; he knew that it must be something important if Thunderbolt would leave headquarters at a time like this.

"Very well," Leni said at last. "I will be returning to the Baron's shortly. Load the stun panels and *find* Thunderbolt," he added coolly. "Or I will find someone else who can."

As Kayla scurried away, Leni leaned back and traced his finger along a readout screen. Timing was an issue now. The League was closing in, and if they found the mansion before he was prepared, everything would fall apart. He needed another couple of weeks, at least. Then he could execute Project Nightfall, and the League would be caught in his trap, along with the Vindico.

He would kill the League members and the Baron. With the old man out of the picture, the rest of the Vindico and their protégés would be forced to swear loyalty to Leni or be killed as well. At least, everyone but Hayden.

Now that he'd conducted his own scan, Leni knew that his protégé had the potential to become extremely powerful, maybe even more than his mentor. He was a threat that couldn't be ignored. When the time came for Nightfall, Hayden would have to die.

21

"WE SHOULD PLAY TWENTY QUESTIONS," HAYDEN SAID LATER that night. "I mean, we don't know that much about each other." He turned to Lana, folded his fingers together, and rested his chin on them with an exaggeratedly curious expression. "Let's start with you, Lana . . ." He frowned. "I don't know your last name. Or any of yours, actually."

"Hunter," Lana told him. She put her hand up to block his view. "And please stop looking at me like that."

"Lana Hunter . . . I like that," Hayden said. "James? Wait, let me guess . . . James Eugene Pidwinkle?"

James scowled. "It's James Renwick."

"That was my next guess. Emily, Sam?"

"Mine is Lau," Emily replied.

"Bennett," Sam said.

Hayden stood up and took an elaborate bow. "And *I* am Hayden Matthew Lockwood. Just think: it could have been Hayden Hinnigan."

"All right, Hayden, I have a question," Lana said. "Do you miss your mom?"

"Well, that's not exactly the fun type of question I had in mind," Hayden replied slowly, sitting down again, "but I guess I didn't specify."

Over the last couple of years, Hayden had created a thousand theories of where his mom had been and why she didn't call him anymore. He knew she hadn't died because the courts would have found him, and someone was still paying the bills for his house. A new family had been his best guess, so he hadn't been that surprised to learn it was true. Still, he'd secretly been hoping it was something else. It hurt that he hadn't been good enough for her, but Hayden had learned to put those types of feelings away, especially in front of others.

"I did miss her," Hayden said, "but then I realized the reason my eggs were always burning was because I was using sugar on the pan instead of butter. I thought they were interchangeable." He looked away, biting his lip. "So many wasted eggs."

"Why are you such an idiot?" Lana asked.

Hayden immediately brightened. "That's a better question. I suspect it's my poor attendance record at school. Now, Lana, what type of men do you go for?"

"I'm not answering that."

"But it's the game . . ." Hayden said.

"I don't want to play, then. Pick a new game."

Hayden raised his eyebrows. "Any game?"

"As long as it's not twenty questions," Lana said.

Hayden stood up, wearing a lopsided grin. "You're the boss."

"Why are you smiling like that?" James asked suspiciously.

Hayden turned to him. "I know how we can get to know each other better."

"I can't believe I'm playing this." Lana shook her head.

They all sat around the coffee table, watching Hayden clear off the surface.

"You did say *any* game," Hayden reminded her as he placed a cup sideways on the table. "And this is the absolute best game to get to know each other. Spin the bottle. The original game of chance."

"You mean spin the plastic cup," Emily corrected.

"Right," Hayden said. "Now, since it was Lana's idea to play, I think she should get the honor of the first spin."

"It was *not* my idea," she corrected. "And these are just pecks, nothing more."

Lana looked around the group and saw that Sam was already fidgeting nervously. James was leaning forward, his brown eyes fixated on the cup, while Emily was just watching curiously, as if she had neither seen nor heard of such a game.

I need to learn to keep my mouth shut, Lana told herself, and then spun the cup.

It landed on James. Immediately, his cheeks flushed scarlet.

I suppose he would be the least awkward one to kiss,

Lana thought. *Well, Hayden would probably be the least awkward, but I'm not about to give him the satisfaction.*

"This is so romantic," Hayden said. "Someone dim the lights."

"Shut up," Lana muttered, and then she leaned over and quickly kissed James on the lips. As she sat back again, she noticed that James still had his eyes closed.

"Oh no, James is trapped in time!" Hayden shouted.

James opened his eyes and forced an embarrassed smile, avoiding Lana's gaze.

"I love spin the bottle," Hayden said happily. "And I love it more now that it's Sam's turn. Have you ever kissed anyone, Sammy?"

Sam shook his head, his eyes on the coffee table.

"Well, the wait is over," Hayden said. "Spin the cup, Mr. Bennett!"

Sam tentatively reached out to grab the cup and with a slow, deliberate movement, he spun it.

At first it landed on Hayden, who promptly closed his eyes and puckered his lips.

"I feel so honored," he whispered.

Lana burst out laughing at the horrified look on Sam's face. "Spin again, Sam," she said.

He did, and this time it landed on James.

"Sorry, Sam," James said. "But no kiss from me. I don't know you well enough."

Emily looked at Sam with a sly smile. "If you get one of the boys again, you're going to have to kiss him," she warned. "That will be three strikes."

Sam gulped and spun the bottle again. This time, it landed on Lana.

Lana glanced at Sam, who literally looked like he might get up and run. *If it's his first kiss, I better make it special,* she decided. Calmly, she turned to him, cupped his chin with both hands, and kissed him firmly on the mouth. When Lana pulled away, Sam's eyes were so wide she thought they might pop.

Hayden stood up and started clapping. "That was incredible," he said. "Best first kiss ever. I think I have goose bumps."

"How does Leni put up with you?" James asked.

"Mainly by beating me," Hayden said. "Yesterday he hit me with a block of sand because I asked him if he had a girlfriend."

"Can you move anything with your mind yet?" Sam asked.

"Sort of. I can make the sand move a little, but I can't pick it up or anything. I was actually trying to affect the cup, but no dice."

"What were you trying to do to it?" Lana asked, glaring at him.

Hayden smirked. "I think you know."

James groaned and stood up. "I'm going to the bathroom."

As he left, Hayden jumped to his feet. "All right, I'm going to move something," he announced, walking around the couches. "It's time to become a supervillain." He whirled his cape in a flourish. "Behold, the dreaded Handsome Hayden!"

He narrowed his eyes and then waved his hand at the chessboard. To everyone's astonishment, it shot across the room and smashed into the far wall.

Hayden stood there for a moment, his mouth hanging open. "Did anyone else see that?"

"I thought you could barely move anything?" Lana asked incredulously.

"I couldn't!" he said. "Leni would be so proud." Grabbing his cape, he flung it behind him and strutted around the room. "Handsome Hayden strikes again. No chessboard is safe!"

"What did I miss? What was that crash?" James asked, hurrying back into the common area. He looked at Hayden. "Why are you marching?"

"Handsome Hayden does not answer to peasants! Shouldn't you be tilling your fields?"

"Hayden just used his powers," Emily explained matter-of-factly.

"Really?" James asked, watching as Hayden continued to strut around the room. "I still can't believe they're giving that kid superpowers."

"It is a scary thought," Lana agreed.

"Sometimes I almost forget what we're doing here," Sam said quietly. "That we're going to be a part of this war we've been hearing about since we were little kids. It's like we're in these four walls, and there's nothing really outside. It feels like it's a private school or something, and eventually we'll go home to our parents and everything will be normal again. But even if we're really lucky, and everything turns out okay, and we actually *can* go home when this is finished, we're going to be the first people in history to be *given* superpowers. We're going to be famous. Nothing will ever be the same again."

Everyone fell silent as Sam's words sank in.

Lana looked up at the black symbol over the fireplace, a reminder of what they were supposed to become: shadows instead of people.

Hayden sat down again. "Well, that killed the mood."

"I just don't think it's—" the Torturer started.

"It is step three of my psychological program," the Baron cut in firmly. "And the most important one. They need to be given a choice. It's the only way we can be sure of their loyalty."

All the Vindico members except Leni were gathered in the Baron's meeting room.

Avaria folded her arms, looking unconvinced. "They are already frightened into obedience."

"But that can only last for so long," the Baron said. "They need to consciously *join* us. We will give them two weeks from tomorrow to make a decision. By then, they will choose to stay. I guarantee it."

"And what if they don't?" Rono asked.

The Baron paused. "Those that choose to leave will be killed as soon as they leave the mansion. We can't risk them going to the League and giving away our plans and position. I don't know how much longer we have until the League finds us. We *must* have these protégés ready to fight as soon as possible. In two weeks, they will become full members of this society. Then the war begins anew. And this time, the odds will finally be in our favor."

"PLEASE, SIT," THE BARON SAID THE NEXT MORNING, LEADING them into a classroom. It was very different than the room Leni and Sliver had used: this one was well lit, and the chairs looked plush and comfortable.

James sat down near the front, with Sam and Emily on either side, while Hayden and Lana took the two desks behind them. The pair continued to grow closer every day. Once again, they'd spent last night's entire workout together and stayed up talking after everyone else had gone to bed.

James felt like he had a rock sitting in his stomach every time he saw them together. He'd only eaten a piece of plain white bread for breakfast.

But while he was concerned over Lana and Hayden's increasing closeness, everything else was going great. He'd been taking Genome AP for three days now and spent most of his time lifting weights with the Torturer. Already, the AP was having some effect: yesterday he had added forty-five pounds to his bench press.

The Baron sat down at the front of the classroom in a high-backed wooden chair. He smiled, showing off his crisply white teeth.

"Today you will have your first 'history' session. So far, we have been concentrating on preparing you for the drastic physical and mental changes you will face. But it's time to give you some context for why you are here. It's time you learn who the true villains are."

James sat up a little straighter in his chair. He'd been practically begging the Torturer for more information about the League and the Vindico, but his mentor always put him off.

"I'm sure you all know the official history of the League," the Baron went on dryly. "At least, the version they promote. The glorious 'Four Founders,' banding together to protect justice and freedom the world over . . . propaganda, and nothing more."

The Baron stood up and began to walk around the room.

"As you know, the first of the Four Founders, Captain Courage, discovered his supernatural abilities fifty-four years ago. The other three Founders appeared over the course of five years: the Champion, Phoenix, and the League's current leader, Thunderbolt. Of course, they immediately became the world's biggest celebrities and media darlings. But at heart, they were just normal people: they had no real goals, no ambition. They weren't superheroes by any standards; they simply lived in big houses, fraternized with each other, and went about their lives. That is, until the fifth founding member of the League came along, the one who first proposed the idea of a unified organization: me."

There was an undercurrent of venom seeping into his story now.

"I didn't have any supernatural abilities myself, but I was obsessed with obtaining them. I spent many years trying to unlock the secrets of their mutation. During that time, I became very close friends with the original four, and it was *I* who proposed the League of Heroes. We would fight crime, solve world issues, and serve as a home for any superpowered individuals who came along.

"In time, the League became a symbol of justice: we captured terrorists, dismantled drug cartels, even supervised international peace negotiations. New recruits began to surface around the globe. And most importantly, after many years of research, my experiments were nearing completion. I was ready to begin my transformation and fully join my friends. But alas," the Baron said darkly, "they had other plans.

"For some time, I'd noticed that some of the League members were starting to push me away. I wasn't like them: I wasn't 'chosen' to be a hero. Despite the fact that I had formed the League, that *I* was its creator, they wanted me gone. I knew I had to complete my transformation before they acted and expelled me from the organization.

"But a few days before I was about to begin, Captain Courage discovered the schematics for my chamber. We had a tremendous argument that morning. I argued that my ability to construct the machine was fate just as much as his powers from birth. But he would not see reason. He forbade me from going through with my plans.

"As soon as I stepped out of his quarters, I ran for my laboratory. I knew I didn't have much time. If I could just make the transformation, then it would be too late. They would have to accept me."

The Baron stopped at the front of the room, his eyes looking beyond them.

"But right before I could get in the chamber, Courage, the Champion, and Thunderbolt burst into my lab. They destroyed everything. Twenty years of work, gone in an instant. I had been betrayed by my closest friends.

"On that day, it became my single-minded mission to destroy the League of Heroes. But as the years passed, I realized I had no power to challenge them. Until one day, three years after the destruction of my chamber, the League found a new teenage protégé, one more powerful than any they had ever seen. But there was a problem. He was angry and ambitious, imperious and condescending."

"Sounds like Leni . . ." Hayden mumbled.

"It was. He remained with the League for nine years, but they never saw eye to eye on what the real function of their organization was. Leni wanted to take preemptive action: he wanted to crush dictatorships, punish war criminals with death, and destroy corporations that took advantage of the poor. You see, his intentions were good, but the League did not believe in directly interfering with global politics. Leni was too radical. Eventually, Courage expelled Leni and banned him from using his powers. This was the chance I'd been waiting for.

"I proposed a new venue for his talents, a new goal. Overthrow the weak, corrupt League, take power, and enforce our will on this planet.

"Leni joined immediately, and everything changed. He was the force that I had needed, and we began preparations for war. But we were still greatly outnumbered and outmatched, and time passed again while we waited for the ideal opportunity.

"It was four more years until the pieces of the puzzle finally fell into place. We found three new recruits over that time. Twenty-two years ago, I discovered the first one, the Torturer. He was a mere sixteen-year-old hiding in the woods. His name then was Evan Port."

James recognized that name, but he couldn't place it.

"At fourteen, Evan managed to gain his incredible size and strength through a highly dangerous mix of compounds he stole from his father, an environmental scientist. Why? Because a hated school bully, Jay Junkit, discovered he could fly right in the middle of class. Evan couldn't stand the sight of him taking off through the window as the other kids cheered, not after all the terrible things Junkit had done to him. He swore that he would have powers of his own."

"Jay Junkit? You mean the Sparrow?" James asked, frowning. "But he came from my high school. He's the most famous product of Cambilsford. How could that . . ."

James suddenly realized why the Torturer had chosen him: his mentor was from the same high school.

The Baron continued his story. "Evan's dream was to join the League of Heroes, but he wanted to taste popularity first. He joined the football team and became a school hero, winning both the state and national championships that year.

"His radical transformation soon came to the ears of the League, and one day, Thunderbolt appeared at his front door. Evan was thrilled: he'd had his fun at school, and now he would be admitted to the League. But when Thunderbolt discovered that Evan's powers had resulted from illegal experiments, he refused to admit him and even banned Evan from the competitive sports that had made him a school hero. All his awards were stripped."

James remembered where he'd heard the name. His father had once told him a story about the best linebacker in school history, who mysteriously disappeared after one season.

"Evan was furious, and he ran away from home. He came to my attention, and the rest of the world's, when he famously robbed a bank in Portersfield by smashing the entire building to pieces. It was the first recorded case of a superpowered criminal. When Firefly foolishly came alone to arrest him, he quickly learned that he was no match for the Torturer, and he was killed in the ensuing battle, along with four police officers. Knowing the League would come after him, Evan fled into the wilderness, and it was there that Leni and I found him."

James was completely blown away. He couldn't believe that someone from *his* high school was behind the Portersfield Incident. James now understood his mentor's hatred of Thunderbolt: he had essentially ruined Evan's life. *But Thunderbolt is the good guy,* James reminded himself.

"We found the second recruit a year later," the Baron continued, "Rono, unique in that he has no powers other than an unmatched intellect. He was an advanced technology scientist and created weapons and ships the likes of which had never been seen. Twenty years ago, he offered his services to the League. They took his designs without question and still use them to this day. But, of course, they wouldn't let him join. He had no powers, they said, therefore he had no right. When he demanded his designs be returned, they refused. Rono was furious, and once again, I was there. Our little society was growing."

"That's why he hates them," Emily said quietly.

"Indeed," the Baron replied. "But the League's darkest secret is centered around a man named Derias Tepper, also known as Nimian, the only recorded shape-shifter in history. You probably haven't heard of him; his name has been wiped from the League's records. But he was a powerful man, just as brilliant as Rono. He served the League for many years and probably still would if not for one thing: his wife. Nimian would have done anything for her, but she only wanted one thing—the thing he was forbidden to give. She wanted superpowers.

"For years she asked him, begged him, until finally, he relented. Nimian was perhaps the world's foremost expert on power transformations; the League had him study the process to see if it could be *reversed*. They always feared that the technology would become widespread. With the League's endless resources at his disposal, Nimian managed in a few months what had taken me twenty years. Like I had, he constructed a chamber that used waves of coded radiation to rebuild the genetic strands of the person inside. Using this technology, he could give his wife unmatched strength and agility. But for all his concealment, all his secrecy, his designs did not go unnoticed.

"His wife was in the chamber when Courage and the Champion arrived at Nimian's door to arrest him. But Nimian did not go easily. While fighting with those so-called heroes, he was murdered by Courage.

"As Courage stood over his dead body, Nimian's wife burst from the chamber. When she saw what had happened, she killed the Champion in a fit of rage. Courage barely escaped with his life. She fled, and using my growing intelligence network, I found her a few weeks later, plotting her vengeance in a run-down apartment. When I told her we shared a similar goal, she joined this society without hesitation. She was guilt-stricken and vengeful: because of her desire for power, her true love was killed."

"Avaria," Lana whispered.

"Yes. She brought a new passion to this group, and a new motivation. The League, the good and just League, had murdered her husband. After Avaria joined, our war against the League took on a new face. We became a shadow force, the Vindico, killing League members and trying to overthrow their corrupt regime. It was never our intention to hurt civilians. We only wanted the League.

"Eventually, Courage retired, citing old age, but we knew it was fear: fear that Avaria would find him. He disappeared, and she still tracks him to this day. We've brought in three more members over the past fifteen years. Two have since been killed, but the youngest, Sliver, remains. Leni found him in British Columbia before the League could, living in a Whistler mansion that he'd coerced some wealthy family into giving him.

"As you know, the war reached its pinnacle two years ago with the murder of Phoenix. That particular act," he said, his voice low, "was not *my* order. I never wanted her to die."

He sat down again, suddenly looking tired.

"Leni thought her death would finally destroy the League, but in fact, it just enraged them. They unified like never before and began to track us down. We were forced into hiding, where we've been these last two years. We were still terribly outnumbered, and as we aged, our chances of victory were ever dwindling." He gestured to them. "Which is where you come in."

"Why don't you have powers?" James asked.

"The most common types of naturally occurring powers, superstrength and agility, are in turn the only ones that can be artificially granted. The League has five members with these types of abilities. Elemental powers, as well as flight, are still beyond the reach of science. And in fact, the capacity for MPA is a natural gift, meaning that

Hayden and Sam were actually eligible to join the League, as were Leni and Sliver."

"What?" Hayden said.

The Baron ignored him. "I don't possess the capacity for MPA, so strength and agility were my only options. But by the time I built another chamber, my body was too old to facilitate the change."

He sighed, and James saw the longing pass over his face.

"We are giving you a gift. Everyone deserves the opportunity to have superpowers, a chance to do something great with their lives, to be just as useful to the world as those 'chosen by fate.' We know we can control you here, but when the time comes for your re-entry into society, you will have to choose your own path. And now that you know the truth, I give you a choice. Give us two more weeks to prove that you should remain here. At that point you can all leave, if you wish."

"You would just let us leave?" Lana asked suspiciously.

"Yes. You may choose to live out there with the rest of a selfish, grasping world, or in here, where gifts are being given for free and where all your ambitions will be made to come within your reach. It is your choice, and yours alone. Choose wisely. We'll spend a bit more time on the three theories today: you need to understand them fully."

When the lesson was finished, the Baron sent the protégés back to their common room.

"I can't believe I could have been in the League!" Hayden said as they walked down the hallway.

Lana shook her head. "We can't just believe everything he says. He's the bad guy, remember?"

"I don't know," Emily said. "He just looked sad to me. James, you seem to know a lot about the League's history. What do you think?"

"Honestly, I don't know anymore," he admitted. "The Baron could definitely be twisting the truth. Then again, it seems like the League could be doing the same thing. Either way, I guess we have at least two more weeks to figure it all out."

James's plan had been to help the League capture the Vindico and then join them, just like he'd dreamed of his entire life. But if the League really wouldn't let him be a member, then he had to rethink everything. To be this close to actually *having* superpowers, just to have it all taken away; well, that seemed like a cruel "choice of fate" to him.

23

AFTER THE BARON'S LESSON, THE DAYS CONTINUED TO PASS SO quickly that the protégés could barely distinguish one from the next. It was always the same routine: they ate breakfast, went to a morning group session, ate lunch, spent the afternoon training with their individual mentors, ate dinner, worked out, and then went to bed. But while the days themselves were difficult to pick apart, there was no doubt of the changes from the first to the last. The protégés had entered into more advanced training, and the effects were dramatic.

Under his regimen of Genome AP, James had become abnormally strong: two days earlier, he'd almost broken Hayden's wrist in an arm wrestle. Meanwhile, Lana had been undergoing constant sessions in Avaria's chamber, and her muscles were becoming lean and hard. When Hayden finally recovered from his arm wrestle with James, Lana swiftly beat him as well.

And while James and Lana were changing physically, Sam and Emily were developing other talents. Sam had begun to display the unnerving ability of being to able to read thoughts and emotions, sometimes replying to things before they were actually said. Emily was becoming an expert marksman, often destroying all of the targets in Rono's group sessions before the other protégés even got a chance to shoot.

They were so busy with training that no one even mentioned the Baron's deadline.

Hayden watched as Leni repositioned the black stones between them. They were in Leni's training room, practicing energy projection, and Hayden knew he should be focused. These battles were fast, chaotic, and dangerous. But despite that, his mind kept drifting to Lana.

He had been spending a lot of time with her, sometimes talking for hours after everyone else was asleep. She was unlike any girl he'd ever met. She didn't laugh unless he *actually* said something funny, and she had no patience for compliments or flirty remarks. Lana kept him on his toes, and he liked it.

Without warning, Leni flicked his right hand in Hayden's direction. A wave of energy leapt toward him, made visible only by the black sand and rocks that were swept along with it.

Hayden quickly raised his hands and used his mental energy to make a shield. Leni's wave suddenly buckled against an invisible sphere, and the sand and rocks sprayed around Hayden like flowing water.

Grinning, Hayden launched the sphere at Leni. His mentor deflected the attack, and it slammed into the wall with the force of a truck, shaking the entire room. Leni charged at Hayden, his cape flapping behind him, and he waved his hand again.

This time, the air distorted into an arrow point, and it flew right at Hayden's chest. He managed to partially deflect it, but the edge still hit his arm. He spun onto his back, winded.

Move! he told himself urgently.

Hayden rolled and stuck his hand out in the same motion, catching Leni off guard with a burst of energy. Leni flew backward, and Hayden jumped to his feet, ready to celebrate the victory.

He should have known better.

Leni landed in a crouch, and when his mentor looked up, Hayden knew that he was in trouble. The rocks floated into the air, and at the same time, the sand billowed into two deadly spears. Everything flew at him at once.

Hayden created another shield, and the air around him became a swirling, distorted mass.

"Energy projection is a game of strategy," Leni said, walking toward him. "It drains us faster than thought commands, and as such, it must be wielded more carefully. When fighting others like ourselves, we must be careful we don't lose *focus.*"

Hayden's arms flew to his sides, pulled against him as if bound by rope.

"If you lose focus," Leni continued, "you leave yourself open to the commands of others." He smiled. "When that happens, there is little you can do."

He waved his hand, and Hayden went flying through the air. He landed on his stomach almost thirty feet away.

"And then you die," Leni said calmly, heading into the hallway. "Get up. That's enough for today."

Grumbling, Hayden climbed to his feet. He was sick of losing. But as he started toward the door, he noticed that Leni's black computer was humming in the corner. There was a folder open on the screen.

Curious, Hayden took a quick look at the door and then hurried over to the computer. It showed the left wing basement of the mansion, where a circular room was highlighted in red. Beneath it, a blown-up layout of the room showed a small, adjoining chamber at the far end, with a narrow tunnel that ran out the side. As he read over the blueprint, Hayden realized it was some sort of trap.

"What do you think you're doing?"

Hayden whirled around and saw Leni standing in the doorway. "Just checking if you had Internet—"

He was cut off as an invisible force pulled him across the room. Hayden stopped right in front of Leni, hanging in midair. His mentor didn't look happy.

"*Never* touch my personal belongings," Leni said. His eyes went to the computer screen. "What did you see?"

"Nothing," Hayden replied quickly.

"Don't let it happen again, or you will be punished," he snarled. "Get back to your quarters."

Hayden hurried back to the common room, throwing anxious looks over his shoulder as he ran. He'd never seen Leni so mad, and that was saying something. Obviously, he wasn't supposed to see those designs. But why? Who was that trap for?

"Activate shoulder mount," Emily said, and she heard whirring from the smooth, metallic attachment covering her left shoulder. Two small panels on the front of the mount slid open, revealing fixed plasma weapons, as did another panel on top of the shoulder mount, from which a sleek black missile launcher emerged.

Clutching a heavy rifle in her hands, Emily started forward. Ahead of her, trees and bushes were scattered in an eclectic pattern, and a brick wall jutted out from the left. A rickety wooden fence stood off in the distance.

Concentrating, she scanned her visor readouts while keeping a close eye on the various obstructions. She took a few more tentative steps forward, and then, as expected, there was a flash of movement from behind one of the trees.

Emily dropped to one knee and hoisted her rifle. Before the unknown assailant had even made it four feet from the trunk, Emily narrowed her sight, pulled the trigger, and sent a stream of pulsating red energy directly toward it. The bolt hit the assailant dead on and exploded, spraying fragments all across the room.

A sudden change in the readout flared across the bottom of her visor, and she realized something else was coming out from behind the brick wall. Not having the time to shift aim, she shouted, "Lock and fire!"

As soon as the words left her mouth, a missile erupted from her shoulder mount and streaked toward the wall. The target had just reached the edge when it was struck by the missile and obliterated.

Emily stood up and continued walking toward the roiling black smoke, ready for another assault. However, after just a few steps, the scenery retracted back into panels along the wall. Soon the massive room was empty again, except for the remains of her "attackers" and the lingering smoke.

"Very good," Rono commented from where he was standing beside the controls. "They never had a chance."

Emily lowered her rifle. "Deactivate shoulder mount." As the missile launcher descended back into its panel, she turned to Rono and grinned. "I love the shoulder mount."

"I figured you would. The missile launcher seems to be responding quickly enough," he said, picking up a fragment of the destroyed attackers. "But that's enough shooting for today. We have important work to do tonight. We need to hack into some very secure parts of the League network. The Baron thinks they are closing in on this mansion, and he wants me to find out just how close they are. He's already begun preparing the defenses."

"Have you ever considered making a truce with the League?" Emily asked.

Rono laughed. "They would lock us up on the Perch the second they got a chance, if they didn't kill us first. There's too much history now. This battle will only end when one side destroys the other, Emily. The League has made that clear."

Emily thought about that as they headed out into the hallway. None of it felt particularly right to her, but she was far more sympathetic to Rono than she was to the League, whom she had never met. And thinking of the opportunities and tools he had given her, she felt a certain responsibility to repay her mentor. She knew that she would defend Rono in a fight.

"Then we had better win," Emily said, and noticed the pleased expression on Rono's face. *He almost looked like a proud father,* Emily thought. This was the first time she'd had one of those, and she decided she liked it very much.

Sam shut his eyes, and without thinking, he launched a mental assault back at Sliver, who clearly hadn't been expecting it. Several walls crumbled in his mentor's mind before he managed to compose himself and halt Sam's invasion. They were practicing the second method of telepathic warfare: mental crippling.

Coercion was the more subtle approach, but it was only effective on untrained or unprepared opponents. When facing a worthy adversary, crippling was the only option.

That involved a blunt attack on an adversary's mind, using one's thoughts like a battering ram to overwhelm their consciousness. Instead of adding his mental voice to the current of someone else's train of thought, Sam was supposed to *displace* it with his own, at which point the enemy would become overwhelmed and faint. And if enough force was used, Sliver continually reminded him, mental crippling could also kill. That was exactly how he'd murdered Mind two years ago. Sam didn't like this method, but Sliver forced him to train with it anyway.

Sliver began to push back against Sam's intrusion, and for a moment, neither could penetrate the other's defenses. It was like a physical pressure on Sam's head, diluting his thoughts so much that he could barely hear himself think.

Sam tried one last time to smash through Sliver's defenses, but his mentor had composed himself now, and his barriers were as hard and thick as a granite wall. Sliver turned the attack back onto Sam, and he frowned in concentration, holding his mentor at bay. This continued for several minutes, until finally, Sliver found a hole in Sam's defenses and broke through, freezing Sam in place with a powerful command.

When Sliver released him, Sam sagged in his chair, sweat beading down his face. But he also saw just the slightest bit of moisture on Sliver's forehead, and he knew he'd improved today.

"That was better," Sliver said. "Much better."

"Thank you," Sam replied, his voice slightly hoarse.

This had been a pattern for the last two weeks. Sam had been steadily improving, and as a result, Sliver wasn't berating him as often. Sam could still sense a strong dislike from the man, but it had been tempered somewhat, and at one point during a duel, Sam had even detected a small touch of pride. That was something his family never expressed to him.

In fact, the more time Sam spent here, the more he began to consider his life at home. Besides his mom, no one was even *nice* to him. Even though he was generous and kind to everyone he met, he was still one of the least popular kids in school. His own father ignored him most of the time, and Sam knew that Hugh could barely stand to have him around. But despite that, he still missed them, especially his mom. Sam didn't want to leave his new friends, but if they were actually allowed to go home, he didn't know if he could pass on the chance to see her.

"Tomorrow we'll be trying something else," Sliver said, glancing at the door.

The two of them now used Sliver's living quarters for their training since the control room had a lot of traffic going in and out of the protégés' common area.

"I'm going to be introducing you to something I created a few years ago: an amplifier for our abilities. I haven't been able to use it yet; not effectively, anyway. It amplified my mental voice, but it also left me dangerously overextended. It was too risky to continue. But in the last few days, it's occurred to me that *two* telepaths might be able to use the amplifier. With it, we should actually be able to combine our voices and strengthen them a hundred times. I'm finishing the adjustments tonight."

He leaned forward, lowering his voice.

"For now, I want you to keep this between us. Don't mention the amplifier to the other kids. It's untested, and I don't want them to tell the rest of the Vindico until I'm sure it's going to work. Understand?"

"Sure," Sam replied. He sensed a strange nervousness in his mentor, but he kept that to himself. Sliver didn't like it when Sam commented on his emotions.

Sliver leaned back in his chair. "Good. One more thing. You haven't gotten an announcement yet, as you know. There's a reason for that. Your announcement was something that took a little time to put together, and it's also not something you can hear. It's something you have to see."

"What is it?" Sam asked apprehensively.

"I had one of Leni's operatives set up a camera inside your house to see what your family has been doing since your disappearance. To see how sad they really are. Do you want to see the recordings?"

Sam bit his lip. "My mom would be sad," he murmured.

"Let's go to the control room," Sliver said, and started for the door.

James threw the bench-press bar up and let it crash against the restraints. He was dripping with sweat.

He sat up and walked over to the mirror, which he did after almost every exercise. He couldn't help it: it was like a dream come true. His pale, skinny body had become lined with muscle. His once-shapeless arms now rose and fell with the curve of biceps, and his chest, which used to sink inward, was firm and shaped.

"How does it feel?" the Torturer called. He was doing bicep curls across the room, and it looked like he had about six hundred pounds on either end of the bar.

"Incredible," James replied. "I just benched four hundred and fifty pounds! I couldn't even lift a hundred a week ago. And I feel hard too, like you said." He turned and punched the metal wall, forming a dent. "Didn't even hurt!" he said excitedly, stretching his fingers.

"Good. Within a few weeks, maybe a month, you'll reach your growth potential. You'll be unstoppable."

"What's growth potential?" James asked.

"We can only push our genomes so far," he explained. "Eventually, you can't go any further, or you'll end up killing yourself. I had to stop taking AP because it was starting to feel like I was gonna burst."

"How do you know when that's going to happen?" James asked nervously.

The Torturer picked up the bar again. "Don't worry, I figured it all out by trial and error. You have a ways to go yet. You'll be smaller than me, like I said, so you're in way less danger of going over your growth potential. It's all under control."

James wasn't completely convinced, but there was also no way he was going to stop now. He turned back to his reflection and smiled. For once, he was happy with what he saw.

"I can actually leave?" Lana asked Avaria skeptically as they stood facing each other in the combat room.

Avaria nodded. "If you wish. That was the agreement."

They had been sparring for twenty minutes, but Lana had hardly broken a sweat. She rarely felt tired anymore, not since Avaria started putting her in the strange chamber. It made her skin crawl uncomfortably under the intense red glow, but every time she stepped out, she felt faster and stronger. Already, she could do one-handed cartwheels and backflips, when she used to struggle to do a somersault without hurting herself.

Their fights were becoming increasingly brutal and fast-paced, but Lana could absorb blows even in the unpadded areas with ease. Her body was changing, and though it scared her sometimes, Lana couldn't deny that she loved it. She would never be helpless again.

"You would just let me go and not contact me again?"

"We have all decided that it is unfair to keep you here. The decision should be yours."

Lana softened her fighting stance, her mind racing. *Is she telling the truth?* Lana wondered. *And what if she is? Can I actually just walk away from all this?*

"I don't know what to do," Lana said honestly, and she saw the slightest flicker of surprise cross Avaria's face.

"I thought you wanted to leave?"

"I did," Lana replied. "I do. But I don't know if I can just go back to high school and be a normal kid. Not after all this."

Avaria stared at her, as if considering her words. "I tried that once . . . tried to just be normal, even though I knew there was a chance I could be more. It is not easy."

Lana studied her mentor. "Would you go back if you could and do it differently?"

"Yes," she said softly. Then her expression hardened. "But I want to know if you are planning on leaving. I won't waste any more of my time training you if you're not going to stay."

Lana longed to return to her family, but in a way, she didn't want to face her father yet. She wanted to see her friends at home, but she wondered what Kyle had told everyone about that night. And mostly, she knew she would miss the others here. She was almost certain that none of them would leave. Maybe Sam, but the other three would stay without a doubt. How could she just abandon them?

An hour later, Lana walked back into the common room and found Emily sitting alone by the chessboard. She was staring intently at the intermingled pieces.

"What are you doing?" Lana asked.

"Playing chess," Emily replied, her eyes on the board.

Lana paused. "By yourself?"

"Of course," Emily said, glancing back at her. "How do you play?"

Lana just shook her head. "Where's everybody else?"

Emily moved a black knight forward. "James is still with the Torturer, and Hayden went to console Sam." She quickly took out the knight with the white queen. "He's upset about something, but all he told me was that it was something to do with his mom. Hayden got back a few minutes before you and decided to cheer him up. Oh, bad move." Emily knocked out the white queen, and clapped in triumph. "Checkmate."

"Hayden is talking to Sam about his mom?" Lana asked skeptically. "That can't be a good thing."

Leaving Emily to reorganize the chessboard, Lana hurried to Sam's room and pressed her ear against the door.

"So wait . . . these surveillance videos showed her doing normal things?" Lana recognized Hayden's deeper voice.

"Yeah," Sam replied. "Just her making breakfast, and going out, and having dinner with my dad and brother. Sliver showed me different days, and she . . . she didn't even look sad."

"It could have been edited together," Hayden suggested. "You know Sliver would do that kind of thing."

"I don't think so." It sounded like Sam had been crying. "She doesn't miss me, Hayden. I knew my dad and brother probably wouldn't even notice I was gone, but my mom, she was supposed to miss me."

Lana was just about to go inside and interrupt whatever snide comment Hayden was about to make, but he beat her to it.

"You know, I might not be an expert when it comes to moms," Hayden said slowly. "That said, I do know a thing or two about missing somebody."

Lana stopped, surprised at the tone of his voice.

"You can do two things when you miss someone," Hayden continued. "You can cry about it, and lie in bed, and just feel miserable. Sometimes you have to do that, I think. But when it's bad, when you really, really loved them, all you can do is normal things. You have to, or you just fall apart. So if your mom was doing normal things, I think that means she's hurting way more than if you'd seen her crying in bed. She misses you, Sam, trust me."

Lana heard sniffling. "Thanks, Hayden," Sam said quietly.

"No problem," Hayden replied. "If you ever want to talk about it, just let me know, all right?"

Lana quickly backed down the hallway.

"Hey," she whispered when Hayden stepped through the door.

"Hey," he said, frowning. "What are you doing?"

She reached out and took his hand. "I heard what you said to Sam. That was really sweet."

For the first time since she'd met him, Hayden's cheeks flushed. "Well, he's upset and—"

"You miss your mom, don't you?" Lana interjected.

He hesitated. "Yeah. I do."

Lana leaned forward and kissed him. "You're only *kind of* a jerk, aren't you?"

"Three-quarters," he said.

"It's a start." She kissed him again and then stepped back, slightly embarrassed. "Sorry, that was kind of—" She stopped when she saw James walk around the corner. He met her eyes and then turned and hurried off in the other direction.

BREAKFAST HAD BEEN DECIDEDLY QUIET THAT MORNING, EMILY noticed, shoveling the last bit of bacon into her mouth. She suspected there were two reasons for that.

The Baron's voice had come over the speakers right before bed last night to remind them that today was the end of his two-week challenge. A decision was needed from every protégé: stay until their mentors decided they were ready, or leave and be sent home immediately.

If they chose to leave, the Baron warned that they would have no second chance to return. He also added something that he had failed to mention two weeks earlier.

"We have gifted you with these abilities," he said, "and we have done so without asking anything in return. But if you decide to go home and use these newfound powers, you will attract the attention of the League of Heroes. If they choose to accept you, which they would do only to use your knowledge to defeat us and then dump you again, you will become our number-one priority. If you attempt to join the League, you will be killed."

It was not quite what he'd said the first time, but from what Emily gathered, none of the protégés were leaving anyway. Still, she assumed everyone was reflecting on their decisions to stay, and it was contributing to the somewhat dour atmosphere.

The second reason involved only three of the protégés.

Hayden and Lana were sitting directly beside each other, leaving both ends of their couch vacant. Obviously, something had happened last night. Emily wasn't really surprised, but judging from the angry looks James was shooting at the pair, it seemed not everyone was happy about it.

Hayden put down his plate and stretched. "I can't deal with these early mornings. I feel like I was asleep for an hour."

James scowled and took a bite of his toast, leaving the rest of his breakfast untouched on the plate. Emily studied him for a moment and watched as his eyes flicked between Lana and Hayden. *He must really like her,* Emily thought. *Poor James.*

"Attention," the Torturer's voice cut in. "You have a group session with the Baron today, so be ready in twenty minutes. You will inform him then of your decisions. But first, we have an announcement, this one concerning Emily."

Emily perked up, glancing at the mirror in surprise. She'd been wondering why she had yet to receive an announcement as it had been almost two-and-a-half weeks since the last one. And if Sam had been given his announcement in private, she was the only one left. Emily had assumed it was either because they couldn't find anything good enough or because Rono didn't want to hurt her feelings. The fact that she was getting one now certainly ruled out the latter.

"Emily is an only child," the Torturer began. "And while her parents have always been civil enough to her, they show her no real affection. They've never told her they love her, never even said they're proud of her. Her grandparents mostly ignore her as well, besides sending a small gift on her birthday, though they have forgotten numerous times in the past. All except her grandfather on her mother's side. He is the only person who has ever told Emily he loves her. He means the world to her."

Emily looked at the mirror, frowning. Why had the Torturer mentioned her grandpa? A knot started to wind itself into her stomach.

"Emily doesn't know this, but there is a reason her parents treat her this way. Fourteen years ago, her mother cheated on her husband with another man. When it was discovered, the scandal shook the close-knit family. It was even worse when Emily's mother discovered she was pregnant. You see, the man Emily thinks is her father is infertile. She was the product of that affair.

"Her parents decided to stay together to raise the child, but they would never love her. She was a constant reminder of her mother's infidelity. Only Emily's grandfather, perhaps the one decent person in the family, recognized that Emily had nothing to do with it."

Emily had always assumed she was adopted, so the Torturer's story was not that surprising. Truthfully, she preferred to think she was adopted because that meant there could be loving parents out there who just couldn't afford to keep her. But the constant talk of her grandpa was really starting to worry her, and she just wished the story would end.

"Her parents' search for Emily lasted about two days and consisted of nothing more than a few calls and a police report. They are happily back to their lives now. But Emily's grandfather searched every day since she disappeared, on his own, driving around the city, interviewing her teachers and classmates. He barely slept. He was determined to find Emily, but of course, he could not."

Emily's eyes started to water. The image of her grandfather searching in vain was too much for her. It was the most caring thing anyone had ever done in her entire life. And the fact that he couldn't find her while she'd been having a great time here made her feel very guilty.

The Torturer paused for a long moment, and Emily allowed herself to believe that the story might be over. Unfortunately, he continued.

"This search went on until yesterday, when, after a long day scouring the town, Emily's grandfather returned home, lay in his bed, and died in his sleep. We can only guess that it was from heartbreak.

"That is all," the Torturer finished. "Be ready in twenty minutes."

Emily stood up, tears streaming down her face. She walked in a daze to her room, closed the door behind her, and fell face-first onto the bed.

25

TWO DAYS AFTER EMILY'S ANNOUNCEMENT, THE TORTURER shuffled into the Baron's meeting room, still rubbing the sleep from his eyes. The others were already sitting around the long table, so he quickly settled into a chair.

"Good morning, everyone," the Baron said from the head of the table, his hands clasped on the gleaming wood. "My apologies for the early wake-up, but I've just received information that requires our immediate attention. Torturer, this concerns you especially." The Baron met his eyes. "It seems that a League member has ventured out of Headquarters *alone.*"

"Tell me it's Junkit . . ." the Torturer breathed, suddenly very awake.

"It is. The Sparrow has left the nest."

The Torturer slammed his meaty fist on the table. "He's mine."

"I figured you would say that," the Baron said. "We need

him alive, however. He's far too close for comfort: only a few hours from here, in a town called Fornist. This is our chance to obtain information on the League's next move."

"It sounds like a trap," Rono said. "Why would Junkit come out here on his own?"

"Because he's a fool," the Torturer scoffed. "He's arrogant. Thinks he can just fly away from a fight."

"He can," Sliver pointed out.

The Torturer turned to Sliver, grinning maliciously. "Not if I'm holding on to his leg."

"Make sure you do," the Baron said. "Now, who's going with the Torturer?"

No one answered.

"Oh, thanks," the Torturer grumbled.

"I'll go," Rono said. "It'll give me a chance to stretch my legs."

The Baron nodded. "Very well. I'll have the address dropped off at your quarters. If all goes well, we will have updates on the League's activities by tomorrow morning. If Junkit is this close, the League must suspect that our base is in this area. It won't be long before they find us. Nighthawk's death will have spurred a new lust for revenge, and if we kill Junkit, it will surely be the catalyst for a full-blown League assault. I suspect our timeline will soon become a matter of days rather than weeks. As such, our protégés must be prepared to fight before the end of this week. Will they be ready?"

Everyone nodded.

"Good," the Baron said. "We will reconvene tomorrow.

By that point, we will have Junkit in captivity, and we can begin his questioning."

The Torturer motioned for Rono to follow him out the door. They had preparations to begin and two more members of their team to recruit.

Later that night, James and Emily stepped through the mirror door, where Rono and the Torturer were waiting in the shadows of the control room.

James was wearing an all-black outfit that had come through the panel earlier that day, along with instructions for him to put it on after dinner. He was happy to be out of his peasant clothes, but had no idea what they were doing, and it was making him nervous. It didn't help that he'd been in a bad mood lately.

The excitement of his developing muscles had been soured by Hayden and Lana, who now seemed to be an official couple. James had seen them kissing twice now, and both times, it felt like someone punched him in the stomach. He tried to tell himself that he barely even knew Lana and couldn't possibly like her enough to feel this terrible, but it didn't help. It was the second time in a month that a girl had chosen someone else over him. Hayden had attempted to talk to him about it yesterday with his usual unapologetic honesty, citing once again that he had "shotgunned her," but James had just shrugged him off.

"So, I hope you're ready," the Torturer began, shutting the door behind them. "We've decided that it's time for your first mission."

James glanced at Emily. She'd said very little since her announcement, despite everyone's best attempts to cheer her up, and now James didn't know how to act around her.

"Really?" he asked. "What are we doing?"

"Capturing the Sparrow," Rono explained, glancing both ways down the hallway. "Then bringing him back here." He nodded at the Torturer. "All right, let's go. It's clear."

As they hurried toward the garage, James noticed that their mentors were cautiously looking around, as if expecting something to leap out at them.

"Is he alone?" James asked quietly. A statue of an ebony werewolf watched them hurry past, its protruding fangs catching the light. "And why are we sneaking out?"

"Yeah, it's just him," the Torturer muttered. They crossed the lobby, and the big man scanned the upper balconies. "And we're sneaking out because the others don't know we're bringing you. We told Avaria that we left you personal instructions for tonight, so you'd both be skipping your workout. The Baron wants to keep the fact that we have been training you secret from the League, but once we capture Junkit, he won't be able to tell anyone anyway. This will be good training for you guys; we couldn't pass it up."

James smiled uncertainly. He might have chosen to stay for the rest of the training, but he wasn't sure he was ready to go attacking League members. However, his mentor looked so eager about the idea that James felt he couldn't let him down.

They made it to the garage without interruption, and Rono led them right to the strange black vehicle James had seen the last time he was there.

"Sweet," he said.

Emily looked at him with the faintest hint of a smile, the first he'd seen from her in days. As soon as Rono reached the ship, a ramp descended, clanging down onto the concrete. "Welcome to the Shadow," he said proudly.

They all clambered inside, and James looked around in awe. The central hold had two benches pressed against either wall and a rack stocked with rifles. Everything was finished in gleaming black. There were two doors, and Rono led them toward the one on the right, which promptly slid aside to reveal the cockpit.

A huge, curving window stretched over the two pilots' chairs and past them on both sides. The only thing to mar the view was the control console, which contained dual levers for steering and a huge array of glowing instrument panels and sensor screens.

Rono and the Torturer settled into the chairs.

"Don't worry," Rono said, firing up the controls. "It won't be a long ride."

"How does this . . . move?" James asked excitedly.

"It flies," Rono said, glancing at him. "Fast."

Turning back to the controls, Rono pushed the two levers forward, and the Shadow accelerated out of the parking garage, pressing James and Emily against the back wall. The ship angled upward, and they raced toward the setting sun.

As the Shadow settled into a gentle landing outside the town of Fornist, Emily stared at the streetlights in the distance, trying to hold back her excitement. The last two days had been miserable. She'd continued with her training, but could no longer enjoy herself because it made her feel even guiltier than she already did.

Emily knew she couldn't give all this up now though, even if the Vindico would still let her leave: she *belonged* here, and that was something she'd never felt before. Besides, with her grandpa gone, she no longer had a family to go back to anyway.

But she also knew she couldn't trust the Vindico, not even Rono. If he'd sent her grandpa a message like she'd asked him to, maybe he would still be alive. Emily would never be loyal to someone she couldn't trust.

"All right, so what's the address?" Rono asked.

The Torturer unfolded a scrap of paper from his pocket. "Thirty-four Davidson Avenue." He turned back to Emily and James. "We need to do a little recon, just to make sure this isn't a trap. That's where you two come in. You'll walk by the house, and Emily can use the infrared on her visor to see if anyone's home. Then report back here."

"Put this over your shoulder, Emily," Rono said, handing her a black shawl. "Cover the mount."

She quietly obliged.

"So, go straight up the main street," the Torturer explained as he folded up the paper again, "and take your fourth right onto Davidson."

"Okay," James said nervously, and he and Emily hurried down the ramp and off into the dusk.

They darted away from the ship, picking their way over little mounds and divots in the grass. A cold gust of wind stung at their cheeks. When they reached the main road, they looked back and saw that the Shadow was almost invisible in the distance.

"I don't like this," James muttered as they started down the road.

"We'll be fine," Emily assured him.

A few cars drove by on the way into town, but otherwise, everything was silent. Neither spoke as they walked along the sidewalk, trying to look casual.

"There it is," James whispered, nodding toward a large, two-story brick house with a white fence bordering the lawn.

Emily nodded and pulled out her visor, taking another quick look around. Fitting it into place, she turned to the house and activated the infrared. Everything darkened except for the glowing sources of heat that were represented by various shades of red and orange.

"Only one person," she said. "Looks like they're lying down upstairs."

"You sure there's only the one?"

She scanned the house again, checking the scrolling readouts at the bottom of her vision at the same time. "Yep.

There's another two I can see . . . but it looks like they're in the house behind. It's just Junkit in there, if it is him."

"All right, let's get back," James said, staring up at the darkened windows.

They strolled back down the main street, and when they were far enough away, they scurried across the field to the Shadow.

"He's the only one there," Emily announced as they climbed up the ramp.

"Good work. Now it's our turn," Rono said, scooping up a rifle from underneath the front console. "I'm going to keep the comm on my belt so you can hear what's going on. If something goes wrong, bring the Shadow in. Pull back on the throttle to—"

"I watched you on the way here," Emily cut in.

"Oh . . . good," Rono said. He tucked a stun gun into the holster on his leg. "If there's a problem, just hover over the house, and we'll do the rest. If things *really* go wrong, this red button fires missiles. Just start blowing things up around the house, and we'll use the distraction." He nodded at the Torturer. "Let's move."

Rono breathed in the cool air as they snuck along the back of a strip mall, keeping to the fence. It had been two years since he'd been out on a mission, and he'd forgotten just how exhilarating it was. They hurried across the street and darted from house to house, always remaining hidden in the shadows. They were far more conspicuous than Emily and James.

He felt a little stab of guilt as he thought of Emily. She was barely speaking to him, and he regretted allowing the Torturer to give her the announcement. He'd wanted to hide the news from her as long as possible, but the others had started to rib him about being too sentimental, so he'd had to relent.

Turning the corner onto Davidson Avenue, Rono spotted a couple walking a dog at the other end of the street. He stepped behind a large oak tree, gesturing for the Torturer to stop. As soon as the couple turned a corner, the two Villains continued on to number 34.

"Is he still in there?" the Torturer whispered as they hunkered down behind a bush on the other side of the street.

Rono checked his infrared reading. "Yeah. He's lying down upstairs."

"Good. I'll take the front door, you try the back."

"Right."

They ran across the street, and Rono rounded the house into the backyard. He quietly edged up to the door, removed a tiny magnetic device from his belt, and popped the lock. There was a slight creak under his boot as he stepped into the kitchen, and he paused. Hearing nothing, he made his way to the front door and opened it for the Torturer.

They tiptoed up the stairs. Every movement sounded impossibly loud, but using his visor, Rono could see that the figure upstairs still hadn't moved. At the top of the steps, Rono led them to a closed door and then nodded at the Torturer. The big man wasted no time. He kicked the door right off its frame and then stepped inside and flicked on the light. Rono raced in after him, his rifle aimed at the sleeping man's head.

"Hello, Junkit," the Torturer said. "It's been a while."

For a moment, Junkit didn't move. He was a handsome man with tousled blond hair and high cheekbones, and though he was lying in bed, he was wearing his navy-blue uniform.

Uh-oh, Rono thought.

A smile spread across Junkit's face, and he opened his eyes.

"I thought you'd come alone," he said casually to the Torturer. "Maybe you've gotten a little smarter. But still, not smart enough. Hello, Rono. What a pleasant surprise."

As soon as Junkit finished speaking, the back wall tore open with an earsplitting crash. Drywall, brick, and paint went flying in all directions, and Rono saw huge black ropes snap away from where they had been attached to the corners of the wall. And there, standing in the opposite yard, was Gali, the League's strongman, gripping the ends of the four ropes. There was a flicker of motion as a lithe red-haired woman jumped up onto the ledge, landing in a crouch.

"Two of them," Jada said. "Even better."

Rono pulled the trigger, and a burst of red energy flared toward Junkit. The League member was ready, though, and he flew off the bed just as it exploded, shooting flaming debris in all directions. With a mighty bellow, the Torturer charged.

• • •

The Torturer's shout erupted over the comm, and James turned to Emily.

"Pull it up!" he said. "We have to go!"

Emily nodded and eased back the throttle, lifting the Shadow off the ground. As soon as they were about ten feet up, she pushed the throttle forward, just like Rono had done, and they streaked ahead like a loosed arrow.

"Not so much!" James yelled as they barreled toward the strip mall.

"Sorry," Emily replied tightly, and pulled back again, slowing them down. "Didn't really know what to expect."

She tilted the throttle upward, and they barely missed the top of the strip mall. As soon as they cleared the roof, they saw fire and smoke billowing up from 34 Davidson. A blast of red energy went careening off into the night sky. Emily accelerated again.

"Keep your hand over the missile launcher," she told James.

He tentatively reached out and put his finger over the red button.

Emily glanced at him. "It'll be okay," she said.

"Yeah," he mumbled.

Emily steered the Shadow over the house, toward the backyard and the spouting flames. She pulled the ship into a tight loop and saw that the entire back wall of the house was missing. The fight had spilled into the yard.

"It's Gali," James said, awe apparent in his voice.

The Torturer was grappling with Gali on the lawn, while Junkit flew overhead and occasionally descended to smash a slab of concrete on the Torturer's head. Even from there, Emily could see that the Torturer was being bested. Upstairs in a bedroom, visible now that the wall was gone, Rono was pinned down by Jada. She had a hold on his rifle as he struggled violently to throw her off.

"Fire something!" Emily screamed.

"At what?"

"Anything! Blow the other side of the house up!" Emily angled the ship to face the exposed master bedroom.

"Okay," James said reluctantly. "Here goes nothing." He pressed the button.

Two glowing missiles erupted from the front of the Shadow and exploded into the upper floor of the house, obliterating the entire master bedroom. But the force of the explosion was a little more than they counted on. The Shadow was buffeted by flames, and Rono and Jada went spinning as the bedroom wall blew inward. They both crashed into a shelf on the far side. In the yard, the Torturer and Gali dove to the ground, while Junkit went tumbling out of the air. The night sky lit up with a red glow.

"That worked," James said in disbelief.

"Maybe too well," Emily agreed, her eyes on Rono, who was trying to shakily pull himself to his feet.

Jada was first to recover, and she sprang at him as soon as he got to his knees, sending them both skidding along the blackened floor. Half of the house was on fire now.

The Torturer and Gali stood up again, and they crashed

into each other like two rams. Junkit was slowly sitting up where he'd landed at the far end of the yard.

"Lower us," James said.

"What?"

"I'm going to get Junkit before he gets up. Lower us!"

Emily tilted the throttle forward, and the Shadow dropped to the grass. James took off for the ramp, and Emily sprinted after him, grabbing a rifle on the way.

"Activate shoulder mount," she commanded, and the panels slid back to expose the fixed plasma weapons and missile launcher.

James was already racing across the grass. He jumped and grabbed Junkit's leg just as he was taking off. A look of shock crossed Junkit's face, visible in the flickering fire, and then James whipped him into the fence.

Emily ran toward the house. She needed to help Rono. On the way she passed the two massive men savagely grappling and punching each other, each blow sounding like it had the weight of a train behind it. The Torturer gave Gali a sharp push, separating them for just a moment, and they prepared to charge again.

Narrowing her eye, Emily took aim at Gali's left leg and fired. The burst of red energy struck his thigh, burning right through the blue fabric of his uniform, and he crashed to the ground.

The Torturer smiled at her and then pounced on his downed foe.

Breaking into a sprint, Emily entered the burning house.

Thick black smoke hung in the air, and she put her hand over her mouth as she bounded up the stairs. Emily spotted an open door and burst through it, lifting her rifle into firing position. She was just in time to see Jada viciously punch Rono across the face. He looked dazed.

Jada whirled to face her. "Who are you?"

"My name is Emily," she said, and then she pulled the trigger.

The red bolt lanced across the room and struck Jada's shoulder, sending her flying right out of the house. She landed in a heap on the grass.

"Emily," Rono said, his voice strained.

She rushed over and helped him to his feet. Behind them, the fire was spreading along the hallway.

"We have to jump," Rono said, walking to the exposed ledge. He looked down at the grass. "This is going to hurt."

The sound of cracking wood caused them both to spin around, and then Rono gripped her arm. "Collapse and roll!" he shouted, then took a quick step and jumped off the ledge.

Emily paused for a moment and then leapt after him. The ground came up very quickly, and her legs buckled as she hit the grass. She threw herself forward, trying to roll, but her ankle twisted on impact, and agonizing pain raced up her leg.

Rono bent over her. "Are you all right?" he asked, concern etched into his face.

"My ankle," Emily groaned. "I rolled it."

Rono heaved her up and propped her against his shoulder. As he led her away from the collapsing house, Emily noticed that Jada was already gone, as was Gali. The Torturer was sitting up, rubbing his forehead.

"They got away," he mumbled. "Jada hit me with a brick when I wasn't looking, and they took off."

"Where's James?" Emily asked.

They scanned the yard and saw that a huge hole had been smashed into the fence.

Just then, James came walking through the hole with Jay Junkit slung over his shoulder.

"Ha!" the Torturer yelled triumphantly. "James, you got him!"

Sirens ripped through the air, and a section of floor gave way in the house, spewing smoke and ash into the yard.

"Time to go," Rono said quickly. "Everyone into the Shadow. Torturer, help Emily."

The big man lifted Emily and gingerly placed her on one of the benches in the central hold.

"Nice shot, by the way," he said. "Don't worry, we'll get him next time."

Then he turned and clapped James on the shoulder as he was lowering Junkit's unconscious body to the floor.

"I can't believe you got him!" the Torturer said. "This is the best gift you could give me!"

He scooped up Junkit, sneered at his limp body, and then opened the door at the other end of the hold. He cast

Junkit inside and closed it again. "Well, we got what we came for," he said, "and almost had more! A success, I would say."

Emily smiled weakly, trying to take the weight off her already-swollen ankle.

"We'll get you patched up," the Torturer assured her, and then went into the cockpit. "Lift her up, Rono!"

The Shadow leapt into the air, and the sirens soon faded away. Emily leaned against the wall, every muscle in her body aching. James sat down beside her.

"That was interesting," he said.

"Yeah," Emily replied, wincing. "We are officially supervillains."

26

LANA WAS JUST NODDING OFF ON HAYDEN'S SHOULDER WHEN
James burst in through the mirror door. He saw them together and pointedly avoided her gaze.

"Where have you been?" Sam asked, rubbing his eyes.
He'd fallen asleep on the couch next to them. "We were
waiting for you. Where's Emily?"

James dropped onto a couch, grinning. "We just completed our first mission." For the next ten minutes, he
recounted the story of Junkit's abduction. Then he sat
back, smugly putting his arms behind his head. "And now
Emily is getting her ankle fixed up. She rolled it jumping
out of the house, just before the floor collapsed."

"That's awesome," Hayden said, for about the tenth
time since James had started telling the story.

Lana hadn't said a word. James was talking about
the mission like it was a video game, and she found it
disturbing.

"Firing those missiles must have been scary," Sam said. He shook his head. "I can't believe you jumped out and attacked a League member!"

James shrugged. "I didn't even think about it at the time. I just knew that I couldn't let him attack the Torturer again, so I had to do something. He almost managed to slip away, but I swiped him right in the head and knocked him out."

Lana couldn't hold back any longer. "You do realize that they're going to *kill* Junkit?" she asked sharply, staring at him.

James looked away. "Why did we take him alive, then?"

"Possibly so the Torturer could, I don't know, *torture* him for information?" Lana replied.

"It would be his right," James snapped. "The League set a trap for the Torturer. They tried to kill him!"

Lana rolled her eyes. "As he and Rono were trying to kidnap and kill Junkit. They were hardly innocent victims."

"Where did they take Junkit?" Sam asked, sounding frightened now. He snuck a glance at the mirror door.

"I don't know," James said. "The Torturer carted him off somewhere."

"So Emily shot two people?" Hayden asked, and Lana glared at him.

James nodded. "Yeah, she told me she hit them both. They survived, though, and escaped."

"Lucky for them . . ." Lana muttered.

James finally turned to her. "You're just mad that we were trusted to go and you weren't. Avaria obviously doesn't think you're ready."

"Or maybe it had something to do with the fact that she wasn't on the mission," Lana replied scathingly. "Listen to yourself. You sound like an idiot."

"Well, I'm trying to tell a story here, and you're getting on my case for no reason," James said. "You weren't there; you didn't see what happened. Emily and I saved their lives, and I'm not going to apologize for it."

"I don't want you to," Lana replied. "I just want you to realize what you did."

"I saved them; that's what. Wouldn't you have done the same?"

Lana shook her head. "I would have let Junkit go."

"So that he could come back and attack me? That would have been smart." James sneered. "You would be captured by the League right now. Or dead."

"You're so arrogant. Now Junkit's going to be tortured and killed because you like having muscles."

"What does that have to do with anything?" James said, raising his voice. He was losing his temper now. "I got asked to go on a mission, and I did. That's it. If you don't like it, keep it to yourself."

The force of his anger surprised Lana, and she fell silent. James had been acting very cold toward her ever since she and Hayden had started spending more time together. Lana had in turn ignored him, feeling that he was being immature. *He has no right to punish me for choosing Hayden,* Lana thought. *He didn't even tell me he liked me, so how was I supposed to know?*

Lana looked around, and saw that Sam was fidgeting

uncomfortably with his hands in his lap. Hayden was just sitting there, and for once, he had nothing to say.

"Fine," Lana whispered. "I will."

She stormed off to her bedroom, slamming the door behind her. *Now it's going to be even more awkward between us,* she thought. But James was turning into something she didn't like, and she had to at least point it out. If that's how he was going to act, she didn't want to be friends with him anyway.

Leni shifted impatiently, watching through the thick glass as Sliver probed Junkit's mind.

The captured League member looked determined as he waged his mental war with Sliver, who was bent forward motionlessly in the chair across from him. This had already gone on for over twenty minutes.

Leni clenched his gloved fist at his side. He wanted answers from Junkit so that he could determine the time frame he had for enacting Nightfall.

If the League knew where the mansion was, they might launch an immediate assault, either to rescue Junkit or avenge his death, and Leni needed at least a few more days to complete the trap.

To make matters worse, Gali and Jada would have warned the League about the two kids that attacked them. He glanced at the Torturer. The fool had jeopardized everything by bringing James and Emily along. Now the League had confirmation that the Vindico was behind the teens' disappearances, and the protégés' skills proved that they weren't just being held captive. They were learning to fight.

"Junkit seems to be resisting the probes," Leni said, breaking the long silence. "Perhaps a different strategy would yield results."

"League members are well trained," the Baron reasoned. "Let's give Sliver a little more time. I'm sure he's making progress."

"What did you have in mind?" the Torturer asked, turning to Leni.

It was just the three of them watching; Rono was still receiving treatment from the Baron's nurse, while Avaria remained in the surveillance room, keeping an eye on the perimeter. The mansion was heavily fortified against an air assault, with five heavy plasma cannons situated around the property, but it was susceptible to a ground attack through the forest. Sensors and cameras could detect intrusion, but it was nearly impossible to build real defenses across such a wide area. Walls wouldn't slow down the League.

"I don't mean having Sliver stop," Leni said, "but perhaps a distraction might speed up the process. Pain might weaken Junkit's mental resolve."

"It might also distract Sliver," the Baron warned.

"I doubt it," Leni replied. "Sliver can use the distraction to bypass Junkit's walls. I'll do it from here."

Leni found Junkit's legs with his mind and squeezed. Junkit's eyes flew open. Leni squeezed harder until the captured League member reached out with shaking hands and clasped his legs, as if trying to pull them free of a vise.

Leni gave one last vicious squeeze, and Junkit howled with pain. As he screamed, Sliver leaned toward him.

Suddenly, Junkit slumped over, his eyes rolling back in his head.

Leni stopped the pressure. "Much better," he said, clasping his hands behind his back.

"Yes," the Baron agreed quietly. "It seems you were right."

Five minutes passed, and then Junkit spilled onto the ground in a heap. After a moment, Sliver stood up.

"Junkit revealed everything," he said, looking concerned. "And it's not good."

The next morning, the protégés filed into Leni's classroom and quickly found their seats.

"There will be no group session today," Leni said, looking them over. "You will spend the rest of the day in preparation. Last night, we interrogated Jay Junkit, and he has revealed some disturbing information. The League knows that our base is in this area. Worse, they now know about you."

Hayden heard the others shifting uncomfortably around him.

"Thunderbolt was scheduled to return to League headquarters in two days to discuss the situation, but Junkit managed to convince Gali and Jada to lure out the Torturer to weaken us and find out more on their own. They did not have Thunderbolt's permission, and now their plan has backfired. But Junkit also revealed that the majority of the League wants to sweep this area *now,* and he believes that

Thunderbolt will finally agree. He expects the League will find us within the next few days."

Hayden sat back in his chair, alarmed. *Fight the entire League?* he thought. He wasn't sure if he was ready for that.

"That's not all," Leni said quietly. "The League has found two new candidates. Junkit doesn't know what they can do, but Thunderbolt has been training them for weeks at a League base in Canada. Apparently, Thunderbolt believes that with these new recruits, the League can destroy us." He paused. "We cannot allow these candidates to join the attack. We must get to them first."

James sat up a little in his chair. "We're going to attack their base?"

"Yes. We're going to kidnap those candidates before they can make it to League headquarters. We leave tonight, and all of you but Emily will be joining us. She will stay here with Rono and the Baron to build up the mansion's defenses."

"I want to help," Emily protested.

"You would only be a liability with your injury," Leni replied coolly. "Now, for those coming, spend the remainder of the day resting. It's going to be a long night."

With that, he stalked out of the classroom.

"That's okay, we don't have any questions," Hayden muttered.

They all filed back to the common area, and James, Emily, and Sam went to their rooms to get some sleep. After they'd gone, Lana led Hayden to her room, and they lay down. She rested her head on his chest.

"I don't think I'm ready for this," she said.

Hayden ran his fingers through her hair, gazing up at the ceiling. "It'll be fine," he replied. "I'll take care of you. I will be wearing a cape, after all."

"That's a comforting thought," she said. "Why am I with you again?"

He looked at her. "Are you saying we're official?"

"No," she replied quickly. "This is only a supervillain-training fling."

"Damn," he said. "I hate those."

"Sorry. You're not my type." She shrugged. "I never liked caped men."

Hayden frowned. "Are you making me choose between you and my cape?"

"What if I am?"

"Then I need some time to think."

Lana punched him on the arm.

"Okay, ow," Hayden said. "Remember how you can punch through walls?"

"Sorry," she replied playfully. "I forgot how weak you were. Want me to kiss it better?"

"Well, I actually bit my lip when you hit me, so you better start there."

Lana rolled her eyes, but then shifted up and kissed him.

"Still hurts," Hayden whispered, his lips on hers.

She kissed him again, and Hayden forgot all about the mission.

SAM FELT A BEAD OF SWEAT SLOWLY CREEP BETWEEN HIS EYES.
It ran down to the tip of his nose and then paused, as if
building up the courage to jump. He quickly wiped it away.
It wasn't warm in the Shadow's hold; in fact, the cold night-
time air was seeping in through the metal. Sam was just
terrified: they were attacking a League base, and as if that
weren't bad enough, he absolutely *hated* flying.

He and James were sitting on one of the benches in the
Shadow, while Lana and Hayden sat across from them on
the other. Leni, Sliver, Avaria, and the Torturer were all
gathered in the cockpit, where they'd been since takeoff
about two hours ago.

They had all been given black jumpsuits to match the
one James had worn on his first mission. At first, Hayden
had complained that there was no cape, but after he slid
his on, he made a point of showing everyone how good his
butt looked in it.

We look like the black silhouettes over the fireplace, Sam thought miserably.

The cockpit door slid open, and Leni stepped out. "We have the base sighted on the scanners. There's a forest that surrounds the entire property, so we can make our entry through the trees. We'll land as soon as we find a big enough clearing. James and Sam, you'll stay with the ship so Sliver can contact you if we need a quick escape. We land in a few minutes. Prepare yourselves."

Leni returned to the cockpit, and Hayden stood up and started running on the spot.

"What?" he said when he saw the others staring at him. "Don't want to pull a hamstring on the entry."

"Idiot," Lana muttered.

Sam was in no mood to laugh. He felt sick to his stomach. He kept thinking of his mom, and what she would say if she knew he was about to attack a League base. What if he never saw her again? What if he didn't get to say good-bye?

The Shadow abruptly dropped, and Sam clutched the bottom of the bench in terror. Just when he was sure he was about to vomit, the ship slowed, and gravity settled in again. They felt a thump as the bottom fins hit the grass, and then the Shadow powered down.

"Game time," the Torturer announced, grabbing two plasma rifles off the rack. He gave one each to Lana and Hayden.

Avaria and Sliver took rifles as well, and each had another smaller gun strapped to their right thighs. Avaria also had a black cylinder strapped to her left leg, and she wore Rono's visor. Leni came out last, bearing no weapon. He wasn't wearing a cape for the first time since Sam had seen him, and his hair was tied back in a ponytail.

"Let's move," Leni ordered. "James, Sam, to the cockpit."

Avaria triggered the ramp, and it descended into the long grass. The night was dark and starless, and a cold breeze swept up into the hold as soon as the door opened. Sam shivered.

"See you soon," the Torturer said to James before bounding down the ramp, the other three Vindico members hurrying after him.

Hayden and Lana exchanged a quick glance and then turned to James and Sam.

"Be careful," Sam said.

"Don't worry, *I'm* on this mission," Hayden replied. "What could go wrong?" He started down the ramp. "We better go. I think we're being abandoned."

Lana hesitated for just a moment and then took off after him.

James quickly withdrew the ramp, shutting out the bitter wind. They hurried to the cockpit and peered out the window.

Six shadows were moving swiftly along the edge of the clearing. The lead shadow made a hand signal, and the group turned and plunged into the woods.

They raced through the underbrush like hunting cats, whipping in and around the trees. Branches were grasping at them from all sides, hidden in the darkness, but they brushed harmlessly off their padded outfits.

Lana was in the rear, easily keeping up with Hayden. Before her transformation, she probably would have stumbled into a tree or tripped on the uneven surface, but now her feet danced over the ground, and she made her way through the forest with ease.

As much as Lana hated the idea of kidnapping anyone, she had to admit this secret entry through the woods was kind of exciting. The crunch of their boots on the fallen leaves, the rustling branches, the wind howling over the canopy; it felt good to just be *outside.* After almost a month confined to the mansion, even the frigid air on her cheeks was refreshing.

The group soon came to a halt, and Leni's hushed voice sounded from the front of the line. "The forest ends just ahead, so we'll stop at the tree line and scan the house. Hopefully we can spot our targets before we move in."

At the edge of the woods, they all fanned out and studied the estate in silence.

"What do you pick up?" Leni whispered.

"Almost twenty people," Sliver replied, "but I think most of them are servants. I only pick up the traces of four guarded minds. It's tough to catch the voices, but I'm pretty sure one of them is Thunderbolt."

"Avaria, what does the infrared show?" Leni asked.

"A large group of heat signatures in the left wing of the house. Probably the servants' quarters. A smaller group nearby: maybe two or three people. A few roamers. And in one room upstairs in the right wing, two signatures."

"Sliver?" Leni said.

"Those are definitely guarded minds. I haven't encountered them before."

"Can you break through?" the Torturer asked.

"No," Sliver replied. "Not without alerting them to our presence."

"Very well," Leni said. "We go for those two. If it's not them, we head for the smaller group. Let's move."

He took off across the enormous lawn. Manicured gardens were visible as dim silhouettes in the moonlight, which had finally broken through the clouds. The estate looked like an almost perfect replica of the Baron's.

Following their mentors' leads, Lana hunched as she ran, and they made it within forty feet of the wall before ducking behind a large hedge.

Leni began speaking just as Lana reached the group. "All right, there's a door straight ahead. I'll open it, just keep running. Lana, Hayden, you'll stay at the doorway to keep watch. One facing out, one in. Go!"

Leni rounded the hedge, and as soon as he approached the door, it flew open. Without slowing, he ran right through the opening, the other three Vindico members close behind him. Hayden and Lana stopped at the entrance.

"In or out?" Hayden whispered.

"In." Lana wanted to get out of the eerie moonlit yard.

She walked into what looked like an unused guest bedroom. Leni already had the hallway door open, flooding the room with light, and he was looking in both directions.

"Clear," she heard him whisper, and then they disappeared around the corner.

Despite herself, Lana was actually a little concerned for Avaria. They were far from friends, but now that they possessed the same abilities, there was a connection between them that Lana couldn't share with anyone else.

"Now we chill," Hayden whispered from the doorway. "Want to play I spy?"

"Shut up and keep watch," she told him.

"Yes, ma'am," he said, spinning back to the yard. "No squirrel or rabbit is going to get the drop on me."

Lana shook her head. She was going to have to keep half an eye on the outside entrance as well.

The Vindico members tiptoed briskly down the hallway, and Avaria continually scanned the mansion for heat signatures with her visor. So far, no one had moved.

While the layout was the same as the Baron's mansion, the decor was vastly different. The floor was polished hardwood, and the walls were painted navy blue, the same color as the League's uniforms. The only similarity was the gold trim along the ceiling, which was matched by the gold-framed paintings lining the walls. Many of them were portraits of former and current League members, and they watched the intruders as they crept by.

Leni led them to a winding staircase and cautiously began to climb the steps. Lifting her rifle, Avaria followed, her every sense on high alert. Distance readouts scrolled across the bottom of her vision, counting down as they approached the two glowing bodies.

"How much farther?" Leni asked softly as they reached the top of the stairs.

"They're at the far end of this hallway," Avaria replied. "On the right side."

They slunk down the corridor, quickly reaching the last door.

"Sliver, attack their minds and keep them quiet," Leni said. "I'll make sure they don't move. Avaria, Torturer, knock them out and take them. Ready?"

They all nodded. At a sharp wave of Leni's hand, the door flew open.

Two kids who looked no older than Sam were sitting on the edges of their respective beds. They were illuminated only by the moonlight streaming in through the windows. One was a dark-skinned girl with curly black hair and a round face, and she had her hands calmly folded across her lap. The other was undoubtedly her brother, with the same round face and hair.

"Hello," the girl said. "We've been waiting for you."

"She sensed you when you first landed your ship," the boy added. "She followed you all the way here."

She nodded. "We were warned you might try to kidnap us once the Sparrow was taken. I was told you had a powerful telepath among you, and I felt you probing, Sliver."

"That's enough," Leni snarled. "Take her."

The girl closed her eyes, and Sliver immediately

stiffened. Using the distraction, Avaria stepped around him and charged. She didn't make it very far. A blast of invisible energy erupted from the boy, and the Vindico members all went flying backward. The drywall smashed under the impact, sending up clouds of dust and debris, and the Torturer sailed right through into the hallway.

Leni scrambled back to his feet, half-blinded by the dust, and launched a blast of energy back at the kids. The young boy stood up with outstretched arms and met the assault head-on. The entire room began to shake.

Avaria aimed her rifle at the boy's chest and fired. Pulsating red energy burst from the nozzle, but it seemed to warp and distort as it crossed the distance between them and fizzled out before it got there. The boy smiled confidently.

Growling, the Torturer charged across the hallway. But as soon as he entered the room, he went spinning away again, deflected by the unseen forces battling each other.

"They are strong indeed," Leni managed. "But not as experienced. Get ready, Sliver."

Sliver said nothing, locked in mental combat with the girl.

The walls began flaking, and the debris started to close in on the children. For the first time, the boy's confident expression faltered. An expanding crack split the ground beneath him.

"Call the others!" he yelled to his sister as he barely managed to avoid falling through the floor.

"Stop her!" Leni shouted.

"Too late," Sliver said. "Avaria, Torturer, go and meet them!"

They took off down the hall and were halfway to the staircase when someone rounded the corner. There was a brilliant blue flash, and a blast of electricity streaked toward them.

Avaria threw herself against the wall, dodging the attack. She heard a loud thump as the Torturer did the same.

Thunderbolt stepped into the middle of the hallway, and Avaria saw him wrap his hands into a ball. Thrumming blue energy collected around them.

"I don't think so," Avaria whispered, and opened fire.

Thunderbolt managed to leap through a doorway just before the deadly lasers struck him, and they exploded at the end of the long corridor.

Another man rolled out of a doorway farther down the hall, and he lifted his gun and fired in one smooth motion. Avaria dove under the scarlet bolt and returned fire, forcing the man to retreat back the way he had come.

Smiling, Avaria slid the stun pole off her leg. She pressed a button on its side, and the cylinder extended into a four-foot staff. If she was correct, the man who had just fired at them was Septer, the League's weapons specialist. The last time they'd fought was four years ago during a raid on a secondary League base in Melbourne, but their battle had been cut short by the arrival of Phoenix. Septer wouldn't be so lucky this time.

Avaria sprinted down the hall, laying down covering fire at the doorway Thunderbolt had leapt into.

"Take him!" she shouted behind her.

"Gladly!" the Torturer called back, and then crashed right through the wall, ignoring the door.

Avaria stopped about ten feet from where Septer had retreated and backed against the wall, her rifle trained on the doorway. "Is that you, Septer?"

"Hello, Avaria," he replied. "It's been a while. Since Melbourne, right?"

"That's right," Avaria said, slowly walking toward the doorway. "You won't get away this time."

"We'll see. We knew you would come for them."

"You should have prepared better," Avaria replied, her finger tightening on the trigger.

"Perhaps we're more prepared than you think. You better kill me fast."

"You're sure someone's coming?" James asked, anxiously scanning the night sky.

"Yeah," Sam said. "There's a ship on the way with League members, I'm sure of it. Sliver taught me how their guarded minds would feel, and even through that, I can tell they're excited."

James grabbed the controls, trying to think back to when Emily flew the Shadow. He'd been so scared that he hadn't really been paying much attention, but he had a general idea how to fly it. "We have to do something."

"What can we do?" Sam whimpered.

"I don't know! Blow up the ship, blow up the base, something! Lana and Hayden are going to get hurt down there!"

Sam nodded, looking queasy. "You think you can blow up their ship?"

"I don't know," James replied. "I know how to shoot missiles, so I guess so. Let's wait until they land. I'll get them on the ground."

Sam closed his eyes. "I hope Hayden and Lana are okay," he murmured. "I can feel that they're scared. What do you think they'll do?"

"I don't know. Nothing, hopefully. They should let the Vindico do the fighting."

Sam was quiet for a moment. "Somehow, I doubt that Hayden is just going to stand there."

James sighed. "Yeah, me too."

"But they told us to watch the door!" Lana shouted, running down the hallway after Hayden.

Hayden spotted a staircase and bounded up the steps, projecting an invisible shield in front of him. Lana quickly caught up, and they ran into the upstairs corridor. The air felt alive with electricity.

To the left, Hayden spotted Leni and Sliver standing in the hallway, facing a blown-out wall. Neither was moving. To the right, Avaria was locked in combat with Septer, she wielding a staff and he a gleaming blade. They were attacking and defending with incredible speed.

"Help Leni and Sliver!" Lana told Hayden, turning toward Avaria.

Hayden ran left but had only gone a few steps when a huge blast of electricity exploded out of the wall in front of him. The Torturer flew out with it, crashing to the floor. He lifted his dust-caked head. "Is that the best you got, old man?" he shouted.

"Looks pretty good to me," Hayden commented. "Need some assistance?"

The Torturer nodded. "Couldn't hurt. He's dangerous, though, watch it."

"Who's there?" said a deep voice.

Hayden crept to the corner of the freshly blown-out hole and saw a white-haired man leaning against the back wall, clutching his side.

"Hayden Lockwood," Thunderbolt said, straightening up. "I was wondering when I'd see you again."

Hayden stepped into the room, frowning. He had his rifle aimed right at Thunderbolt's chest. "How do you know my name?"

Thunderbolt looked past him to where the Torturer was slowly pushing himself up again. "How do you think they found you? They stole your file from our network, yours and Sam's. We knew it was no coincidence that you two were among the missing children." He shook his head. "You were both League candidates."

"Candidates?" Hayden replied in disbelief. "Why didn't you contact us, then?" He kept a close eye on Thunderbolt's hands; Hayden knew he could shoot electricity with a flick of his finger.

"Sam is too young. When he was twelve, we were going

to come for him." Thunderbolt hesitated. "And you *were* a candidate, but I decided not to train you."

Hayden lowered the rifle slightly. "Why not?"

Thunderbolt glanced at the Torturer again, who was back on his feet. "Because you reminded me of Leni," he said quietly, meeting Hayden's eyes. "You had just as much potential, and just as much reason to be angry. We couldn't risk another rogue member."

"You didn't even give me a chance," Hayden said. "How is that fair?"

"I did what I thought was best," Thunderbolt replied. "It was the safest decision for everyone."

"There's always an excuse," the Torturer growled, and then he charged again.

Thunderbolt sent another burst of electricity at him, which the Torturer mostly absorbed, but it slowed the big man just enough that Thunderbolt was able to leap out of his way. He was still in midair when Hayden stretched out his hand, and Thunderbolt went flying backward with startling speed. He hit the wall and crumpled to the floor.

"Nice work," the Torturer said, walking over to the unconscious body.

"Did I kill him?" Hayden asked tentatively.

"Nah, just knocked him out." The Torturer scooped Thunderbolt up by his collar. "You better go help the other two; those kids are strong."

Hayden took a last look at the old man dangling from the Torturer's fingers and then ran down the hallway toward Leni and Sliver.

Reaching them, he saw a boy and girl standing in the middle of a swirling ring of debris, expressions of determination on their faces.

"Hayden," Leni managed, sounding strained. "Attack!"

Hayden stuck out his hand again, channeling his thoughts toward the kids. He could feel Leni's mental energy closing in around them, but the boy was responding with incredible power of his own, and Leni couldn't break through. Hayden forced his energy into a single spear and plunged it into the fray. The boy was not ready for another attack.

The spear broke through his defenses and hit them full-on. The two kids flew into the wall and collapsed against each other.

Lana twisted to the side, narrowly avoiding a silver knife that embedded itself into the wall behind her. It had missed her arm by less than an inch.

Avaria swung at Septer's outstretched arm, but he blocked the attack with the sword in his other hand and pushed her back. There was another vicious exchange of blows and counterblows. They were perfectly matched, and Lana knew it was up to her to end the fight.

She hoisted her rifle. "Get down!" she screamed to Avaria.

Her mentor instantly dropped onto her stomach. Septer tried to dive out of the way, but he was a second too slow. Lana pulled the trigger.

The red blast caught him in the chest. She saw his eyes

widen in shock, and then he fell backward, lifeless. Smoke rose from the wound.

Avaria climbed back to her feet, smiling. "Well done," she said. "Your first kill."

Lana lowered the rifle. She suddenly felt cold.

"Let's move," Avaria said. "Septer hinted that this was a trap."

She grabbed Lana's arm and literally pulled her down the hallway. The others were already running toward the staircase from the other end of the mansion, and she saw that Thunderbolt was draped over the Torturer's shoulder. Two unconscious children were floating behind them as well.

"Where's Septer?" the Torturer called.

"Dead," Avaria told him, the satisfaction evident in her voice.

Hayden glanced at Lana, but she didn't meet his eyes.

"Good," Leni said as he started down the staircase. "Sliver, signal Sam."

"I can't . . . he's blocking his mind," Sliver said. "That, or he's very focused on something else. He's not listening."

"Try harder!" Leni snapped. He ran down the main hallway and took a sharp left into the bedroom they'd come in through.

"I am!" Sliver replied. "There, I got him. He's upset . . . uh-oh. We have trouble."

"I know," Leni said quietly as the rest of the group caught up with him in the bedroom.

Through the open doorway, Lana could see a white ship

descending to the grass, the League crest emblazoned on its side. It was the Defender, their flagship. As soon as it landed, League members began streaming down the ramp.

"We're in trouble, all right," the Torturer muttered.

"Everyone spread out . . ." Leni started, but he was interrupted as two missiles suddenly exploded into the side of the white ship. The impact blew the *Defender* sideways, causing it to roll, and the League members went flying through the air.

The Shadow appeared over the forest, streaking just a few feet above the treetops. It dove toward the lawn and just barely pulled up before it hit the ground. The ramp was already down.

The group sprinted toward the Shadow, the floating bodies of the captured children hurtling after them. As soon as they were all inside, the ship leapt into the air. A flurry of red blasts dinged off the hull, but the Shadow turned sharply and accelerated into the clouds. The Torturer managed to close the hatch, shutting out the raging wind, and the hold fell into silence.

Hayden sat down next to Lana and took her hand. She leaned against his shoulder, her eyes on the floor. She didn't say anything the entire trip home.

WHEN THEY RETURNED TO THE MANSION, THE PROTÉGÉS QUIETLY filed into the Baron's classroom, where the old man stood in front of a large blue schematic of the estate projected onto the wall. Emily was already waiting at her desk, and she gave them a relieved smile when she saw that they'd all returned safely.

"Welcome back," the Baron said. "I'm sorry we haven't given you the chance to rest, but we have to begin planning immediately. Fortunately, the Defender was too damaged to give chase, and so the exact location of this mansion remains a secret. For now. The League knows we're in this area, and they will find us soon. We must prepare for their assault.

"But before that, let me be the first to congratulate you. Leni has informed me of the success of your mission, and I am extremely impressed."

James glanced at Lana. Her eyes were locked firmly on her desk.

"You managed something we have never been able to do: capture Thunderbolt. And not only that, but you did it in the League's original headquarters."

"*That* was the League's original headquarters?" Hayden asked, frowning.

The Baron nodded. "Did the house look familiar to you?"

"Yeah, it was pretty much the exact same as this one," Hayden said.

"It is." He clasped his hands behind his back, staring at the schematic. "When I first proposed the League of Heroes, I also offered up my home as the headquarters. I'd had it built years earlier in the middle of the wilderness for privacy as I conducted my experiments. But when my war with the League began, I was forced to give it up. Courage raided the mansion in the early days and converted it back into a League base. I was furious, but there was no way to take my home back, and hold it, with our limited manpower. So, I secretly began the construction of a replica. I changed some of the decor, as you may have noticed, but otherwise, it's identical."

He gestured around them.

"Its existence has long been a secret. The materials were all diverted from cover projects, and the construction workers were imported. Rono even installed a fake broadcast signal so when a satellite scans the area, all it sees is trees. This has been the headquarters of the Vindico for years. I suspect the League already had an idea

I was in the area: they uncovered one of my fake construction projects and tracked the materials to this state. Now with the Torturer's excursions to nearby Cambilsford and Fornist, that suspicion must have been confirmed.

"They will soon begin more detailed reconnaissance on this area. In Thunderbolt's absence, their next in line for command would be Meirna, and she's cautious. She'll wait until they have the exact location and information on our defenses before making a move. This should buy us some time."

He turned to the schematic again.

"The focal point of their attack will come right at the front entrance," he continued, pointing to the circular lobby. "It's an obvious point of entry, but it's also the weakest area of the entire mansion. There are two large windows and a lot of exposed wall. We need to set up shooters on the balconies, and the Torturer will lead the first charge from the hallway . . ."

After the Baron's strategy session was over, the protégés all walked back to the common room, discussing the impending attack.

"Where's Lana?" Sam asked suddenly.

James turned around and saw a flash of blond hair disappear into the lobby at the far end of the hallway. For a moment, they were all too stunned to speak.

Finally, James snapped out of it. "Lana! Wait!" he shouted, running after her.

He heard the rest of the group start after him but didn't bother looking back. He ran into the lobby and saw that the front doors were still closed. *Lana wouldn't go for the front doors anyway,* he realized. *She's too smart for that. The garage.*

James sprinted down the right wing of the mansion. Skidding to a halt in front of the door, he flung it open and stepped inside. The garage was dimly lit, so he stepped forward uncertainly, his eyes adjusting to the darkness. It was completely silent.

The others ran in behind him, their footsteps unnaturally loud.

"Lana! Are you in here?" Hayden shouted, his voice echoing around the room. "See anything?" he asked James.

"Nothing," James replied, puzzled.

"Let's go check outside," Hayden said, and he started back toward the hallway. "She must have gone out the front door."

James was just turning away when the garage door started sliding into the ceiling. He jumped, startled by the noise, and then he saw it. The Shadow was lifting off the cement floor, wobbling in midair. The ship hovered there for a moment, and then sped out of the garage.

29

"I'M GOING AFTER HER," AVARIA SNAPPED, JABBING A FINGER at the Baron. "Right now."

"Of course," he agreed. "I'm only saying we need to be careful. She's in the Shadow: we can't catch her. The best I can do is get a helicopter in."

Avaria paced around the meeting room, livid. She should have known Lana might do something drastic. She had seen the horrified look on Lana's face after she killed Septer and the way she was staring at the floor on the flight back. She'd looked broken, defeated. Avaria had pushed her too far, and now Lana had snapped.

"The League will capture her in no time," she said. "The Shadow is far too obvious in the middle of the day, and the media will be at her house the second they find out one of the missing children is home."

"What happened?" Rono asked, rushing into the room. Sliver was right behind him.

"Lana left," the Baron explained, "in the Shadow. I'm calling for the helicopter."

Rono shook his head. "A helicopter will be too slow. We'll take my new ship, the Arrow. I haven't finished all of my tests, but we don't have much choice. We better move fast; the League will hear about the Shadow very soon. It's done too much damage lately."

"Let's go," Avaria said, and she sprinted out of the room.

She's going to get herself killed, Avaria thought furiously. *And if I catch her before the League does, it won't be much better.*

Lana lifted the Shadow higher up into the thin cloud cover. It was a relatively clear morning, which was not to her benefit. The black ship would be easy to spot.

The full weight of what she had just done was pressing down on her, but she had to stay calm. If Lana allowed herself to realize the implications, she might start to panic, and that wouldn't help. She knew Avaria would find her soon, even if the League didn't.

But Lana couldn't face another battle. She couldn't face the League, knowing she'd murdered one of them. She couldn't bear the thought of having to kill again.

So when she left the Baron's classroom, she'd had only one thing on her mind. She had to see her family. She knew she might be bringing a lot of trouble down on them, but she had to. Even if it was just one more time.

She pushed harder on the levers, sending the Shadow hurtling across the sky. There was a blank screen beside the controls, and she tried to activate it, searching for a map or GPS. Then she remembered something Emily had told her: almost all of Rono's devices were voice-activated.

"GPS system activate," she said, and a map immediately popped onto the screen, with a little glowing dot representing the Shadow's position.

Fortunately, Lana had followed her instincts, and she was flying in the right direction. She was heading northwest and only had to make a slight adjustment to get on a straight track to Maine.

"How long until arrival in Maine?"

A message popped up at the bottom of the screen: AT CURRENT SPEED, THIRTY MINUTES.

She leaned back in the chair, biting her lip. In thirty minutes, she would see her family. Lana knew she wouldn't have very long. Both the Vindico and the League would be right behind her.

The worst part was that she wasn't sure who she wanted to catch her.

"I can't believe she took off!" James said again, slapping the coffee table. "Stupid!"

"What do you think they're going to do?" Sam asked.

Hayden was pacing back and forth behind the couches, his expression unusually serious. "I don't know," he said. "If they think she's going to the League, Avaria might actually kill her."

Hayden was guilt-stricken. He'd been so busy talking about the battle, he hadn't been paying attention to his own girlfriend. How could he be so stupid? Of course she wouldn't want to fight the League again. Not after seeing Septer die.

"The League might kill her too," James mumbled. "Or take her to the Perch."

"We can't let that happen," Emily said, turning to the mirror. "Hey! Is anyone listening?" She stood up, hobbled over to the mirror, and proceeded to bang on the glass. "Hey!"

"They're busy chasing Lana," Hayden said, stepping up beside her. "But you're right. We have to do something."

James frowned. "What do you have in mind?"

"Where's your visor?" Hayden asked Emily, ignoring James.

"In my room," she said, and took off for her bedroom.

Hayden paced along the mirror. "First, we're going to have to go to Rono's target range to get some rifles."

"You're not serious," James said. "We're going to attack them? They'll kill us. We're not that strong yet, and they—"

Hayden spun around to face him. "Whose side are you on?" he asked sharply.

James put his hands up, taken aback. "I thought we were all on the same side."

"Not if they hurt Lana," Hayden replied. He knew James was just being reasonable. But right now, he really didn't care about reason.

"We should at least just *ask* them not to hurt her first," James pointed out. "We don't know anything yet."

"We'll ask," Hayden said, "but if they try to hurt her, we fight."

"And we all get killed." James sighed. "All right, I'm in."

Emily hurried back, wearing her visor and shoulder mount. The missile launcher was already protruding from the top.

"Sam, who's still in the mansion?" Hayden asked.

Sam closed his eyes. "Sliver is gone. I don't sense Avaria or Rono, and . . . no, I don't sense Leni either. Just the Baron and the Torturer."

Hayden nodded. "The others must have gone after her, then. Well, we can take those two easily enough, but what good will that do?"

"They won't do anything to Lana out there," Emily said. "They won't have time; the League will be after them, if they haven't already gotten to Lana first. The Vindico will bring her back here."

"And then we can be ready," Hayden agreed. "We'll just have to hope the League doesn't attack at the same time."

"All right, so the target range, then," James said. "But where do we find the Baron and the Torturer?"

Emily glanced at him. "They'll probably be in the monitoring room. Rono and I spent some time in there while you guys were at the League's base. But they'll be in direct contact with the ship, and Leni and the others will know if we attack. Let's go to Rono's lab first; I can shut off the signal."

"Good call," Hayden said. He waved his hand, and the

mirror door flew backward, snapping off its metal hinges. It smashed into the far wall of the control room, and the glass shattered everywhere.

"Couldn't you have just opened it?" James asked.

"Probably," Hayden replied, and then he hurried through the doorway, stepping around the blanket of shattered glass. "All right, guns first, then the signal, then the monitoring room," he listed.

James shook his head. "This is trouble."

"Lots of trouble," Sam agreed quietly as they crept down the hallway.

"Looks like the teachers are about to be taught a lesson," Emily said. "If you turn a bunch of kids into supervillains, you can't expect them to follow the rules."

Lana brought the Shadow down, angling toward her street. There was a crop of trees nearby and, within it, a small park. She aimed for that, not wanting to alert the whole neighborhood by setting a ship down in front of her house. Lana just needed to get home and have as much time with her family as she could before someone came and took her away.

She rotated the Shadow so it landed at the edge of the trees, with the entrance facing away from the playground. Lana lowered the ramp and sprinted through the narrow patch of forest, leaping over a creek.

She emerged onto her street and kept running, ignoring the stares from passing cars. Lana sprinted down the sidewalk, ran right across her lawn, hopped a flower bed, and threw open her front door.

"Mom! Mom! Are you here?" Lana heard noises upstairs. "Mom! Dad! Jer! It's me!"

Her mother appeared at the top of the stairs, her hand pressed over her mouth. "Lana!" she shrieked, and ran down the steps. "Lana!"

"Mom!" Lana buried her face into her mother's shoulder.

"Baby, baby," her mom whimpered. "Where have you been?"

"I was kidnapped," Lana said, tears pouring down her cheeks. "I wanted to come back, but I couldn't."

"What do you mean? Who took you?" She began to sob. "I thought I lost you."

"The Villains. They're coming for me, Mom, they're coming here." Lana met her eyes. "They'll be here soon."

"The Villains?" she gasped. "What do you mean, they're coming here? Did they take those other children too?"

"Yeah," Lana said, glancing back at the door. "They took us to train as their protégés. They changed me, Mom. I've . . . done things."

Her mother took Lana's face in her hands, looking confused. "People were saying they might have been involved, but I didn't believe it," she murmured. "What do you mean they changed you?"

"They made me strong and fast. I . . . I killed a League member, Mom. I killed Septer."

Her mother pulled back. "You killed Septer," she

breathed. "No. How could that be? What do you mean they made you stronger?"

Lana wiped her eyes. "Watch." She took her mother's shoulders and easily lifted her four inches off the ground.

"They put me in a chamber—" Lana broke off as she lowered her mother again, unable to speak.

"It's okay, baby, it's okay," her mom whispered, but Lana saw fear in her eyes.

"I didn't mean to kill him," Lana said, almost pleading. "There was a fight, and I didn't know what to do. But I don't have much time. They'll be here soon. Where's Jer? Is he at school?"

"What are you talking about?" her mother asked, fearfully looking at the door. "I'll call the police." She ran for the phone, but just as she was about to grab it, the base suddenly blew off the wall and went careening into the living room.

Leni strode through the front door, Avaria right behind him. Her green eyes flashed with anger when they met Lana's.

"Who are you?" Lana's mother screamed. "Stay away from my daughter!"

She charged Leni, her arms flailing, but she was stopped dead in her tracks, as if frozen.

"Now, now," Leni said, his finger absently pointing at her. He turned to Lana. "You'll be coming with us now."

"Let her go," Lana warned.

"You're in no position to make demands," Avaria hissed, starting toward her.

Lana threw a savage kick at Avaria's head, and though she managed to block it, the force of the blow sent her reeling backward. Hooking her fingers into claws, Lana lunged at her, but she was knocked sideways in midair and sent crashing into the wall.

"Enough," Leni commanded. "We don't have time for this."

But as soon as Lana hit the wall, she rolled onto her feet and rushed at Avaria again, who blocked her punch and viciously backhanded Lana across the face. Lana staggered to the floor, and she vaguely heard her mom screaming.

"Resist again and I kill your mother," Leni said coolly. "I should do it anyway as punishment."

"No," Lana wheezed.

"Then stand up and get in the ship. Now."

Lana shakily got to her feet, never taking her eyes off Avaria. Then she turned to her mom. "I'm sorry, Mom. I love you."

"No!" Lana's mother screamed. "Get away from her, you monsters!"

"Now, Lana," Leni snapped, and then glanced at Avaria. "Sliver just informed me they have League vessels on the radar."

Avaria grabbed Lana and forced her out the door. Lana saw that another black vessel, larger and sleeker than the Shadow, was parked in the middle of the street. Cars were backed up in both directions, and her neighbors were all watching from their lawns. The Shadow was hovering overhead.

"Get in," Avaria hissed, and Lana climbed the ramp, feeling the last touch of a breeze before she was thrown headfirst into the hold.

"Two ships on the radar," Rono called from the front. "Definitely League. You in?"

"We're in," Leni replied, closing the hatch. "I have left your mother alive for now, girl, but I placed an explosive on the roof of your house. If you misbehave again, your family will die."

The protégés huddled together outside the monitoring room door, clutching the heavy rifles they'd grabbed from the target range. Emily had already turned the signal off, and now there was only one thing left to do.

"Surprise," Hayden whispered, and then he pressed the control panel. The door slid into the ceiling, and the Baron and the Torturer spun around, eyes wide.

"What is the meaning—" the Baron started.

"Where's Lana?" Hayden asked, cutting him off. The protégés stepped into the room, keeping their rifles trained on the two men.

"She is being retrieved by the others," the Baron replied. "Everything is under control. Now put the guns away, and go back . . ."

James shook his head. "Not until we know she hasn't been hurt."

"That is very unwise," the Baron said, "and unnecessary. Of course they won't hurt her. She's too valuable."

"We want to make sure," Hayden replied. "No offense, but by nature, you guys are not very trustworthy."

"How did you agree to this, James?" the Torturer asked, scowling.

James said nothing. Sam shifted uncertainly, the gun feeling heavy and unnatural in his hands. The Baron turned to him.

"Sam, why don't you just go in my mind and get the answer yourself? You can tell them."

"We'll wait until they get back," Emily said sharply.

"And then what?" the Baron asked. "What will you do then? Did you really think about this plan?"

Hayden narrowed his eyes. "Nice try, Baron. Then we take Lana, and if anything happens to her, you deal with all of us."

"You'll be squashed like ants," the Torturer snarled.

"I understand you're upset," the Baron said, "as you should be. But let's put down the weapons and speak as equals, so that—"

"No," Emily interrupted. "You're not talking us into anything."

The Baron stared at her for a moment. "And what happens when Leni removes your weapons? What do you expect us to do then with this mutiny? We don't have time for this. We have to prepare for the League. The two of us will forget this ever happened. We won't tell the others."

Sam could sense James wavering, and he felt his own resolve, which had never been very firm, vanish completely.

Hayden was not so easily swayed. "Sure, as soon as we know Lana is safe."

"Except Leni will know you led this little rebellion," the Torturer pointed out, "and he's not going to be very happy."

Hayden nodded. "You're right. Leni will be angry. He'll probably throw me through a wall or beat me with some trees. Fortunately, I have a plan."

He abruptly fired a fizzling blue stun charge right at the Baron, catching him in the midsection. The old man collapsed to the ground.

"Why did you do that?" James shouted, whirling on Hayden.

"It was the only thing he could do," Emily said as she walked towards the Torturer. "He'll need three or four."

"Don't even think about—" the Torturer started, but he was cut off as Emily fired right into his chest. Hayden followed with another blast.

The Torturer staggered against the wall, looking scandalized, and after another shot each, he collapsed as well.

"Emily, do you know where the cells are?" Hayden asked, lowering his rifle.

"Yeah, I've been helping Rono reinforce the security systems. They're in the right wing basement. What's your plan?"

"We need reinforcements," Hayden explained, "and I know two really strong kids who don't like villains."

"Aren't you the one who knocked them out?" James asked.

"I'll just have to explain the situation. I can be very charming, you know."

Emily scanned the monitor that the Baron and the Torturer had been watching. "The comm signal is down, but there's still a reading on the ships' locations. They'll be back in twenty minutes."

"We better move quickly, then," Hayden said, gesturing with his rifle at the Torturer. "James, you drag the big lug. I'll take the Baron. We'll throw them in a cell and find the kids. Sam, maybe you should come too, and Emily, you keep an eye on the ships, maybe figure out how we can ambush them in the meanwhile. Cool?"

"We're dead," Sam said, staring down at the crumpled bodies.

Hayden waved a hand in dismissal. "Don't worry about it! This is how you graduate from supervillain school: you take out your teachers. Congratulations, the diploma's in the mail. Now, unless we all want to end up being mentally whipped by Leni, we should get moving."

30

"HOLD ON!" RONO SHOUTED AS HE SENT THE ARROW INTO A spinning, breakneck dive.

The repaired League ship, the Defender, was right behind them, firing red blasts wildly overhead. Rono pulled up hard on the controls, and the Arrow just narrowly missed plunging into a hillside, its hull skimming the long grass. The blasts from the pursuing League ship exploded uselessly into the ground, sending up plumes of dirt and smoke.

"Where's the Shadow?" Leni asked, peering into the sky.

Rono snuck a glance at the radar. "It's still in one piece. We need to—"

The Arrow was suddenly rocked by a direct hit, almost spilling Rono from his seat. He clenched the throttle and angled the ship toward the sky again.

"Look out below," he whispered, pressing a button on the weapons display.

A remote explosive dropped out the back of the ship, and they all watched on the sensors as it fell toward the climbing League vessel. When it was within twenty feet of the target, it exploded, and the Defender plunged right into the massive fireball.

"Got him!" Rono shouted triumphantly. "That's a new trick that . . ." He stopped when he saw the blackened Defender emerge from the explosion, still intact. "Damn," he muttered. "It's damaged, but they're holding together."

"They're firing everything they can at Sliver," Avaria said, pointing to where the Shadow was weaving in and out of a furious barrage of laser fire from the other League ship.

Leni glanced at the sensors. "We have to hold on for a few more minutes. We have no choice but to give up the mansion's location. Signal the Baron, and tell him to ready the antiaircraft cannons."

Rono triggered the comm. "That's weird."

"What?" Leni asked.

Rono tried again. "There's no signal from the mansion. Either it's down, or we're being jammed."

"The League doesn't want us to send warning," Avaria said.

"It seems that way," Leni muttered. "But there's nothing we can do. There's no point in turning to fight when we can just lead them back to the mansion. The Baron will have warning enough when he sees the League ships come into range. They'll be forced to pull back and come in on foot."

"So how do we wake them up?" Sam asked curiously, looking at the girl.

"I have no idea," Hayden said. "I kind of assumed they'd be awake."

After depositing their mentors in one of the heavily reinforced cells in the basement prison, they'd found the captured siblings, as well as cells containing the unconscious bodies of Thunderbolt and Junkit. James had been extremely relieved to see that Junkit was still alive.

Now they stood over the two prone kids, who were laid out across separate metal tables.

"I'm sure there's a way to wake them up," Hayden continued, looking below the tables. "This is probably the same stuff they used on us." He shook the boy's leg.

"That did it," James said sarcastically. He glanced down the corridor. "They're going to be back soon."

"We're going to be killed," Sam whispered.

"Don't be so pessimistic," Hayden said. He bit his lip, staring at the unconscious bodies. "Wait. Sam, you can do it, right? You can wake them?"

Sam frowned. "What gives you that idea?"

"You're a telepath; just tell them to wake up in their minds! You told James to stroke Lana's hair, right? Just do the same thing. Start with the girl; she's a telepath too."

"I don't think it works like that . . ." Sam said.

"Just try it!"

"Okay," Sam said hesitantly. He laid his hands on the

girl's arm and closed his eyes. A minute passed, and then he began to tremble.

"Uh, Sam?" James asked, reaching for his shoulder.

A sudden wave of panic swept through James, and he toppled to the floor. Slowly pushing himself up again, James saw that Sam and Hayden were lying flat on their backs beside him. The girl was sitting on the platform, looking at them suspiciously.

"That was unexpected," Hayden groaned, climbing to his feet. He managed a weak smile. "Good morning."

"*You*," she said. "You're the one who attacked us." She narrowed her eyes.

"Wait!" Hayden said quickly. "We're friends."

Sam blinked and sat up, rubbing his forehead.

"Where am I?" the girl asked.

"You're in the Vindico's mansion," Hayden replied, gesturing at James and Sam. "We're their protégés, but we've had a bit of a falling-out."

"Their protégés?" she murmured. "Yes, Thunderbolt mentioned something about you."

"Yeah," Hayden said slowly, "Thunderbolt. Well, here's the deal . . ." Hayden briefly ran through Lana's escape and their subsequent rebellion. "Now the rest of the Vindico are coming back, and we have to ambush them so they don't kill us. And we need your help. You and your brother's."

She raised her eyebrows. "You want us to help you even though you're the one who attacked us?"

"Yeah, sorry about that," Hayden said, sounding guilty. "Sort of a spur-of-the-moment thing."

"Hmm," she said, glaring at him. "And what happens after we ambush the Villains?"

"I don't know," Hayden conceded. "You two can leave if you want. See the thing is, we can't just make peace with the League either. Basically, we're going to start our own group, I guess." He looked at the others, shrugging. "Right? Something like that. You're free to join if you want."

"And what are you going to do with your mentors?" she asked.

"I don't know, lock them up?" Hayden glanced at the hallway, looking increasingly anxious. "I hate to rush you, but they could be back any minute, so you know, the after-planning isn't as urgent."

She looked them over for a moment and then sighed. "Well, we don't have any choice, do we? You seem honest enough. I'll wake Lyle."

She turned to her brother, and after a moment, he jerked awake. As soon as he saw Hayden, he lifted his hand.

"They're friends," the girl said.

"That's not how I remember it," he snarled.

Hayden forced a smile. "First impressions were never my strong suit, but I grow on you. Just ask these guys."

James snorted.

"We don't have time for this," Sam pointed out. "They'll be back soon."

"Right," Hayden agreed. "Listen, Lyle, and . . ."

"Deanna," she said.

"Deanna, we need your help to save our friend Lana

from certain death." Hayden paused. "Well, we think. Not clear on that. It doesn't matter. Will you help us?"

"Where are Thunderbolt and Septer?" Lyle asked.

"Thunderbolt is in a cell down the hall," Hayden explained, "and Septer, he, uh . . . he's dead."

"Dead?" Lyle whispered, getting to his feet. He exchanged a disturbed look with his sister. "They'll pay for that. Let's get Thunderbolt."

Hayden shifted uncomfortably. "Yeah, we'll do that after, I think. He *may* not be too happy to see me." Lyle seemed wary, and Hayden met his eyes. "I know you don't trust us, and I don't blame you, but if we're not ready when the Vindico get back, we all may be killed."

Lyle glanced at his sister. "All right," he said. "What's the plan?"

There was a moment of silence.

"Getting you two was kind of as far as I got," Hayden admitted.

James sighed. "Some leader you are. Deanna, can you guard your minds so Sliver doesn't know you and Lyle are awake?"

"I think so."

"Do that. Let's get back upstairs. We'll ambush them in the garage, where there are lots of things to hide behind."

"And lots of things for Leni to throw at us," Hayden objected.

"Well, make sure you throw them first," James said. "Sam, contact Emily and tell her to meet us there. Let's move."

"You're so dreamy when you take charge," Hayden purred.

James just shook his head and led the group to the garage. Emily was already waiting there.

"Emily," Hayden said, "meet Lyle and Deanna, who have kindly agreed to help us."

"We can do introductions later," James snapped. "How long do we have, Emily?"

"About four minutes. And there are two more ships behind them. I think it's the League."

"Oh, that's good," Hayden muttered.

"I figured out how to activate the antiaircraft weapons," Emily said. "They'll fire at the new ships if they come too close."

"You better not kill any more League members," Lyle warned.

"We won't," Hayden assured him. "But we have to worry about saving Lana first."

James nodded. "We'll take cover around the Shadow's usual landing spot. When they come down the ramp, Lyle and Deanna will attack Leni and Sliver with Hayden and Sam's help. Emily and I will stun Rono and Avaria. There are six of us: this *should* work. Hopefully Lana will be awake, and she can help."

"Brilliant strategy," Hayden commented. "Very clever."

"Do you have something better?" James asked.

"Nope."

"That's what I thought. Let's go."

James hurried to where the Shadow was usually parked. It was a big space, so he assumed they could probably land both ships right next to each other. He turned back to the group. "All right, make a perimeter around this spot. Get behind cover, and make sure it's on the side *away* from the garage door."

"What happens if they don't park both ships here?" Emily asked.

James hesitated. "Then we'll just have to deal with that when the times comes."

He crouched down behind a sleek red sports car and watched the others fan out around the opening. Deanna and Lyle hid behind a black SUV next to him, and after a few anxious minutes, the garage started to open.

Daylight flooded into the room, and the Vindico ships appeared. The Shadow was spewing smoke, and both were covered with black scorch marks. Fortunately, the two ships set down right where the Shadow usually parked.

James heard the ramps sliding down and then the shuffle of feet as their mentors quickly exited the ships. He waited another couple of seconds.

"Now!" he shouted. Then he rolled out from behind the car and opened fire.

31

LANA WAS BARELY OUT OF THE SHIP WHEN EVERYTHING ERUPTED into chaos.

Fizzling blue stun blasts leapt toward them from every direction, as if they'd walked into a lightning storm. She and Avaria instinctively dove to the ground, but Rono didn't move fast enough and took a blast to the shoulder. In desperation, Leni threw himself across the garage, and she saw his flapping black cape disappear behind a van. Sliver managed to duck under the first wave of stun blasts, but he soon stiffened under a mental attack.

Time to do your part, Lana thought. Beside her, Avaria flipped back onto her feet, narrowly avoiding a stun bolt that dissipated against the concrete. She tried to run for cover, but Lana kicked out her trailing leg and sent her toppling back to the ground. Lana attempted to follow that up with a stomp to her mentor's stomach, but Avaria was too fast. She rolled as soon as she hit the ground and then swept Lana's legs out from under her with a vicious kick of her own.

Lana hit the concrete with a thud, and Avaria sprinted into the ring of vehicles. James attempted to shoot her down, but his stun blasts all sailed wide.

You're not getting away so easily, Lana thought. She pushed herself up and took off after her.

Sam's rifle dropped from his hands and clattered off the concrete. He was having a hard time keeping track of his own thoughts. He knew he wanted to shoot Sliver, but another powerful voice had told him to drop the gun, so he had.

We need to overwhelm him, Deanna said into Sam's mind. *Push!*

Sam found Sliver's consciousness and extended himself toward it, trying to displace it with his own. But Sliver was not giving up easily.

Help me, Sam! Sliver's voice said, sounding strained now. *I'm your friend! Cripple the girl!*

Sam pushed harder, and he could feel Deanna joining him, their combined strength bearing down on Sliver. Sam could almost feel his mentor's knees buckling, and Sliver's anger became colored with fear and betrayal.

Your mother forgot about you, Sliver said desperately. *I'm all you have left! And you would betray me?*

You just used us, Sam replied, pushing back against the voice.

There was a sudden flare of rage, and Sam felt his

mentor gathering his energy. Now it was Sam's turn to be afraid. Sliver was preparing a violent attack, and Sam wasn't sure he could stop it. His mentor was going to try and murder him.

Pull back! Deanna warned. *He's going to—*

Abruptly, Sliver's mind went dark. Sam opened his eyes just in time to see Sliver fall face-first onto the concrete, unconscious. Behind him, James lowered his rifle.

"Not fun getting hit in the back, is it?" James said, looking down on Sliver's limp body.

Sam and Deanna exchanged a relieved smile, and then she turned and ran after Lyle and Hayden. "I'm going to help my brother!" Deanna called. Ahead of her, Sam saw a motorcycle fly through the air, only to stop suddenly and go spiraling across the room.

"Be careful . . ." Sam muttered.

Across the garage, Emily fired another salvo of stun blasts, forcing Rono to duck behind the van again. She was using the Arrow as cover, and she knew Rono was at a disadvantage. His left arm was limp and useless from where she'd shot him, and he was struggling to use his rifle accurately with one hand.

Emily peeked out from behind the ship and fired again, just missing Rono's head. She could switch to kill shots and blow the van apart, but she didn't want to hurt him. She just needed to expose him somehow so she could stun him.

Emily heard rapid footsteps behind her and turned to

see Sam running toward the ship. He huddled next to her, awkwardly clutching his rifle.

"Need any help?" he asked.

Emily laid down some cover fire. "Yeah," she said, glancing at him. "Can you get to the Shadow? Start it up, and ram the van. I'll pop out and stun him."

Sam nodded and ran toward the Shadow.

"What do you want, Emily?" Rono shouted. He obviously knew he was about to be cornered.

"We want to make sure Lana is safe!" Emily said. She fired again for good measure, and Rono pulled back.

"Mission accomplished, I think! How about talking this out?"

Emily leaned against the hull, shaking her head. "Don't trust you! Sorry! We'll talk once you're disarmed!"

"How do I know you won't just shoot me?"

"You don't!" she replied loudly.

The heavily damaged Shadow thrummed to life, shooting out another cloud of smoke. It floated off the ground, wobbling unsteadily, and headed straight for Rono.

Emily risked a glance and saw that Rono was staring at the ship, wide-eyed. The Shadow rammed the van, exposing him. At the same time, Emily stepped out and fired. Rono didn't even move. The stun blast caught him in the chest, and he collapsed to the ground.

Hayden ducked as a tire whizzed over his head. It reversed directions and headed for him again, but this time he flicked his hand and sent it spinning away.

He and Lyle were tracking Leni through the maze of parked vehicles, many of which had been destroyed during Leni's repeated attempts to dispatch them. A black, half-destroyed motorcycle barreled toward Lyle, but the boy managed to divert its path and it crashed into a limo, shattering the windshield.

"Face us, coward!" Lyle screamed.

Hayden winced. Calling Leni a coward was probably not a good idea.

A wave of mental energy erupted from Leni's hiding place, and Lyle went flying through the air. He smashed into an SUV and dropped to the floor, dazed.

"Now it's me and you, traitor," Leni's voice rang out, echoing around the garage.

"Yep," Hayden said with false confidence. "Now the student challenges the master and all that."

"Fool. You don't stand a chance against me."

"Maybe," Hayden said. "Only one way to find out, I guess."

Marshaling all his energy, Hayden decided to do something very rash. He ran toward the source of Leni's voice and propelled himself through the air, just as his mentor had done. He sailed right over an SUV, completely out of control. But sure enough, Leni was standing on the other side, and Hayden could tell by the disbelieving expression on his face that he had definitely not expected this.

Probably because it was a dumb idea, Hayden thought. As he flew over his mentor's head, Hayden sent a wave of energy downward and watched in satisfaction as Leni crumpled to the ground.

Hayden looked up just as he was about to hit a large truck. He mentally pulled himself back to slow his pace, but he couldn't reverse his trajectory in time. He smacked right into the side and dropped to the hard concrete.

"Yep, not smart," he muttered. Hearing footsteps, he fearfully glanced back, expecting to see Leni walking toward him. Instead, it was Lyle.

"You all right?" Lyle asked.

Hayden pushed himself to his feet. "Yeah. Where's Leni?"

"You distracted him long enough. Deanna attacked his mind as soon as he hit the ground, and he blacked out."

"Nice," Hayden said, heading back to the ships. "We better check on the others. This didn't go as smoothly as I envisioned."

"So now what?" Sam asked nervously, looking around the group.

The unconscious Vindico members were laid out on the ground. Hayden, Lyle, and Deanna had returned with Leni and thrown him next to Sliver and Rono. Soon after, James and Lana had emerged from the other end of the garage, dragging Avaria behind them. They both looked worse for the wear, wincing and limping.

"Well, putting them in a cell would be a good start," Hayden said, "so that they don't wake up and kill us all.

Then we should probably get ready for the League's attack . . . so they don't kill us all."

"Good times," James said, shaking his head. He scooped up Sliver and threw him over his shoulder. "I can't believe we beat them, even with the element of surprise."

"Yeah, we are pretty great," Hayden agreed. "Where are the League ships now, Emily?"

"They came under fire from the antiaircraft cannons," she replied. "I had the feed relayed to my visor. They both pulled back and landed somewhere outside the perimeter. No one's crossed it yet. I had the perimeter sensors relayed to my visor as well, so we'll have at least five minutes' warning when they do."

"What would we do without you, Emily," Hayden said. He stuck his hand out, and Leni and Rono floated off the ground, their limbs dangling below them. Lana grabbed Avaria, and they all started back to the hallway.

James shifted Sliver so he could fit through the door. "We need to figure out what we're going to do now. The League might be here any minute."

"Maybe you can just make a truce," Lyle suggested. They reached the stairs to the basement prison, and the thick metal door slid aside.

"Maybe," Hayden said, "but that depends what they're going to do with us. If they think we're going to the Perch, *any* of us, then we fight."

They reached the bottom, and Lana turned to the rest of the group. "I didn't get much chance to tell you during all that, but thank you," she said quietly. "I wish I hadn't put you all in danger. I'm sorry. It was selfish of me, and now I messed up everything."

"We're just happy you're back," Hayden said. "Supervillain school isn't the same without you. In fact, it was so terrible that we decided to graduate." He gave her a quick kiss. "Did you miss me?"

She smiled. "Slightly. But it was just a passing thought."

"Remember how the League of Heroes might attack at any minute?" James asked sourly, walking past them. He opened a cell and tossed Sliver inside.

"You used to be more romantic," Hayden said to him as he floated Leni and Rono through the cell door. "But I suppose you're right. Let's call up the League."

"But if they know the Vindico have already been captured, they'll just attack right away," James argued, stepping back as Lana threw in Avaria. "They might be grateful we captured them, but that doesn't mean they'll let us go. We need a guarantee they won't send anyone to the Perch *or* ban us from using our powers."

"How do we do that?" Sam asked.

James locked the cell door and turned to Deanna. "I have an idea."

32

DEANNA STOOD ALONE IN FRONT OF THE COMMUNICATIONS
relay, staring at the blank screen. The rest of the teens were
waiting out of sight by the doorway, listening as she keyed
in the signal code for League headquarters.

"I hope this works," Hayden murmured.

"Yeah," James said softly, "me too."

"Deanna?" a deep voice asked, sounding shocked.

"That's Gali," James whispered.

"Where are you? How are you—" Gali continued.

"I don't have much time," Deanna interrupted. "I'm in
the Vindico's mansion."

"Have you escaped? The Defender just contacted us;
they said they came under heavy fire at the perimeter of
the estate. We have no choice but to come in on the ground.
The rest of us are leaving now to join the assault. If you can
get out of the building, hide in the forest and contact—"

Deanna cut him off again. "We haven't escaped. The

Vindico are still here, but one of their protégés is guarding me. He brought me here to contact you." She lowered her voice. "He says the protégés are willing to help you capture the Vindico, but they have terms."

"What terms?" Gali asked suspiciously.

She hesitated. "They want your assurance that none of them will be punished in any way."

"Impossible," Gali said. "They have willfully attacked League members, and they will serve the required sentence."

The protégés exchanged nervous looks.

Gali continued, sounding agitated. "And they will *all* be banned from using their powers. You know the law, Deanna. If they want to go home when their sentence is done, their abilities must be kept a secret or it's life on the Perch."

James didn't need to hear any more: whatever loyalty he'd still had to the League was now gone. This war wasn't over yet.

"But they won't help then . . ." Deanna argued.

"Where is the boy who's guarding you? Can he hear us?" Gali asked, lowering his voice.

"He's in the hallway."

"Tell them we agree," Gali whispered. "Do you think you'll be able to get back to the relay to send us another message?"

"Yes," Deanna said quietly. "I think so."

"Tell them to go ahead with the rebellion and that we'll coordinate our attack. Set up a time, and then call headquarters again. I'll have it relayed to the ship. We'll capture everybody in one swoop. You'll be a hero, Deanna."

"Yeah," she whispered. "I'll get back to you soon."

Deanna ended the signal. Then she turned to the others, who were all standing there in silence.

"Well," Deanna said coolly, "who's ready for another ambush?"

Hayden stepped into the large, circular room, and the others filed in after him. The floor, walls, and ceiling were all finished with gleaming black tiles. The room's only contents were a pool table, a leather couch, and a flat-screen television.

"Here it is," Hayden said, gesturing around them. "*This* is our answer."

Lana frowned. "A lounge is our answer? How is this possibly going to help?"

"And why do the Vindico even *have* a lounge?" Emily asked curiously, walking over to the pool table. She ran her fingers along the green felt. "They don't seem the type."

"They aren't the type," Hayden agreed. "And they don't have a lounge. Last week I saw a file open on Leni's computer. They were blueprints for something called 'Nightfall.' This is it."

Hayden started toward a bare wall at the far end of the room. He ran his fingers along the black tiles for a moment and then stepped back and stuck out his hand. There was a click from somewhere within the wall, and a narrow door eased open.

"This entire room is a trap," Hayden told them. "I think Leni was going to lure the League to the mansion and then draw them in here. When he got them all into this room, he would step through this door, and these"—he pointed at the black tiles—"pull objects in when activated, like an electromagnet, and stun them."

"Why didn't you say anything about this before?" James asked in disbelief, poking his head into the hidden chamber on the other side of the door.

Hayden shrugged. "I didn't think it was that important at the time. I mean, we knew they were trying to capture the League. I just didn't think we would be trying to eventually as well. So, this is what I'm thinking. We stage our rebellion, like Gali said, and then, just like Leni planned, we lead them to this room, get into the chamber, and capture the entire League at once."

"So many things can go wrong with that plan," James pointed out. "Like, literally every part of it." He paused. "But before you ask, no, I don't have any better ideas."

"So we're trapping the League, then," Lana said. She glanced at Deanna and Lyle. "You sure you're on board?"

"Punishing you guys for being kidnapped is wrong," Deanna said. "Lyle and I are with you."

Lyle shifted a little. "But how are we going to make the League believe there's a rebellion happening when your mentors are locked in a cell?"

"I know how," Emily said casually from where she was inspecting the black tiles across the room. "We let a few of them out."

"What?" Hayden and James asked at the same time.

"We only let out a few of them," Emily repeated. "Not Leni or Avaria, obviously. We'll tell them that if they help trap the League, we'll let them go free. They'll jump at the chance to finally destroy their enemies." She smiled. "We just won't tell them that we're going to force the League to agree to our terms. We'll act like we want to kill them too."

"Well," James muttered, "it's completely crazy, but that hasn't stopped us lately. Let's go recruit the Villains that we literally *just* betrayed. This should go over well."

"Yeah," Hayden said slowly. "Everyone bring your guns."

"Why should we help you traitors?" the Torturer asked coldly, staring straight at James. He, Rono, and Sliver had been taken out of their cell as Hayden and Lyle stood guard by the doorway.

"Because," James told him, his rifle aimed at the big man's chest, "you want to finish the League off, and so do we. And if you help us, then you're all free to go, and we can put this behind us."

"Your protégés all figured you should be given the chance," Hayden added. "I don't really want Leni here since he's probably going to kill me the first chance he gets, and Lana doesn't want Avaria for the same reason. We left the Baron locked up because he knows the ins and outs of this mansion better than anyone, and it was too risky to have him running around on his own. He might try something."

"What will you do with them?" Rono asked, glancing back at the cell.

Hayden paused. "Leni and Avaria will stay where they are until we figure something out. We'll let the Baron go after we're done with the ambush."

"I see," Rono said slowly. He seemed to consider their offer. "I guess we don't have much choice, do we?"

"Not really," Hayden said. "We'll come get you as soon as the perimeter sensors are tripped." He put his hand over the door controls. "Ready, Lyle?"

Lyle positioned himself on the other side. "Ready."

"In we go, then," Hayden ordered, pressing the button.

The three Villains filed back into the cell, where Leni, Avaria, and the Baron were watching suspiciously, and then the door slid shut again.

"Deanna?" Gali said eagerly from the relay screen when Deanna called him back twenty minutes later. "What did they say?"

"The protégés are rebelling," she replied, her voice breathless and rushed. She looked back toward the door. "They're fighting the Vindico right now . . . you better hurry. I don't know how long they can hold out."

"Lock yourself in the room. We'll be there in ten minutes."

Deanna ended the signal and watched as the screen went black. "I guess it's a go," she said nervously.

James hoisted his rifle. "Let's move."

33

THE TORTURER LOWERED HIS HEAD AND CHARGED STRAIGHT AT James, who barely managed to dive out of the way. On the other side of the room, Hayden yelled something incomprehensible and flung a marble statue in the Torturer's general direction, but it intentionally flew about ten feet wide and smashed into the wall. Near the lobby's towering front entrance, Deanna was lying on the ground, pretending to have been knocked over.

James got to his feet and rushed toward his mentor, who spun around and clipped him painfully in the ribs. James winced and threw a punch at the Torturer's arm, but he just laughed and beat it aside. The big man swung at him, and James swiftly ducked under the counterpunch and kicked him in the torso. The Torturer swore and tried to grab at him, but they were both knocked sideways by a wave of Hayden's mental energy, who was screaming some sort of war cry.

James had just scrambled back to his feet when both of the enormous windows on either side of the entrance shattered in one cacophonic moment.

They spun around to see multiple figures jump, run, and fly through, and then the front doors burst open. An enraged Gali stood on the threshold.

The Torturer took off down the left wing hallway, just narrowly avoiding a stream of laser bolts aimed at his departing form. James bellowed and ran after him, shooting some purposefully wide blasts. Hayden followed, flinging statues and paintings. James risked a quick glance back before he rounded the corner, and he saw Gali pulling Deanna to her feet.

Leaving the rest to her, James continued the chase. A second mock firefight had erupted in the left wing, and the Torturer sprinted right past Lana and Lyle to join Sliver. Both Villains bolted down a staircase.

James had just reached Lana and Lyle when he looked back to see that the League members were already in pursuit. The Flame was wielding a rapidly expanding fireball. *This had really better work,* James thought. Together, he, Hayden, Lana, and Lyle raced down the stairs in pursuit of their mentors before wheeling toward yet another mock firefight.

Blue stun blasts rocketed back and forth across the long corridor in front of them, forcing James to press against the wall as he ran. One bolt sizzled disturbingly close to his arm. The Torturer and Sliver had by now joined up with Rono, and all three Vindico members were firing back at the protégés from the trap room door.

The first of the League members descended the stairs, and at the sight of them, all three mentors fled into the room.

"After them!" James shouted for dramatic effect.

Everyone but Emily and Sam, who had agreed to stay behind and fire on any League members who didn't enter the trap room, rushed in after them. As soon as James was inside, he fired up at the ceiling, and blazing sparks rained down. On the far side of the room, the Vindico members were already heading into the hidden chamber.

James had a sudden flash of suspicion. "Hayden!" he shouted. "Keep that door open!"

Sure enough, James saw Rono immediately lunge for the control panel to shut the door and trap the protégés in the room with the League. But Hayden blocked the door with an invisible barrier, and he ran into the chamber. James let everyone else go through the door ahead of him while he stayed at the entrance to the trap room to cover them.

Just as the last person ran through the hidden door, the League members stormed into the circular room. James turned to run, realizing with a surge of fear that he might have waited too long.

He sprinted for the trap room door as fast as he could, dodging a fierce barrage of lasers. Just as he was sure he would be shot down, he felt an invisible pull that yanked him across the room. James skidded into the shadowy chamber, and the door slid shut.

"Thanks," he said to Hayden.

"You can hug me later," Hayden replied, turning to the control panel. "It's time to spring the trap."

He pressed a green button.

James stood up and watched through a window, obviously a fake tile, as the door to the trap room closed behind the League members. Meirna, an older woman with dark, wrinkled skin and short black hair, suddenly turned right toward them, comprehension on her face.

Hayden pressed a red button. Nothing happened.

"Let's try that again," Hayden muttered. He pressed the button harder. Again, nothing.

"What's wrong?" Lana asked, leaning over his shoulder.

"That's a good question," he replied, pressing the button repeatedly.

"Did you test this thing?" Rono shouted.

Hayden paused. "Well, not really."

"How could you not test it?" James snapped.

"I just assumed it was finished! It looked finished."

"You idiots," the Torturer said, shaking his head. "James, how did you let this moron take charge?"

"He seemed confident," James said quietly.

Inside the room, the League members were walking purposefully toward the hidden chamber. Meirna pointed, and the entire wall began to tremble. Behind her, the Flame was still wielding an ever-growing fireball between his hands.

"This wall isn't going to last long," Sliver said nervously. "Is there a way out of here?"

"There is now," the Torturer growled, and he turned, lowered his head, and charged right into the wall behind them. There was a loud crunch, and then he toppled backward.

"I'm pretty sure we're underground," Hayden said. "But yes, there is a way out. I saw it in the designs."

"Now you tell me," the Torturer grumbled, climbing back to his feet.

Hayden pressed another button, and a door slid open beside them, leading into a dark corridor. "I think this leads back upstairs, in case something goes wrong," he explained. "Like the rest of the plan not working. We better regroup with Emily and Sam and figure out a new strategy."

The vibrations grew stronger, shaking the ground beneath their feet.

"Run!" Lana screamed, and they all took off down the corridor just as a massive fireball hit the chamber, sending cracks splintering along the wall.

Lana led them down the corridor about forty feet until they came to a crude, concrete staircase. She raced to the top of the steps and pushed against what looked to just be a wall. A square section swung outward, and hurrying through the opening, they found themselves right back in the opulent main hallway.

"Now what?" James asked, glancing back down the steps.

"Deanna, can you contact Sam and Emily?" Hayden said.

"I already did," Deanna said. "They're on their way."

"Oh." Hayden shrugged. "Well, that's all I've got. Can we fight them?"

"We need to release Leni and Avaria," Sliver told them. "It's the only way we'll have a chance."

Emily and Sam came up the first staircase they'd gone down and hurried over. Emily's limping was growing ever more pronounced. "What happened?" she wheezed.

"The trap room wasn't quite finished," Lana explained, glaring at Hayden.

"You didn't test it?" Emily asked him.

Hayden held up his hands. "Well, where were all you people an hour ago?"

"How you kids managed to ambush us, I'll never know," the Torturer muttered. "Hey, where are you going?"

Sliver was sprinting down the hallway. "To get the others!"

"Wait," Hayden said, and then took off after him. "That's a bad plan!"

A massive, echoing explosion sounded from the secret corridor, and voices filtered up through the opening. The League was already through.

The Torturer hastily closed the wall segment again. "That should hold them for about one second. Let's go."

They ran after Hayden and Sliver but had just reached the lobby when the hidden wall segment exploded. League members spilled out into the hallway.

"Hurry!" James shouted.

They broke into a wild sprint across the lobby. Emily

was lagging, so James dropped his pace to keep up with her. Stun blasts flew around them. The Torturer was hit in the back, but he just stumbled and kept running. Lana was the fastest, and she led them through the reinforced metal door and down into the basement prison. James waited until Emily had gone in, just narrowly avoiding a blue flash, and then he hurried after her. He closed the door and fired right into the panel, shorting out the controls.

James had just reached the bottom of the stairs when the first League members began pounding on the door. Farther down the prison corridor, Sliver was pinned against the wall, held up by an invisible grip. Hayden was calmly standing in front of him as Lana explained the situation.

"So you're saying we do in fact need to let Leni out?" Hayden asked.

She nodded. "Yes."

Sliver dropped to the ground, and the Torturer strode over to the cell door. As soon as it opened, Leni stalked out with Avaria and the Baron close on his heels.

"You," Leni hissed, starting toward Hayden.

"Hey, Teach," he mumbled.

"You're going to pay—"

"Later," Rono said. "The League is here. We have to do something."

"How about kill them all?" Avaria suggested, narrowing her eyes.

"You can't do that," Lyle objected.

Leni turned to him. "I suppose you wouldn't like that, would you? Very well." He waved his hand, and Lyle and Deanna flew into the cell. Avaria closed the door.

All the protégés protested at once, aiming their rifles at Leni's chest.

He slowly raised his hands. "It needed to be done. Unlike *some,* they wouldn't have fought their own teachers. Why would they? They won't be arrested or killed, so they have no need. We'll release them after the battle, and they can do as they please. Right now, we have more pressing issues. It's time we end this war."

With that, he walked toward the stairs, ignoring the rifles that were still pointed at him. James glanced at the others, but none seemed willing to shoot.

The rest of the Vindico followed Leni, leaving the protégés alone.

"I'm scared," Sam murmured. His hair was matted against his sweating forehead, and his brown eyes looked watery. "I just want things to be normal again. I want to go to school tomorrow."

"Me too," Hayden said, and everyone looked at him. "Well, not really. It just seemed like the right thing to say."

James sighed. "Let's get this over with."

They all started for the staircase, and each step was accompanied by another pounding blow on the door, like a war drum calling them to battle.

34

"HAYDEN, COME HERE," LENI SNARLED, BECKONING HIM TO the door.

Hayden pushed his way through and stood beside Leni, two or three feet back from the reinforced metal door. Already, the center was beaten in only a foot from their noses.

"What's the plan?" Hayden asked.

"Gather all the energy you have," Leni told him. "Combine it with mine, and then we will blow this door open and charge."

A massive boom shook the door again, and the dent inched closer to their faces. Hayden almost fell backward, but Leni didn't even flinch.

"And then what?" Hayden said, straightening up again.

"Then it's everyone for themselves. Are you ready?"

"Not really."

"Prepare yourself!" Leni said sharply.

Muttering under his breath, Hayden began to collect his mental energy. He could feel Leni's forces brewing beside him, swirling and expanding, and he merged into it. The fluctuating mass doubled, and the thick walls around them began to vibrate. Hayden had never felt so much power, even during Lyle and Deanna's kidnapping. Leni's wrath toward the League was heightening his strength.

Just when their combined energy reached a breaking point, Leni and Hayden stuck out their hands and released it.

The metal door burst off its frame and went careening into the hallway, smashing right through the far wall. A stunned Gali went with it. The concrete frame around the door had ripped apart as well, and chunks of debris flew toward the rest of the League members. Some of them were hit and went down. But the majority managed to avoid the attack, and they fell back in both directions, screaming out orders over the noise.

Leni ran through the opening and turned right, spraying debris in front of him in a thick, impenetrable cloud.

Hayden dashed to the left, and with a sharp wave of his hand, he sent Jada spinning through the air. The others streamed out behind him, and laser fire erupted everywhere.

Lana somersaulted underneath a blast of fire, feeling the heat singe the back of her legs. She rolled back onto her feet, grabbed the Flame's arm, and launched him down the hallway. As she did so, something hard smacked her across the back, and Lana tumbled to the ground.

Glancing back, she saw the young League member Ceri walking toward her, clutching a long white staff. Ceri had just raised her weapon, ready to deliver a blow to Lana's head, when Avaria appeared behind her. She took a running jump and kicked Ceri in the back, sending her flying right over Lana.

"That's twice I've saved you," Avaria reminded her, and then went after the League member.

As Lana climbed back to her feet, she saw Renda, a burly, muscular woman with superstrength, charging right for Sam. Sam didn't notice the danger; he was locked in mental combat with Sinio, one of the League's telepaths.

Lana tossed her rifle to the floor, not wanting to shoot anybody again, and tackled Renda. They landed in a tangled heap, with Lana on top, but Renda placed her thick legs on Lana's stomach and pushed violently. Lana hit the ground ten feet away. Managing to roll, she landed in a crouch, her hands flat against the carpet.

"We don't want to fight you!" Lana shouted over the noise.

"You should have thought of that before you joined them," she hissed.

"Joined?" Lana said. "We had no choice! We were kidnapped!"

"Were you forced to attack Sparrow?" Renda asked. "Or help abduct those children?"

Lana hesitated. The truth was they hadn't been forced. The Baron had given them the option to leave, and they had all stayed. Without even realizing it, they had chosen to join the Vindico. They had chosen to be the bad guys.

"That's what I thought," Renda said coldly.

But as she started toward Lana, a red blast struck her in the thigh, burning right through her uniform. She pitched forward to the floor, shrieking, and Rono shot Lana a thumbs-up before plunging back into the fray.

Lana watched the black smoke rising from Renda's leg. Just like it had from Septer's chest.

What have I become? Lana wondered, standing up again. But as soon as she did, she was blindsided by a wave of invisible energy, and she crashed into the wall.

The Baron's lobby was a scene of carnage. The walls, the statues, even the curving staircases were all being destroyed as flames, laser blasts, and invisible forces hurtled back and forth, obliterating the mansion.

James heard an explosion and looked up to see the massive diamond chandelier dropping from the ceiling. He took a running leap to get out from under it and then watched as it shattered into a million pieces, the glass fragments biting into his exposed cheek.

Wiping the blood off his face, James aimed his rifle and fired a stun blast at Meirna, who was fighting with Leni in the corner. The bolt dissipated in a haze of blue particles. She glanced at him, and in that moment Leni gained ground, pushing her backward.

Let him deal with her, James thought. He spotted Emily trying to shoot down Peregrine by the front entrance, but the flying woman was too quick. James was halfway to Emily when he was hit in the ribs by a powerful stream of ice-cold water.

In his shock, he dropped the rifle and saw a pale, slender woman with blue hair facing him from across the room. It was Blue, the League member he'd had a crush on since he was eight. *This isn't how I pictured our first meeting,* he thought.

Blue lifted her hands, and another blast of water rocketed toward him. This time, James ducked under the jet, and in the same motion he scooped up a big piece of drywall from the floor. Cocking his arm, he threw the chunk at her. It struck her in the right shoulder, exploding into dust, and she gasped and fell to her knees.

James picked up his rifle and jogged over, prepared to stun her. She looked up at him with wide, ice-blue eyes, and he hesitated.

"Are you going to kill me?" she asked, the fear evident in her voice.

"No," James said, taken aback. "I'm not a killer."

"Then why are you fighting with them?"

James thought about that for a moment. He could see Emily grappling with Peregrine now as the League member tried to rip the gun from her hands. James shot one last look at Blue, and then he raced toward Emily.

• • •

Sam bent over, feeling sick. He had just waged a terrible mental battle with Sinio, neither able to gain any ground. Only an errant blast had ended the duel, striking Sinio in the arm and breaking his defenses. Sam had easily flooded in after that and overwhelmed him. His mental scream still echoed in Sam's head.

This isn't for me, Sam thought numbly. *I'm not a Villain.*

Before Sinio had fainted, Sam had glimpsed a vivid image of the man's family in his mind: his two young daughters and wife, gathered around the kitchen table.

It was like he was saying good-bye, Sam realized. *He thought I was going to kill him.*

The nausea rose up again, and Sam teetered over to the wall to support himself. A few bodies lay strewn about him, including the Baron, who had taken a stun bolt to the head as soon as he came out of the doorway. Farther down, he saw Lana shakily getting to her feet, covered in dust and blood.

They met eyes, and Sam could tell that she was thinking the same thing. It was time to end this, and not the way they planned. Sam had an idea. He sprinted down the hallway, heading for Sliver's quarters.

"Let . . . go," Emily managed, desperately holding on to her rifle.

Peregrine abruptly shifted her weight, but Emily still held on, and they circled each other, meeting eyes.

"You're the one who helped kidnap Junkit, aren't you?"

Peregrine hissed. She tried to knee Emily in the stomach, but Emily leaned back, avoiding the blow. "You'll pay for that."

A red blast sizzled only a few feet from their heads, and they both instinctively ducked. Smoke and dust spewed around them as the blast erupted into the wall.

"I . . . had no choice," Emily said. Peregrine was stronger than she was, and Emily's fingers were slowly slipping along the metal. She kicked at the League member's ankles, but Peregrine stepped over her foot.

"No excuse," she replied, and finally ripped the rifle out of Emily's hands and spun it toward her. "You can have your sentence when you wake up."

But before Peregrine could pull the trigger, there was a blue flash, and she pitched face-first to the ground. Emily stepped aside, letting her fall.

"Thanks," she said as James ran up to her.

"Anytime," James muttered, his eyes on the body.

Emily studied the ongoing battle. Sliver and Rono were propped against a huge, half-destroyed statue of a dragon, exchanging fire with someone down the left wing hallway. Avaria was circling a now-unarmed Ceri, the Flame already lying dead or unconscious at her feet. Leni had Meirna pressed flat against the wall, her arms pinned against her sides. But the Torturer and the Baron were nowhere in sight, and neither were Hayden, Sam, and Lana.

"We should find the others," Emily said anxiously, starting for the right wing.

James grabbed her arm. "Emily, are you sure we're on the right side?"

She looked back. "Not really."

"Me either."

"Where's Sam?" Hayden shouted over the noise.

He deflected a blue blast into the wall and gestured sharply upward. Jada flew headfirst into the ceiling and was immediately knocked out. As soon as her limp body hit the ground again, the other member he'd been fighting, Noran, blanched and retreated upstairs.

"I don't know," Lana replied, leaning against the wall. Her forehead was caked with blood. "He ran off a minute ago, and I haven't seen him since."

"Are you okay? You've looked better."

"Thanks. So have you."

"Really?" he said. "I thought exhaustion and gnawing guilt were attractive qualities."

"Yeah," Lana murmured. "This doesn't feel right to me either."

"It should, since we're winning. And personally, I'm kicking butt. But somehow I felt better attacking our mentors."

"Me too." She met his eyes. "We have to stop this. Do you think we can beat them again?"

Hayden shook his head. "I doubt it. We caught them off guard the first time." He paused. "You know, if we do happen to get out of this alive, we should go on a date."

"A date?" she asked in disbelief. "You really need to work on your priorities."

"That was always a problem for me. What do you say? A real one, outside of supervillain school."

"Fine," Lana said, "one date. But that's—"

She stopped in mid-sentence, and Hayden turned to see Sam come barreling down the staircase, clutching an odd silver device. Two handles were attached to a wide metal cylinder, and a box covered in blinking lights stuck out from the top.

"Sam, what are you—" he asked.

"No time to talk!" Sam shouted, and ran down the stairs to the basement.

James and Emily rounded the corner from the lobby and made their way through the scattered bodies.

"Listen—" James said.

Lana cut him off. "Yeah, we know: we're fighting on the wrong side."

"What should we do?" Emily asked, glancing back at the lobby. "Unfortunately, we figured this out *after* we took out most of the League."

"It seems our brightest member already has a plan," Hayden said. "Look."

Sam and Deanna emerged from the blown-out opening to the basement. Each was holding one of the handles on the silver device, and the box was spinning and blinking. Lyle came out right behind them, and Hayden could feel the protective shield he'd placed around the two telepaths.

"What is that?" Hayden asked, frowning.

"It's an amplifier," Sam mumbled. "Now we can put the Vindico to bed."

The three of them slowly walked into the lobby, and Hayden noticed that the sounds of fighting had stopped. He glanced at the others and then followed them into the devastated room. Piles of rubble lay everywhere, fires were burning around blackened scorch marks, and bodies were strewn across the floor.

By the dragon statue, Sliver was glaring at Sam furiously, but he had lowered his rifle and seemed unable to move. Rono and Avaria were similarly immobile, and even Leni was standing frozen on the other side of the room, his arms at his side.

And then, one by one, they closed their eyes and toppled over. Leni was the last to fall, and he managed to pivot and shoot them a final venomous glare before crumpling to the floor. Hayden heard a loud thump from inside one of the walls, and he guessed that the Torturer had gone down as well.

Sam and Deanna lowered the device onto the floor.

"That's that," Sam said, quivering with exhaustion. "I wish I thought of that earlier. Sliver taught me how to use this amplifier last week but made me swear I wouldn't tell anyone about it. We even practiced locating the other Vindico members' minds specifically. I think he was going to use this against them at some point." Sam managed a smile. "And now he did."

The few remaining League members looked around in

shock and then turned to face the young group. There was a moment of awkward silence.

"Drop the guns, and don't move," a commanding voice said from behind them.

They whirled around and saw that Thunderbolt was standing in the doorway, Junkit beside him. Blue electricity was coursing along his body and crackling at his fingertips.

"Lyle and I let them out," Deanna whispered. "Sorry."

The five protégés looked at each other, and then Emily, James, and Hayden dropped their rifles. The rest of the League gathered around, though there were only three still capable of walking, and formed a loose circle.

Hayden smiled weakly. "So . . . remember that time we won the battle for you guys?"

Thunderbolt turned to the remaining League members. "Get the Vindico in the ship before they wake up. I'm going to have a talk with their protégés." He glared at the young group. "Deanna, Lyle, come with us. You all have a lot of explaining to do."

"AND THEN YOU APPEARED, AND HERE WE ARE," HAYDEN finished, having recounted the entire story. It had taken him almost twenty minutes to get through, even skipping many of the details.

They were all seated around the Baron's meeting room table, with Thunderbolt at the head, listening quietly.

"I don't think you kids understand the gravity of the situation," Thunderbolt said.

"With all due respect, yes, we do," Sam replied, and everyone turned to him in surprise. "But we didn't have a lot of choices."

"I disagree. You should have helped defeat the Vindico when they kidnapped Deanna and Lyle. And you most certainly should not have released them once you had captured them."

"Well, we weren't too keen on being arrested," Hayden pointed out.

"And what would you have done once you had the League captured?"

They all looked at each other. "Well . . ." James began.

"We were going to arrange a peace conference?" Hayden suggested.

"We were just tired of being used," Sam said, meeting Thunderbolt's eyes, "and being stuck in the middle of *your* war."

Thunderbolt leaned back in his chair. "A war that you've ended. For now, at least. But your actions cannot go unpunished. It is illegal to artificially grant yourself powers, on punishment of life imprisonment. Twenty-one years ago, I made an exception with a young man named Evan Port, and we all know how that turned out." He looked around the table. "However, your situation is somewhat unique since you were coerced."

"It was horrible," Hayden said dramatically. "You wouldn't believe what they put us through, and—"

"How Leni put up with you, I'll never know," Thunderbolt snapped. "But the fact is that you five attacked the League numerous times, almost killed a member, and then attempted to capture the entire League, resulting in—"

"Wait," Lana cut in, sitting up in her chair. "*Almost* killed a member," she breathed. "Do you mean Septer?"

He nodded. "Yes, I just spoke with Meirna. He was in critical condition for a while, but he pulled through."

Lana sat back, staring at the far wall. Tears formed in the corners of her eyes, and Hayden put his arm around her, grinning.

"He's alive," Lana said softly.

"Yes, well . . . it was fortunate," Thunderbolt said. "But regardless, there have been a lot of very serious injuries today, and that makes you as much enemies as the Villains who taught you. As such, we should treat you the same." He paused. "However, I'm not sure that would be a fair assumption. No doubt you at times went along willingly, and even eagerly, but I suppose that is to be expected with the thrill of new powers."

Thunderbolt sighed.

"It was foolish of the others to demand your arrest. Gali was enraged by Junkit's capture; he didn't have Meirna's approval for those demands. She never would have made them. A compromise would have saved us this embarrassment. We were overconfident and spiteful."

Thunderbolt leaned forward again, clasping his hands on the table.

"And of course, it was Sam's quick thinking that won the battle. Without him, we would all be dead, or worse, and we are grateful. With all this in mind, here is your sentence. First, you will all go home."

Emily started to protest, but he quieted her with a hard stare.

"For now. You each have abilities that a normal person shouldn't possess, and I recognize the issues associated with that fact. I doubt that you could go on and live normal lives now, having experienced what you have. And because of that, for the first time in our history, we will consider allowing you all into the League of Heroes."

James exchanged an ecstatic grin with Emily and Hayden, but Sam and Lana looked uncertain.

"Perhaps, by doing that, we can make amends for our past mistakes, of which there are many. Because of your special situation, you five would be the first and last exceptions to that rule." He pointed around the table. "*However,* you must return home for at least six months before any decision can be made. That means all of you. I think a little more growth as people, before the media spotlight, will do you all some good. At that time, you will be introduced to the public as having naturally acquired your abilities."

Hayden opened his mouth to say something, but Thunderbolt cut him off.

"Yes, even *you,* Hayden," he muttered. "I will enjoy the peace and quiet as much as I can until then."

Hayden turned to Lana, grinning. "You're going to be dating a celebrity."

"Second," Thunderbolt said sharply, "you will not speak of what occurred here to anyone outside this room. The League will impose a ban on any media contact with you and release a statement citing that the Villains discovered you were candidates and abducted you before you could join the League. Even your families *must* believe that story. We cannot have the public knowing that these types of powers can be artificially granted. It would be chaos. That's a very strict rule, and anyone breaking it will not be admitted to the League. Got it?"

They all nodded.

"Good. Third. You have these abilities now, but you are

not free to use them at will. If we hear even a rumor that one of you has done something supernatural, particularly if it's something morally questionable, you will not only be banned from the League, but we'll take you to the Perch."

"Why is everyone looking at me?" Hayden asked.

"And lastly, while the League cannot ban you from speaking with one another, we can ban you from forming your own little superpowered group. Same consequences. I would say those are excellent conditions under the circumstances, as I'm sure you'll all agree."

Thunderbolt stood up.

"Lyle, Deanna, you'll come back to headquarters with us. Unlike these five, your parents provided consent for your training, and you both made a well-informed choice to pursue this calling. They will be given the time at home with their families to make an equally well-informed decision. You can see them again when they join, *if* they do." He started for the door. "Now, let's get you all home."

"One more question," James asked. "What about the Vindico?"

"Foiled by children," Leni snarled. "Wonderful."

"An ironic end," the Baron agreed, shifting on the hard floor.

They were sitting in the holding cell of the Defender, which was taking them to the Canadian north. There, the Perch was waiting.

"Can you believe they double-crossed us again?" the Torturer said, leaning up against the wall. "I mean, come on."

"We were so close," Avaria whispered to herself. She sat alone in the corner.

"You know something," the Torturer said, "I hate them, but in a way, I'm strangely proud. They really screwed us. They might be little bastards, but that's what we were going for, right? I mean, overall, we did a pretty good job."

"What a consolation," Leni muttered.

"Well," Rono said, "we'll have many years to reflect on it."

"Maybe not as long as you think, Rono," the Baron replied with a sly smile.

"You have a plan?" Leni asked sharply.

The Baron's cold eyes sparkled. "I don't need one. Eventually, our former protégés will free us."

Leni barked with laughter. "Now you've lost it old man. Why in the world would they free us?"

"Because," he said, "they'll soon find out that it's far more fun to be a villain."

36

THE FIVE FORMER PROTÉGÉS STOOD ALONE IN FRONT OF THE Baron's mansion. Lyle and Deanna had already left with Gali to resume their training.

They had all been watching as Sam said good-bye to Deanna, and Hayden whooped out loud when Sam quickly gave her a hug. The farewell to the siblings had been sad, but it was nothing compared to the one they faced now. They were being split into two groups to get dropped off by two different ships.

"So," Hayden said, looking around at their sullen faces, "that was an interesting month. But hey, we'll be together again soon. That is, if you guys are going to join?"

"I am," Emily replied immediately.

"Maybe," Sam said. "I'm not sure if I'm cut out for this yet."

Lana shook her head. "I don't know if I'll join either, to tell you the truth. I have six months to decide, I guess."

"I will be," James said firmly.

"Well, you all should. It would be sweet. Though the League doesn't look nearly as fun as us. We could always start our own group . . ." Hayden suggested.

"No," Lana said. "Can you at least *try* not to get us all thrown on the Perch?"

"I don't want to go home," Emily murmured. "I have no one to go home to."

Hayden smiled at her. "Yes, you do. I have a couple spare bedrooms in my house. I'm sure the League could take care of the paperwork once they find out how bad it is at your place. We'll just tell them you feel more evil when you're at home."

"Really?" Emily asked, her eyes lighting up. "I can come live with you?"

"Really."

Emily hugged him, and it almost looked like she was about to cry.

"I know," Hayden said, rubbing her back, "I'm the best."

"I just hope my mom didn't forget about me," Sam muttered.

Lana waved a hand in dismissal. "She didn't, trust me. And now you have Deanna," she added, winking, "who definitely won't forget about you."

"Well, she did say she would come visit," he replied, looking embarrassed.

"And what are you going to do about Sara?" Lana asked James.

He smiled. "I'm just going to walk up to her and take my shirt off."

They were still laughing when two white ships touched down on the driveway.

"I guess this is it," James said.

"Everyone keep in touch," Hayden added. "Group hug?"

They all groaned, but leaned in and hugged each other.

"I'll miss you guys," Sam whispered.

"We'll miss you too, Sammy," Hayden replied. "But we'll see each other soon, I'm sure."

"Hayden, get your hand off my butt," James said resignedly.

"Oh, that's your butt?" he responded with mock surprise. "My mistake."

"That's it, I'm out of here," James announced, breaking off the group hug.

"Homeward bound," Hayden agreed. "Let's go grab your stuff, Emily. We're the only ones headed west." He turned to Lana. "I know you agreed in the heat of battle when you weren't sure you would survive, but I'm holding you to that date."

They walked down the steps toward the waiting ships and split into two groups. James saw Lana give Hayden a kiss, and he was surprised that he didn't feel as jealous anymore, not with everything that had happened. They were a good match, he had to admit. He climbed on board with Sam, and Lana soon joined them.

James gazed at the dwindling mansion as they lifted

away and then at the other ship as they flew in different directions into the clouds.

Later that night, James fell onto his bed. After all the screaming, hugging, and crying, he was exhausted.

But now that he'd answered his family's countless questions about his disappearance and drastic physical change, trying his best to hide the exact details, everything already seemed to be settling back to normal. Dinner was on the stove, he was upstairs alone, and tomorrow he was going to school.

But James knew that he wouldn't be happy in Cambilsford, even if people started to like him. His real friends were scattered across the country now, and those were the only people he wanted to see.

Across his bedroom, the poster of Thunderbolt was staring at him. He remembered being six years old, gazing at that poster for hours and desperately dreaming of becoming a League member. Now, finally, it hit him. The road had been much different than he'd imagined, but he had actually gotten there.

He was going to be a superhero.

ACKNOWLEDGMENTS

As with most university graduates who decide to forgo an established career in favor of pursuing their dreams (particularly ones involving teenage supervillains), I have a number of people to thank just for putting up with me. First and foremost, to my parents, who believed in me enough to look past my late nights and later mornings and allow me to live at home rent-free (which was important, since I had no money) as I completed my first four novels. While they occasionally passed along the obligatory parental reminder to "get a job," I always knew they were firmly behind me, and I cannot overstate the reassuring effect that had each time an agent turned me down. So for that, and much, much more, thank you.

To my wonderful girlfriend, Juliana, who never doubted that this story could one day become a novel. In retrospect, I'm not even sure she had to read it. She just had unflinching faith in my ability to do this, which seems to be a common thread here. Sometimes we don't know how lucky we are until we sit down and write about it.

To my fantastic agent at Writers House, Brianne Johnson, who somehow found the potential of this story in the overlong, disjointed manuscript I first sent her. Her endless enthusiasm and determination to sell this book carried us both through almost a year of rejections, and her humor and general zest for life made even that enjoyable. It didn't take long for my new agent to become a trusted friend. And to Susan Cohen, the Writers House agent whom I first submitted this to, who allowed Brianne to take it on and subsequently gave me the best partner I could have asked for.

To Shauna Fay, my editor at G. P. Putnam's Sons, who saw the humor and personality of my ragtag characters and loved them enough to tackle that unwieldy manuscript. I always thought authors were supposed to be at creative odds with their editors, but that couldn't be farther from the truth. Her organized, methodical approach was the perfect match for my often rambling imagination, and together we were able to reshape the story to really bring these characters to life. And to Jen Besser, who also saw the potential and let Shauna run with it.

And finally, to my family and friends at large, whose encouragement was vital to my writing this book. Thank you for being the best support network anyone could ask for.